Goemon motioned the girl to enter.

'Close the door,' he added as an afterthought.

'Remember you are a samurai!' Okiku whispered his favourite exhortation to him as they watched the maid approach. She stopped to kneel, but Goemon motioned her closer. She knelt and bowed, then asked, 'Is there something. . . ?'

Goemon looked her up and down for a moment, making up his mind. There was a mild cough from Rosamund. His chin firmed and he took a breath.

'Lie down and spread your legs!' he barked abruptly.

For a moment the four froze in a tableau. The maid's eyes swung from one to the other, the rich nobleman, his small concubine, and the other, the strange woman that looked like something out of a dream: yellow hair and round eyes. Her lips parted as if for a scream or a protest. But years of training and of service in the inn took over.

'Yes!' she coughed. She lay back and spread her legs, her eyes closed.

CHAMPIONS OF DESIRE

Anonymous

A NEXUS BOOK
published by
the Paperback Division of
W. H. Allen & Co plc

A Nexus Book
Published in 1990
by the Paperback Division of
W. H. Allen & Co plc
Sekforde House, 175/9 St John Street
London EC1V 4LL

Copyright © 1988 Blue Moon Books, Inc.

Typeset by Avocet Robinson, Buckingham

Printed and bound in Great Britain by
Cox & Wyman Ltd, Reading

ISBN 0 352 32569 0

Chapter One

The flickering of the tiny oil lamp barely illuminated the smoothness of her bare skin. She trembled slightly, less at the kiss of cold air on her exposed back than from tension and fright. The symbols that decorated the walls of the tiny hut, the brass and wood and paper objects scattered about — cauldrons, weapons, scrolls, inscribed boards — all spoke of power. Before her, the cold, handsome man regarded her impassively. Outside, the last cold winds of winter howled like beaten wolves driven before the sun. It was the thaw of the sixth year of the Genwa period, almost twenty years since the Tokugawa clan had become the paramount clan in the islands of the Japans, and their head had been named Shogun by the All under Heaven. Across continents and oceans, other men of strange appearance, with red hair and barbaric ways (and, some said, tails) reckoned it as the year 1621 of their saviour.

The man moved at last. He had a thin, handsome face, and his glittering eyes were sunk deeply into their sockets. He pointed to his lap with one hand while the other performing an intricate flexing of the fingers: a *mudra* of power.

· 'Undo me,' he said. His voice had a peculiar resonance to it. It expected immediate obedience. Nothing could stand in the way of a will such as the one that owned that voice. She knelt before him. Her long hair fell over her shoulders. Small breasts swung forward, their finger-thick nipples puckered by the cold. She wished he would grab them, grab her, do something that any other man would do in the circumstances.

She undid his robe, then the loincloth beneath. His cock lay flaccid in a nest of black hairs. She cupped the limp thing in her hands. It seemed as if it were the only warm thing in the room. Shivering with cold, she clutched it to her.

3

Without his urging she bent further. Her breath blew cool against the shrivelled skin. The tiny pink tip of her tongue peeped forth and barely touched the warmth, then hurriedly fled back into the coolness of her mouth. She opened her moist lips, and the lower softness caught the tip of his strength. She sucked him in, enjoying the soft, almost helpless feel of him in her mouth. Her liquid tongue laved the length of his fleshy extrusion.

With a suddenness that almost caused her to leap back, his cock expanded in her mouth. The long shaft filled the cool, sweet cavern, and the tip pushed against her uvula. She struggled to control her gag reflex, overcoming it only when he moved her head back. But he stiffened slightly, and she sensed his displeasure. In expiation, her tongue laved the length of the shaft as far as she could reach. She moved her head back and forth, the ring of her lips milking the length of the warm pole. Sucking on the end like a hungry honeybee, she began frigging the length of his cock, from hairy ballbag to her own chin.

His lips pursed to a thin line, and his hands dropped lightly to her shoulders. He stroked the muscles of her neck, digging thumbs into the muscles of her jaw, and she gasped in pain through her full mouth. She moved uncomfortably, and his movements eased. Again she stroked the feverish shaft. Her cheeks hollowed, and she sucked ravenously at the plum-shaped knob. A faint salty taste permeated her mouth. Her sucking pressure increased, as did the speed of her hands. His hands were resting lightly on her head. She could tell by the contraction of his scrotum that his climax was near. She wished he would let her get some relief too. The taste and smell of his crotch brought on her own randiness, and she rubbed her thighs together as she crouched before him.

He raised her, and she stood trembling. Her smooth skin was unmarked. Thin hips accentuated her flat belly and small erect breasts. Only the thick legs of a peasant marred her perfection. He stroked the length of her flank, then leaned forward to study the dew on her bushy mound. His thumbs parted the lips and slid the length of her labia. She

4

shivered, her channel of love running with her moisture. One thumb penetrated her cavern, and she jogged herself forward and back on the digit. He regarded her movements curiously, then spread her legs farther apart. With the tip of his finger he began tracing signs on the soft flesh of her thigh, then drew her down to kneel before him again. She trembled as he worked, her hands reaching blindly for his smooth, powerful chest, then dropping down in search of his ready erection.

He drew mystic symbols on her skin, his sharp nails marking the golden surface with a flushed line that lingered as if written in fire. He traced the character for *beginning*, the unknown one for the female principle, marks of power of various sorts. She writhed in his arms. Her breathing was agitated, and a moan escaped her lips.

'More, more, lover!' she whispered in the dark. Panting with desire she sought to force him back and mount him. He resisted powerfully, though his fingers continued their tracing. He returned to the burning cavern of her lower mouth. He twisted the hairs that surrounded it into the seven braids, then pinched the slick lower lips between two sharp nails.

She was almost howling now. Her teeth were flashing, and her hair tossed about. At last she succeeded in forcing him backwards. He fell flat on his back, the pole of his erection jutting into the air. With a howl of hunger that matched the winds outside, she impaled herself roughly on the waiting member. He bore her wild ride patiently, obviously uninterested even when she climaxed and squeezed him to a climax of his own.

He rose, and she bowed deeply to the floor. She looked up, expecting a pleased face to look back into her own. His eyes were indifferent as he motioned her to leave the room.

'She will not do,' he called down the mountainside.

Below, in a larger structure, an unseen figure in the dark responded with a disappointed cry.

'Find me another!' commanded the ascetic in the hut, and closed the door. He returned to his meditations while below him his followers filed down the mountain. Salvation was not yet to be.

The young man ran wildly through the streets of Miyako. Formerly the capital, and still residence of the All under Heaven, the town was unused to such tumult. The grey-tiled roofs seemed to lower their displeasure at this rowdy behaviour. The youth's topknot, usually smooth and straight, was falling askew. He had hiked up his robes, and his bare legs flashed in the summer sun. One of his straw sandals fell off as he ran, but in his hurry he did not pause to collect it. He entered a maze of crooked streets faced with blank grey wooden walls. Housewives about their daily business, cleaning the outsides of their houses or dickering with tradesmen, paused and recoiled at his rush. Some gathered their children protectively to their skirts as he passed by. One at least caught a flash of golden thigh and licked her lips thoughtfully, lost perhaps in a daydream.

At last he reached a narrow way bordered by the clay or brick walls of modest villas pierced by thatched-roof gates: the houses of middle-class samurai. The villas themselves, neither large nor ostentatious, were set off behind small gardens. He paused before one and leaned on the gate for a moment to catch his breath. Suddenly noticing his own disarray, he hurriedly straightened his grey robe and let the skirt fall from his hand.

Each doorpost bore a simple wooden sign. Black ink characters on one bore the name MIURA. The other, incised into a small slab of wood, said simply, LESSONS. The young man pushed open the door and took a deep breath. He knew the master of the house only vaguely and had reason to be apprehensive in the man's presence. But he knew that this was the one place where he could get the help he needed. And the mistress of the house was kind. . . . He pushed open the gate and stepped inside, walked down the flagstoned path, and stepped into the earth-floored anteroom.

'Forgive me for disturbing you!' he called out formally in a loud voice.

There was an answering cry from inside the house. A young, plump woman rushed up. She knelt on the wooden floor of polished boards that served as barrier between the anteroom and the house proper.

'What can I do for you, please?' she asked her head near the floor.

He admired the sweep of her neck between her upswept hairdo and the stiffness of her collar, and the plump lushness of her buttocks as they tightened the fabric lower down.

'Is Teacher Miura or his wife home? It is urgent I see them!'

She looked up quizzically at the tension in his voice.

'The master is here. He is in the back. I will call him.'

'No need — I know the way,' he said forcefully. He turned and ran out the door and around the side of the house. The pale green plumes of giant bamboo wove a pleasant canopy over his head. He looked around. At the far end of the garden, against a wall, stood a small open hut. Before it on a tiny raised platform sat a man in deep concentration. The visitor ran through the small grove. Spots of sunlight moved about in the imperfect shade of the bamboo. Stray leaves, twirled by occasional breezes, moved restlessly.

The visitor slowed as he approached Miura. From close up the man was a giant. His stolid face was topped by a wealth of hair that was brushed smoothly back, then rose into a topknot that was bent forward over his head. His hands were in his lap. Beside him on the platform was a large two-hand sword. In his belt rested another, shorter one. He seemed to be gazing sleepily at the ground before him.

A slight breeze swirled some leaves. One of the oblong brown slivers passed through a shaft of sunlight. Another followed. The giant's hands moved suddenly. A tiny dirk — a *kozuka* — that had been hidden in the scabbard of the short blade in his sash suddenly appeared in his hand. It flipped through the air, passed through the spotlit leaf, and pinned it to the ground. His hands returned to his lap.

He looked up at the young visitor. 'You are Matsuo, are

7

you not? Osatsuki's man?'

Matsuo bowed, then fell to the ground on his knees and buried his face in the leaves.

'Yes, master Miura. But please hurry. They have come and taken her! You must hurry and help her!'

'Mistress Osatsuki? What has happened to her?' The giant rose leisurely. He thrust the two-hand *katana* back into his belt, then bent to pick up the *kozuka* and restore it to its hiding place.

'What has happened to her?' he repeated to the grovelling figure at his feet.

Matsuo raised a tear-streaked face. 'Several men. They came and took her. They would have killed me, but she told me to run and hide. You must come. She has told me before that no one but Miura Jiro and his wife could help her if necessary.'

Jiro nodded his head slowly while he slipped on his sandals.

'Was she expecting trouble?'

'No, no. It was all so sudden.'

They walked to the house, and Jiro called to the maid. She came out and stood looking at them shyly. Under her bowed head she peeked at Matsuo, seemingly finding his appearance very pleasing.

'My wife is away, visiting a friend at the moment. I will have to leave her a message; then will come with you.' With a bold hand he wrote a message and handed it to the maid. She bowed, and Jiro indicated that Matsuo should precede him. They turned towards the other side of the city, where Osatsuki had her abode and place of business.

The Gion quarter was on the way to the famous temples that littered the mountains east of Miyako. It was gradually being given over to an entertainment quarter. Party entertainers, who now called themselves geisha, teahouses, discreet eating places were all to be found there. And of course, courtesans.

Satsuki's house was a discreet two-storey affair. Heavy wooden bars protected the upper-floor windows and afforded the residents a view of the street without being seen.

There were numerous passersby. Residents of the area seemed to hurry past, averting their glances. Casual visitors just sauntered on, unknowing and uncaring.

Jiro and Matsuo arrived before the house. Matsuo was sweating from the exertion. He had run far and returned in haste. Jiro strode along at unaltered pace. A lounger was leaning against the wall near the entrance to Osatsuki's house. He was dressed in a loud blue-checked robe tucked up into his loincloth. His shins were wrapped in black cloths as if ready for a journey, and there was a short sword stuck in his sash. He looked at passersby arrogantly under lowered brows. Most people, recognising his type by the unkempt hairdo and general air of bravado, avoided his eyes. He was tunelessly whistling a popular air.

Jiro made as if to enter. The lounger stuck out a hand automatically to bar his way. Seeing the massive build of the samurai, Jiro hesitated.

'Can't go in there,' the man said in rough tones.

'Oh?' said Jiro civilly. 'Why not, if you please?'

'Boss, he owns the house, he says so.' The man's face twitched.

'I happen to be a friend of the owners. I'm sure there'd be no objection. Where is Mistress Osatsuki, by the way?'

'The boss took her to . . . Hey, wait a moment, you a friend of that woman Satsuki?'

'Yes,' said Jiro, smiling faintly, 'Of course. She's the owner.'

'Getoutahere!' said blue-checks with a snarl. He put a hand on the hilt of his sword to emphasise his words.

Jiro's smile broadened. His hands flashed up twice. Blue-check's head rocked from side to side, and he fell with a cry.

Jiro rolled him over, then placed a sandalled foot on the man's chest. 'Tell me about it,' he commanded softly.

Blue-checks tried to rise.

Jiro leaned forward, and the man collapsed with a shriek. 'Tell me!' commanded Jiro again, leaning forward. 'This boss, where is he? Where did he take Osatsuki?'

The man on the ground groaned but did not speak until Jiro reached for his great sword.

9

'Yasaka shrine. Behind Yasaka shrine. His name is Uchibei. Everyone knows him.'

Jiro grinned. 'I'll tell him you sent me.' He turned and entered the house. The ruffian scuttled to the side, then rose to his feet. He considered for a moment, then, realising his predicament, headed away from Satsuki's house at a lope, moving northwards. The Yasaka shrine was to the south, and he was anxious to put some distance between himself and his boss. He could have lied, he supposed, but the massive samurai looked like a man who would not take kindly to such a ploy.

'We'll go up and have a look,' said Jiro.

The place had been thoroughly wrecked. It was not likely that Osatsuki had put up a fight, so the wrecking had been done as a matter of spite. Items of value had been pillaged, and Satsuki's robes were scattered about, torn and trodden on. Matsuo looked at the destruction, tears in his eyes. Jiro was more controlled. He did not know Satsuki well, but he had great respect for her beauty and charm.

'Matsuo, I shall follow her kidnappers. You must restore the house to its former condition. If there is any trouble before we are back, run and call Okiku. She will know what to do. I will follow the kidnappers to Yasaka shrine.'

The search took Jiro almost half the day. There was a maze of small streets and tiny neighbourhoods around and behind the famous shrine. They were the result of the growth of the city since peace had come to the land. No one seemed to know the mysterious Uchibei. A lounger, quite elderly, his straggly hair barely held in a knot, had been following Jiro with his eyes. Jiro sat down beside him and jingled some coins suggestively in his sleeve.

'Is there anything I can get the honoured samurai? A drink? A smoke? A woman, perhaps?'

Jiro smiled and didn't answer, merely taking out a small string of copper coins. The man's face brightened. 'That's a rather small store of cash for such a large samurai as your honoured self,' he said, half-fawning, half-sneering.

'There is more,' Jiro said laconically, jingling his sleeves again.

'Is there something the honoured sir is particularly interested in?'

'I've heard of a man named Uchibei in these parts. I have some business with him.'

'Elder Brother Uchibei is not generally pleased when someone tells of his whereabouts. . . .'

'With cash, a man can be far from trouble.' Jiro drew another string of copper coins. The old man reached for them with a dirty claw.

'Uchibei? You do mean Uchibei? The big man? His mansion is right behind the temple. I will tell you. . . .' With many side glances and mutterings the lounger described Uchibei's mansion. Jiro nodded his understanding, then paid over the string of cash.

Uchibei, he knew, was one of that vast mass of 'mean people' who infested all cities, preying on the weak and the helpless. He would have to be careful, as one should be careful with any pack of stray dogs.

Chapter Two

Satsuki considered her bonds ruefully. They would undoubtedly cause unsightly bruises on her skin. She was tied tightly and efficiently with a rope of some rough substance she did not recognise. She tried to make herself more comfortable, but the bonds were too tight. The room she had been dumped in was dirty, the tatami mats worn, brown, and old. Moving her legs, she found she could arrange her robes in a more elegant fashion, draped carelessly over her legs, the several contrasting layers showing pleasingly. She contemplated the effect for a while. There was little else to do.

She had been brought bound and gagged from her home in the Gion. The ride had been painfully uncomfortable, and the palanquin closed and stuffy. The ruffians who had seized her and rubbed their hands over every exposed and some unexposed portions of her skin. Not that she'd minded. She had left the safety of her life as a noblewoman with the object of finding a more exciting life for herself. That the excitement was of a rough and perhaps unpleasant sort worried her but did not faze her.

There were heavy steps from the outer room, and the torn sliding door that had once been elegant was thrust roughly open. Four men stood in the opening. She recognised three of them as members of the kidnap party that had seized her and ruined her home. The fourth was a heavyset, unshaven man of indeterminable age. He was dressed in a rich brocade robe open to the waist. A massive chest and a heavy belly showed themselves to the world.

They stood at the door for a moment, savouring her helplessness. One of them spoke at last. 'What shall we do with her, Boss?'

'I'm surprised at you gentlemen!' These were the first words she'd uttered and the attention of her captors focused on her. 'At your ages you should know what to do with a woman, surely?' She lowered her lids modestly. The sentence had been wrung from her involuntarily. She was ashamed of her outburst. After all, it was not her place to lecture these men.

The heavyset man who had been addressed as Boss stepped heavily into the room. The ancient brown tatami trembled under his tread.

'So you want it, eh? That's nice. Stupid of you to set up business without paying me a fee. But I see you're ready to make up for that. We'll get right down to business.' He parted his robe, exposing a rather worn silk loincloth, which bulged outwards furiously. In a quick move he was naked and his erect dark cock leered at her from beneath the curve of his massive belly, which overhung a mass of black hairs.

The other three whooped and rushed forward. One pushed her shoulder back onto the mats. Each of the other two seized an ankle roughly and pulled her legs apart; then one of them flipped her robes open, exposing the length of white thighs and their dark-haired juncture.

'Really, there's no need for that,' she murmured — unheeded. She decided that she needed to learn more about these rough commoners. True, she had left her previous life — that of the pampered wife of a nobleman — behind her by choice and had chosen to associate with commoners, but most of her customers had been well-to-do merchants with a yen for refined living. This was her first encounter with *real* commoners. She was still trying to decide whether she liked it, when the boss stretched himself out on her and entered her warm crack forcefully.

Out of habit and a sense of professional neatness, she raised her hips high to accommodate him. He grunted as he sank slowly into her. The soft, moist tissues of her canal gently clipped the length of his stubby thick cock. He rested there for a second, admiring her face, which was composed but watchful. The other three ruffians roughly pinched her arse and tits. One of them squeezed her erect nipples brutally, and she could feel another jerking his naked cock against her calf, leaving a trail of moisture on the sensitive

16

skin. However, her attention was on the boss as he started moving back and forth in her. She was alert to his every move, attempting to anticipate him and bring on his crisis. Her tight cunt squeezed and contracted at each entry to extract the greatest amount of pleasure for her customer.

He pounded quickly on. The pressure of her cuntal walls on his prick was the most exquisite he had felt. His motions speeded up. His eyes never left her face while his hands roved bruisingly about her body. One hand knocked against the scrabbling paw of one of his henchmen. He roared at them, and they let go. She breathed more easily, arching her body in response to his motions, cushioning his loins and belly on her own.

It was all over very suddenly. Before he had a chance to change his tempo, his imperious balls emptied their contents into her waiting cunt. Gobs of sperm boiled out of his sack and splashed heavily into her channel, flooding her insides. His head dropped onto her shoulder, and he breathed deeply for a while.

He rolled off her and squatted at her side, regarding her somberly for a moment from his pig-like eyes.

'Well, sweety, I don't mind saying that was the best I've ever had. I'm Uchibei, by the way. While I rest, the boys will have you.' There was stirring among his men when he said that. 'Then I'll have you again. This time was too quick. Anyway, from now on you'll be working for me. All the other women do. But I'll keep you for a while, yes I will.

'Take off those ropes!' he concluded, roaring at his men. They obeyed hastily. 'We don't want those pretty limbs marked in any way, and from the looks of it you enjoy it as much as we do. . . .' He laughed, and his belly shook while his men snarled at one another for the right to be first. He cuffed them impartially and one of them settled himself leisurely on her body.

The man's hands grabbed roughly at her tits. With a dirty thumb he forced the nipples into the pale, soft mounds of flesh. He nibbled at the side of her neck and grunted into her shell-like ear. All this time she could feel the length of his prick rubbing roughly the length of her soft, wet lower

17

lips. Unable to find the entrance he coveted, he grunted in frustration and his rear end bobbed in the air to his companions' laughter.

'A moment please, dear sir,' she whispered in his ear, well knowing the delicate nature of most men. Her soft hand slid between their two bodies, and she positioned the thick heart-shaped head of his prick at the entrance to her gluey channel. He sighed with satisfaction and rewarded her with a hard jab at the softness of her cunt. She eased his passage by raising her hips to meet his, and her dimpled knees held on to his hairy thighs. He drove into her, sweating and grunting. She felt the tides of lust rising in his stringy long poker. His hands squeezed her breasts with ferocity as his body came down on her soft flesh like a pile driver. Again he grunted, and she murmured regret at not understanding his words. His eyes were closed and his teeth were clenched as a tide of thick juice spurted rapidly from his cock and flooded her interior.

She raised her head to await the pleasures of the other men, only to see that their attention was directed outside the room. There were the sounds of a commotion, some muted screams and heavy thumps from inside the dilapidated mansion. Unchibei was rising from his seat by her side, when the doorway through which he and his men had entered was filled with a threatening figure.

'Ah, Uchibei!' it said, but the ready, blood-dripping sword was not meant as a greeting.

The man who had just left Satsuki's overflowing cunt twisted his neck and stared, then scrabbled to one side. 'The *yamabushi!* They've found us!' he cried in disbelief.

The *yamabushi* was rough featured, his long moustaches untrimmed. Long hair was pulled back, pate unshaven. He was dressed in a fantastic costume. His robe was printed in a bold pattern of blue checks. It was tucked into wide bloused trousers that ended at the knee. His calves were wrapped in leggings, his feet encased in wooden sandals that raised his height considerably. Incongruously, his neck was bedecked with a garland of red pompoms attached to a brocade yoke that hung down in front and back. On his head

18

perched a tiny black pillbox hat, tilted rakishly over his forehead.

There was little time for inspection. The intruder called out, and Uchibei and his men rose, scrambling for weapons and clothes. The wooden walls of the room burst open, and men in variants of the intruder's costume leaped in. They screamed and leaped, seemed to be everywhere. Uchibei and his men had no chance to return a blow. Uchibei's head flew from his shoulders after a savage blow from the leader of the intruders. The thin man who had slobbered over Satsuki's breasts sought refuge behind her, but a long lance shafted him from behind.

Satsuki covered her eyes, trying to ignore the sounds and the activity around her. Something wet splashed against her foot, and she recoiled. At last the sounds of activity and screaming died down. A figure stood threateningly over her kneeling form.

The mansion, when found, lay behind a rotting, crumbling wall. The gate was uncharacteristically open, showing a vista of desolation and lost grandeur. Jiro stepped inside. The garden that met his eyes was full of melancholy and the signs of genteel decay. It also contained a dead man, face down in the dirt, his blood pooling around him. Jiro explored cautiously. There were several more bodies. One of them groaned and muttered something. Jiro rolled him over. His belly had been gashed, and his entrails were spilling out.'

'Water . . . water,' the ruffian begged.

'You will die of it,' Jiro cautioned.

The man laughed rackingly. 'What d'ye think I'm doin' now, eh? Get me some water. Sake is even better.'

Jiro rooted in the mess, only some of it made by the attackers, whoever they were, the rest the result of the piggish habits of the inhabitants, and found a filthy bottle half full of some liquid that smelled alcoholic. The wounded man grabbed at the bottle as Jiro knelt by him. The samurai jerked it out of reach.

'What happened here?'

The wounded man eyed the sake bottle hungrily, clutching at his stomach.

'Bastard, I'm dying.'

'What happened?'

'*Yamabushi* attacked us.'

'Why?'

'A drink, you animal!'

'You'll die with the first swallow. Why?'

'We've been competing with them for women and for territory.

'There was a woman here. . . .'

'Some *woman*, too!' The man's eyes lit up in memory. 'They took her. She was a first-class bitch from the Gion area.'

'Where did they take her?'

'How should I know? They are heading south, that's all I know. I swear it. South. Maybe to Koya-san. . . . The bottle — give me the bottle; that's all I know. . . .' The wounded bully was sobbing now.

Jiro handed him the bottle, and he gulped several times gratefully, then gave a great cry and expired. Jiro rose and headed south. The flies tended to their own, buzzing happily.

Chapter Three

The Yamato plain is a basin bordered by mountains. Jiro passed the city of Nara in the centre of the plain by a side road. Meeting a professional messenger on the road, he had sent a message to Okiku, but inasmuch as there was little real news to tell, he only asked her to alert their friend Goemon and meet him at some well-known spot. He chose Koya-san, knowing little about his quarry besides their possible connection with that well-known monastery. He had inquired along his route, gleaning a hint here and there. *Yamabushi* bands were not uncommon, many travelled with women, and they all seemed to be heading south. Still, Osatsuki's beauty and charm were striking, and Jiro was not a man to give up easily.

He marched the entire day. Well-tended straight-sided rice fields stretched out to the wooded mountains that rose steadily before him. He made inquiries along the way, with little hope. No one had seen any sign that could be interpreted as a kidnapped courtesan. The ground rose with the setting of the sun, and by the time the sun was in the far west, Jiro decided to call it a day. He was in a rural area. Small hamlets and occasional isolated houses dotted the landscape. He headed towards one of the nearer hamlets across the fields and fruit groves. A road led through the hamlet, and it looked as if it might have an inn, or at least the house of a wealthy farmer who would offer him shelter for the night.

He passed through a small peach orchard and came suddenly upon a small farmhouse. Before it, a spring bubbled from between two rocks. One of them was carved with the words 'water god,' to indicate its sacred nature. A young woman knelt by the water's edge, at the small artificial pool. She was bare to the waist, and her breasts dangled suggestively over the water. She was combing her

23

hair, and spots of moisture on her back seemed to indicate that she was in the final act of a rustic bath.

She raised her head at Jiro's approach, saw his tall figure emerging from the trees, gasped, and rose to flee. Her straw sandal caught in a tangle of brush, and she crashed to the ground, yelping in pain. Trying desparately to rise, she cried out. Jiro stopped at the other side of the pool as she frantically sought to cover her breasts and crawl away from him at the same time.

'I won't hurt you,' he said. To demonstrate his peaceful intentions he knelt and drew some water in his cupped hand.

She tried to rise and fell back. Panting heavily, she managed to hide her breasts. He rocked back on his hams and looked at her.

'I was only passing through, on my way to the hamlet.' He waved casually at the gathering gloom behind her.

His tone and immobility rather than his words seemed to reassure her. She rolled to her knees and bowed.

'I am sorry, Mr Samurai, but I am not used to strangers. My mother and I are alone here since — *Oh!*' Her hand flew to her mouth in consternation.

'Ah, you're not supposed to say that, are you?' He laughed and waved a hand. 'Don't worry. I'll be on my way. I won't take advantage of your situation.'

He rose to go, and she rose with him, moaning a little. She turned to pick up a heavy wooden bucket but could not put weight on her sprained ankle. She cried in pain.

'Let me help you?'

She tried to refuse, awed by her proximity to what was to her a mighty nobleman. He insisted gently and was at last allowed to carry the heavy bucket. He marvelled at these simple country girls, able to carry burdens that would make a man look for other employment.

The house was a small peasant's cottage. The interior was divided by wooden and matting screens into several rooms. Bare rafters, huge beams of twisted aged wood, rose in the gloom. Farmer's tools were scattered about. Over all was an air of abandonment and poverty. Tools seemed unrepaired, and the matting was old, the wood warped.

24

She begged him to rest, and Jiro gratefully sat on the wooden platform, his feet still in sandals on the pounded earth floor of the entrance hall. He removed his sword from his sash and accepted the fruit she offered.

'How did you get here, sir?' she asked with country ingenuousness.

'I am looking for a friend,' he answered absently. She was quite pretty, he decided. Flat, round face with fine eyes. Thick ankles below the hem of her soft dress, but a nicely rounded body. 'I was hoping to find an inn in the hamlet. . . .'

'There isn't one,' she said. 'It's a very poor village. There is an inn, I have heard, several miles away. Perhaps you could try that?'

'No. I'll just have to sleep on the veranda of some shrine. The kami are always hospitable.'

She laughed. Then her brows ceased in thought. 'Actually, why don't you stay here for the night? I'm afraid we have little to offer, but at least a mat and some protection from the elements . . .'

He waved his hand in refusal. 'I could not impose on your parents. . . .'

'No, only my mother. She is not here now. She has gone to sell some akebia-vine baskets. My father died some years ago. That is why we are so poor.' She looked mournfully at the dilapidated cottage.

He bowed his thanks.

Supper was a simple stew of mushrooms, wild vegetables, and taro cooked in a pot over a small fire. It was held by a straw rope threaded through a wooden post in the shape of a fish. She served him, not eating until he had had his fill. While she was eating he leaned forward and poked idly at the fire. His hand snaked forward into the ashes.

'Look — you must have lost this. . . .' There was a small string of square-holed copper cash in his hand. Her bowl almost dropped from her hand. She laid down her chopsticks and stared at the money. He laid it down in her lap.

'It must have dropped there from your father's sleeve,' Jiro said. He was almost penniless now, but there would always be some way to proceed. She hugged the string to her breasts.

Just then they were interrupted. 'I am home!' a strong female voice called from the entrance hall. 'Etsuko, come and help me.' The girl hurried to her feet and rushed to the entrance, calling, 'Welcome home!'

The mother was in her early forties, Jiro estimated. She had the girl's country good looks, not yet turned stringy with age, her face only slightly wrinkled with care. She cast a suspicious look at Jiro, then at her daughter. Seeing nothing apparently amiss, she bowed at the samurai. Jiro introduced himself, and uncomfortably, with thin lips, she bade him welcome. After a few moments she motioned her daughter aside. Jiro, impassive by the fireside, could hear muttered accusations and bitter protest. The two women reentered the room. Etsuko, the daughter, was drying her eyes and casting appealing glances in Jiro's direction. Jiro knew the source of the argument. Many samurai, he knew, treated peasant women as their chattels. They took them where and when they wanted, and pretty farm girls were prime targets. Wandering, lordless samurai such as himself were the worst: they not only raped, but also robbed and killed on the slightest pretext. Though the law was usually severe and swift, that was little consolation to the dead and none to the peasant who feared officialdom more than he feared death.

Jiro rose and bowed to the mother. 'If you will excuse me, I will leave. I am sorry to be such a bother.' The mother made some protest, but it was clear she was relieved to see him go. The daughter, Etsu, looked on with a blank face.

Jiro stepped out into the cool night air. He would have to sleep the night on the ground after all. He shrugged mentally. It would not be the first time. He walked away from the house, through small gardens of beans and squash and other vegetables ripening in the summer warmth. The path was worn, and it meandered as it neared points of importance to the peasants. He passed by a bamboo grove, the plumes of the plants glinting in the moonlight. The sky was clear, and the lunar illumination cast a glow over everything. There was a large tree in a clearing near the grove. Jiro marked it from afar for future reference. Such trees sometimes indicated shrines, and if the shrine was large enough, it would be his hostel for the night.

He slowed down as he approached. His trained senses told him of someone lurking in the shadows. Without turning his head he watched the dark cautiously. Suddenly he was distracted. A group of men came up the path. Some of them bore lanterns. Their feet were bare, but they were in a hurry. They saw him in the moonlight, and one of them called out, 'There he is! I told you there was a samurai there!'

Jiro stood in the clearing to await developments. The lurker in the shadow of the shrine did not move. The excited villagers surrounded the giant samurai like hounds bringing a wolf to bay. There were eight of them armed with improvised weapons — sickles, flails, rakes, and wooden poles.

They dithered around him for awhile, and one, braver perhaps than the rest, stalked up to Jiro. 'Well, Mr Samurai, what are you doing here, eh? Had your fun with our widow, huh? Don't think you can get away with it. We've had enough of you people. We pay the landlord, and that's enough.'

'Matagel, cut the chatter and let's finish him,' another rough voice broke in.

'I was merely looking for shelter for the night, but it proved inconvenient for the household,' Jiro replied mildly. 'Now get out of the way, please. It would be a bother reporting your death to the authorities.'

'Bastard! Report my death to the authorities?' The apparent leader of the peasant youths raised his staff. Jiro's left hand rested lightly on his sheath. One of the peasants sniggered 'Shelter for the night. Bastard!' Others raised their makeshift weapons. Jiro kept his eyes on the leader. He knew from the sounds and small rushes they were making that they were not ready to attack — yet. As soon as their courage was up they would, and he would have to act. He grinned to himself. He had never been trained to run away. A defect, Okiku often told him, in a perfect character. Run

27

away and fight again was his mate's philosophy.

'Please don't draw your sword, Mr Samurai. The smell of blood would upset my digestion.' The voice from the shadows was hoarse and adenoidal, though the words and accent were town, rather than country. A massive shadow detached itself from the deeper shadow of the shrine-tree and lumbered forward. Nine faces turned in that direction.

The interloper was shorter than Jiro but outweighed him by a half. An enormous belly extended the front of his robe, which was wrapped by a smart black-striped silk sash. His face was almost as round as the moon but framed in curly sideburns that reached to his fat jowls. He waddled forward and stood with feet planted wide.

'I do think you should disperse, you know. Or at least fight him one by one.'

'Who asked you, horse-head?' Some of the peasants coverged on him, their weapons raised.

'A moment, please.' He raised his hands. 'As you can see, I'm unarmed. Here, look . . .' He extended his arms to the sides, palms upwards. He wore a light summer robe, and there did not appear to be anything hidden in it. He squatted a bit and stamped his feet on the ground. 'You wouldn't want to attack an unarmed man, would you?'

'I don't care if you're unarmed or the samurai here armed. We want you out of here. We don't care for any strangers, particularly those fucking our widow.' There was chorus of assent from his companions.

One of the peasants, a husky young man, spat on his hands and marched up to the fat man. 'I'll deal with him!' he called over his shoulder. 'The rest of you attend to the samurai.'

The peasant's hard bare foot lashed out and connected with a thump to the fat man's crotch. The fat man winced but stood there looking the peasant in the eye. The surprised young man, who had expected the fat man to collapse in agony, stared with his jaw open. An enormous fat hand lashed out and slapped his face. The peasant youth collapsed to the ground.

The other young men yelled their battle cries and charged.

28

Two of them rushed the fat man. The rest charged Jiro, who still had time to see how his unexpected ally dealt with some of his opponents. The fat man leapt forward in a single giant frog hop. One hand smacked solidly into a charging peasant's face, sending him flying. The other seized an opponent's neck and swung him around in a hip throw that crashed him to the ground.

All that, Jiro saw in a flash as the other peasants were upon him. He dodged a pole aimed at his head and slid forward. The butt of his sword slammed into a midriff, and one of the men went down before him. Twisting, he seized another man's sleeve and with a quick move threw him over his own shoulder. He drew the sword, still sheathed, from his sash and parried a hooking cut by an attacker armed with a sharp curved sickle. Skilfully, the man tried to entrap the sword, but Jiro was too experienced a swordsman. His sheath moved with the hook, then thrust forward to the point of the peasant's chin. Jiro turned to his last opponent, and that worthy, trapped between two formidable foes, backed away in terror.

'A moment, please, do not run.' The fat man's hoarse voice sounded again. 'If I may inquire, why are you so anxious to attack us?'

The young peasant, fearful for his life, had lost his former belligerence. He became obsequious as he bowed, trembling. 'Pardon me, sir. We — we feared for our widow. You know, we are poor men, but we must protect our own. . . .'

'Your widow?' Jiro interjected. 'Surely all of you are alive and well. . . .

The man bobbed his head again. 'Our widow, sir . . . that is . . .' He stammered for a second, trying to explain what was to him a commonplace. 'You see, sir, we have a custom hereabouts — I think it must seem strange to you gentlemen. Anyway, when a man dies leaving a wife, the young unmarried men take care of her. Bring her firewood, help with plowing and sowing, repairs, things like that which she cannot do for herself. Of course, we also have to protect her, and someone saw the samurai gentleman entering her house, so we thought . . . we thought . . .'

'You thought I was going to rape her,' concluded Jiro drily.

'Well, yes, sir. And that's no good sir. Besides, it was Kichibei and Saburo's turn to visit her tonight. We came along as a sort of guard, sir.'

The fat man moved impatiently. 'Turn? Explain?'

The peasant bobbed his head again. 'Of course, we take care of *all* her needs. She is very nice to us, and since we cannot enter the houses of girls to visit them, she sleeps with us. A nice woman she is too, sir.'

Jiro and the fat man both laughed.

'Well, I'm sorry I interrupted your friends' turn. I really did leave her there unharmed. Her daughter, too. I suggest, though,' he added in a severe tone, 'that you and your friends refrain from attacking samurai in the future. Your entire village could be razed if that came out.' The young peasant shivered at the words, knowing how true they were. He fell to his knees and bowed to the ground, babbling for forgiveness. Jiro ignored him, and bowed to the massive figure at his side.

'I am Miura Jiro, an unattached samurai and teacher. At your service. Thank you for your help. I would never have succeeded without you.'

'Nonsense!' said the fat man cheerfully and informally. Though dressed as a commoner, he seemed to take Jiro as an equal, if not perhaps even an inferior. 'I am Tatsunoyama, a wrestler from Osaka. I am travelling on pilgrimage. Also, I am scouting for possible candidates for the ring.' He looked up at Jiro. 'A shame we did not find you when you were young.'

Jiro stiffened at the insult, then relaxed. The wrestler was obviously not out to insult him by questioning his profession of arms. He was merely blunt.

'If I may venture a question . . .' Jiro said delicately.

Tatsunoyama bowed slightly.

'You were kicked in a place that normally renders a man unconscious, and yet . . .' The peasant, who had been busy trying to revive his groaning companions, paused to listen too.

30

'It is one of the secrets of our trade,' Tatsonoyama said hoarsely. 'But I can tell you that I can raise my precious jewels at will. Thus it was a painful kick but had no real effect.'

The two men exchanged pleasantries for a time, while the attackers scrambled groggily to their feet. The peasants huddled together for a while, and Jiro eyed them covertly, wondering whether they were planning another attack. One of them, his back bent submissively, crept to the two. The others bowed their heads in a group behind. The spokesman scratched his head and laughed with embarrassment.

'Excuse us, gentlemen, but this was all a mistake. I hope you are not angry?' Encouraged by Jiro's and Tatsunoyama's response, he continued. 'We . . . we would like to make amends. Can we invite you gentlemen to stay the night? I understand the samurai gentleman has no place to go. . . .' His voice trailed off at his own temerity. 'And of course, the wrestler gentleman as well. . . .'

Tatsunoyama grunted, then smiled. 'As for me, I thank you, but I am being hosted by someone in the neighbourhood. I merely went out for a stroll. The gentleman here will accept your offer. Take good care of him.' He flipped an enormous paw in Jiro's direction and rolled off ponderously.

Jiro marvelled how such a mountain of flesh could move so swiftly in a fight. He marvelled too at how the wrestler, a commoner, could treat him, a nobleman, so casually.

The peasant tugged at his sleeve. 'If you please, master, we could repair to the widow's? We have some wine. . .'

The widow greeted her guests gaily. It was obvious that they were desirable visitors. She eyed Jiro with a greater surprise, but one of the young men took her aside, and after a low-voice conversation punctuated with glances toward Jiro, she accepted him and even offered him some of the warmed rice wine in an old cracked cup specially polished for the occasion.

The men lounged around the sunken fireplace, drinking and munching some snacks she had prepared. The widow served them herself, her round cheeks glowing with the heat

31

and the pleasure of their company. Pounded rice cakes and taro were set to bake in the ashes. Etsuko, the girl, was nowhere to be seen, Jiro sat a little apart. The conversation was about subjects and people he knew little of. Gossip mainly, talk of the harvest and a coming festival.

Jiro excused himself — to everyone's evident relief. There was a pallet on the floor in an inner room, laid on the bare boards. The widow offered it to him, with a bow. He noted the sour looks from the young men by the fire.

'Thank you, no. But do you have a hayloft? I noted a barn and thought . . . well, I have not had the pleasure of the smell of newly cut grass in many years. That would be a delight.'

The widow looked at him in surprise. She tried to protest, not too strongly, but finally led him upstairs and through a narrow hatch to a pile of hay that overlooked the empty horse stall.

'We had to sell the horse a long while ago, but this place is well protected and part of the main building, so you should be warm and comfortable,' she said. He bowed his thanks, and she departed back to her guests.

The loft was indeed comfortable, and the soft highland grass fragrant. Jiro burrowed into the grass and found himself ensconced against the loft wall. He was soon dozing, but then he found that a light was shining into his eyes. He blinked sleepily. The light came from a narrow fissure in the wooden floor. He rubbed his eyes and then peered blearily through the crack.

The light came from a candle in the room occupied by the pallet offered him earlier. The wooden sliding door between the room and the kitchen where the young men lounged was closed. On the pallet lay the widow, her hair slightly loose, struggling in the arms of one of the farmers. Jiro snapped awake. The woman giggled and said something in a low voice, and the man relaxed his grip. She sat up on the pallet and languidly loosened the top of her robe. It fell to her waist, and she peered coyly at her companion from beneath the loose strands of hair. He lay back on the pallet, and she wiggled her shoulders. Her plump tits bounced, the nipples prominent dark, dancing at their tips. The man seized her impatiently, and she lay on him while he pulled off her robe. She had a full, muscular backside and thick, short legs. Jiro could see the shadow formed by the dark hairs that peeped like a little beard from between the columns of her thighs. The man grasped her shoulders and rolled her over. Jiro could see his rampant prick, a shiny drop of lubricant decorating its tip.

The man took his cock in one hand and shook it several times. She spread her legs waiting for him. Her dark bush shadowed the lower part of her belly. The plump lips were almost obscured by the thicket. Her hand snaked between her legs, and she teased the lips open, affording Jiro a full look at her red cunt slit. Then the man's muscular body covered hers, and her knees came up slightly. The man heaved into her, and she uttered a sigh. Her face was obscured by the man's untidy hairdo, and then uncovered as he bent to suck at a nipple. Her eyes were closed, and she was breathing heavily as the lusty peasant ploughed into her. His buttocks moved in a rhythm that became rapidly faster. He grunted and she gasped as his passion reached a climax. The man stiffened as she looked reproachfully at his slack face. His arse jerked several times as his pent-up passion siphoned through his cock and flooded her interior.

He lay on her as if dead for a while, until she shook him off impatiently. There was disappointment on her face, but she brightened as a muffled voice called from behind the door. The man rose and wiped himself with his loincloth. He stretched and looked at her with a smile. She lay there, one finger teasing her glistening clitoris, the other behind her head. He left, and another young man came in.

This one dropped his clothes hurriedly and knelt between her parted legs. He pushed forward with a will. A short, stocky youth, he found it hard to thrust deeply into her while holding her breasts. At last he abandoned the attempt and withdrew. She looked at him in surprise. Grasping her hips he turned her over on her face. She protested, not too sincerely, at his mode of entering her. He pulled back for a moment, affording Jiro a clear look at her plump buttocks, bisected by the dark line that shadowed her anus. Below he could clearly see the mossy lips of her cunt, still glowing wetly from the intrusion of the man's stubby cock, which pointed like an arrow at her opening.

The young peasant lad regarded the sight for a moment. Almost shyly he stroked the warm, soft buns. His cock jerked several times in anticipation. The widow smiled at him over her shoulder, then leaned forward and placed her head on her hands. The stocky lad — Jiro thought he could not be older than fifteen — bent forward as if hyptnotised. He bit softly at the woman's prominent buttocks, and she urged him on with a soft cry. His tongue came out, and he licked the twin half moons lovingly. His tongue dipped lower, and he tilted his head, the better to get at the honey between her legs. She whispered at him, and then her hand came out from between her legs and sought his erect cock. She squeezed and rubbed it for a long while as he crouched over her back. He toyed with the plump breasts that hung down before her, and she peered back at his cock, framed by his hands and her own breasts and thighs. At last he gasped and fell forward. His stubby pole sought the delicious entrance, and he entered her cavern.

Jiro could see that the stimulation had proved too much for the lad. His body shook and his buttocks danced as if struck by palsy. He writhed like a hooked fish, and she arched her back, urging more of his meat into herself. She stuck one hand back and massaged her hot clitoris, accompanying him in his frenzy. At last she collapsed forward, panting hard. Oblivious of the world, his face wreathed in a smile, the peasant lad lay over her. Above them both, Jiro gritted his teeth and turned over to try to get some sleep.

A warm, soft body laid itself down by Jiro's side. She slid a hand down his body and whispered, 'Are you awake?'

He responded by reaching for her. They felt one another in silence for a while. Her tits were small and firm, their nipples erect.

'I need it so badly, Mr Samurai — I hope you won't mind.

I watch my mother from the loft, and . . . you know, I have to amuse myself. The young men . . . I like them, but of course they are from the village and one of them will marry me, so they can't . . . they can't . . .'

Jiro stroked her shoulder. 'I understand.' The peasants, he thought, were not proper people. Some expected their women not to have sex before marriage, but in another village they might demand it, and in still others they did not marry at all but mated when lust overtook them. What mean people they were.

Her stroking hand reached the length of his penis, which was squeezed between them, and she gasped as she became conscious of the reality of its size. He stroked the insides of her thighs. The long beard that lay between them was moist with dew. He could tell she had been playing with herself, from the slick state of her fingertips. He fingered the fleshy tip of her small clit for a second. She squirmed against him, her mound pushing roughly into his palm. Her efforts at his staff grew frantic and rough. She jerked at the honey pole urgently and was rewarded with a drop of moisture as his weapon cleared its throat.

He lowered his head to kiss her nipple, proudly erect in the dark, but she moaned, 'No, no,' deep in her throat and pushed his head away. She rolled back onto the hay, spreading her legs as wide as she could. 'Please, now, now!' she demanded feverishly.

He knelt between her legs, looking down for a moment at the picture they made in the dimness. Her pale body was spread in an inviting Y, a dark patch at the juncture of her legs. His massive balls hung down, pulling him by their weight, while his pole projected aggressively forward.

She looked at his face for a moment; then her eyes followed his. The thick end of his pole was pointing her way. She wondered perversely what it would feel like in her mouth, on her tits, then drove such unnatural thoughts from her mind. Impatiently she reached for the source of her pleasure. He lowered his body, and the tip of his pole poised at the hungry entrance to her cunt. She arched her body upwards and pulled ferociously at his buttocks. He came down heavily upon her waiting body. There was a momentary resistance and a gasp from her, and Jiro knew she had been a virgin. Then her arms and legs clamped hard around him and her teeth bit into his shoulder.

He thrust his way well up her lubricated channel, and she grunted at the feeling and the weight. He started a back-and-forth movement, and she held on to his body grimly. He dug his hands through the hay and clutched her firm buttocks. She squirmed in his grasp, but her grip did not slacken. It was obviously up to him to move for both of them, and he set to work with a will. Her channel was tight enough so that every thrust was an effort as she clung to him like a dead weight. Annoyed, Jiro started pummelling her with his cock in earnest. The full weight of his erect penis smashed into her, her hips bruised by the weight of his loins. She began a snorting, stertorous breathing, and he paused, afraid that his violence was killing her. Her hands clamped onto the muscles of his back, then shifted to his arse and dug in, urging him on.

The urgent movement was too much for Jiro. He let himself go completely, pounding into the girl's passive body. At last she began to respond, her hips matching his movements. She threw her head back, and he could see the whites of her eyes and the dark cave of her mouth. He forced his tongue into her mouth, and she barely responded at first, then began to suck at his mobile upper cock with enthusiasm. They twisted wildly in the sweet-smelling grass until Jiro felt his balls twitch in violent orgasm. Streams of sperm jetted out and flooded her hot interior. She responded with an orgasm of her own, as she imagined his cock filling every orifice she had.

She relaxed her grip and smiled at him in the dark.

'That was very good, Mr Samurai. It was wonderful. It was the most wonderful thing that ever happened to me. Now I know what it is to be married. I must be married very soon.'

He smiled in the dark. 'There is more to marriage than that. Perhaps I should teach you other things, too. . . .'

'Oh, no — I am only a peasant girl. This will do very nicely.'

'But there are many other things men and women can learn to do,' he protested half-heartedly.

'I know, Mr Samurai — I have seen my mother through the crack here, many times. But I had rather learn them from my husband. Otherwise he will think I was not a good girl.'

Jiro shook his head in disbelief.

She left him as the sounds of the young men's goodbyes came through the wall. Jiro lay back and prepared for sleep. His cock was pleasantly flaccid on his thigh. He wondered what his friends were doing, back in Miyako. Unconsciously his hand stroked his manhood, playing with it and jerking it from side to side. In a little while, he knew, he would be wondering where Etsu had gone. Since she was unavailable, he thought philosophically, he had better stop playing with himself and go to sleep.

The hatch above his head opened, and a whisper came to him.

'Mr Samurai? Are you awake?'

He grunted assent.

'I just wanted to check that you were comfortable. Can I get you something?' The widow slipped into the loft, unable to see him in the dark. Inadvertedly she trod on his outstretched hand. In trying to avoid hurting him, she stumbled and fell onto his broad chest. 'I am sorry, terribly sorry!'

Her body was warm, soft — and completely naked. She held on to him as if to get her breath back. Jiro leisurely ran a hand down her back and between her buttocks. Her hairs were damp from a washing, and he recalled having heard the sound of sluicing water. She shivered at his touch. His other hand ran down her front, lingering on each tit and its erect nipple. He held her bush with a flat palm, then hoisted her easily over his body. She squealed; then her hands searched out his erect pole.

'Ah, it's wonderfully big?' she breathed. She tried to roll over, bringing Jiro to cover her, but he resisted. He parted her legs, then raised her in the air. The tip of his prick tickled the hairs of her pussy, and she breathed heavily: Fucking for her had been a natural thing, with no artifice. Jiro had

37

experienced experts, and he knew the game of love as none of her previous men had. He teased her crack for a long time, the tip of his cock penetrating her gently then withdrawing. She struggled in his arms, anxious for the morsel of flesh that she knew would spell relief for her demanding cunt. He delayed some more, his mouth seeking out her nipples in turn.

For a moment he poised her unmoving over his cock, then suddenly brought her down the length of his shaft until their hairs mingled. She squealed with delight and grunted as her soft, warm, lubricious interior gripped him. To prolong the pleasure he raised her again until only the tip was left in her. She struggled to lower herself again, her hair and nipples brushing his massive chest. At last he surrendered to her demands, and she straddled him with her muscular thighs, his cock stuffing her belly. She rode him wildly, as if untired by the effort of eight muscular men she had been mounted by before. Tis time she was mounting the man, and the newness of the sensation removed all her tiredness. She experimented boldly, riding high with her back arched and head thrown back, then crouching over him at full length. At times he encouraged her to grind her hips deeply onto him, and she squealed again at the sensation.

His finger slipped behind her buttocks, and she raised her arse slightly as he slid it along her juicy lips. Then, finger moistened, he tickled the brown bud of her anus. She rode him more wildly for that, driving his cock deeply into her until she could not contain her fury. Her cunt exploded with spasms of passion, her thighs clenched his, and she lowered her head to bite painfully at his chest.

Jiro raised himself on his shoulders and heels and drove into her as she forced herself downwards. Her insides were flooded for the ninth time that night as he spurted a diminished load of sperm into her cunt. She lay on him for a while as he played with her bottom and stroked her back. Then, still without a word, she rose from the loft and departed to her pallet.

Jiro fell into a deep sleep.

*

Matsudaira Konnosuke, governor of Miyako, distant relative of the Shogun, had just lifted his mistress's skirt and was smelling the fresh flavour of her cunt when he was interrupted. A low voice on the other side of the transclucent shoji door called out a message he heard only dimly. In any case, he was in no mood to be disturbed. He leaned forward and with his teeth gripped the silky blonde hairs before him, then pulled savagely. His tongue then slid out and bore through the delicate thicket to the slick pink lips below.

The long robe was twitched aside, and his mistress's lovely face looked down indulgently at him. He screwed his eyes upwards but kept on with his licking.

She trembled slightly and spread her perfect white thighs the better to accommodate him, but said, 'I'm sorry love, but Okiku has just arrived, and Oko says she wants to see us urgently.'

He rose, slipping off his loincloth, which hung like a tent over the stiffness of his erection.

'I've had a hard day. I hope this is important. You told Oko to let her in, I suppose. . . .' A vagrant thought crossed his mind. 'There's still plenty of time before she gets here from the postern gate. . . .'

His hand shot out and entrapped one of her large, perfectly shaped tits. He swept his foot forward roughly and pushed with his hips. She fell on her backside with a thump, too startled to use the *yawara* roll he had been teaching her. Parting her thighs roughly, he pushed her torso back with his shoulder, then thrust his cock bruisingly into her still-dry crack. One hand clamped on to her breast through the brocade robe she wore, and the other curved into a claw and gripped her thigh.

She giggled, pleased at the sudden attack; then the giggle turned to a gasp of pleasure as his long meat filled her hungry chasm.

'I want to come *now*, before Okiku arrives?' He thrust at her with every word, and his mouth descended cruelly to her full red lips. She turned her head aside at the last minute, but her reflexes had already taken over before she could say what was on her mind. The trained muscles of her wonderful cunt clenched around the stem that filled her. Ripples of muscular action ran down the walls of her insides, milking the gluey shaft. Her thighs clutched his muscular buttocks. He grinned with anticipation, knowing that just lying there, she could milk him dry in seconds.

'A minute,' she breathed into his ear. 'Why not have Okiku join us? You've not seen her for some time.'

He reared back and slapped her full breasts as he'd been taught. His body rocked on hers. 'That, too,' he agreed. 'But now I want *you!*'

Rosamund clutched at him and her wonderful vaginal muscles set to work again. She sucked at his mouth and tongue as her lower mouth sucked deliciously at his cock. In a few moments it was over. A rush of sperm started from his balls. He writhed and curved over her blonde form, trying to contain the pleasure to the last moment, then burst. Rosamund's insides were inundated with a flood of hoarded male juices. The pleasure was so intense that Matsudaira cried out as her interior muscles milked the last drops from his pole.

Okiku entered the room through a sliding shoji door, to find both her friends sitting demurely and sipping tea. She bowed, then knelt on the proffered cushion. She looked at two of the three people she cared for most in the world. Matsudaira Konnosuke she knew better as Goemon, and preferred him thus. He was dressed in a loose summer robe of white, bordered with a deep indigo pattern of waves and octopuses. His legs were crossed loosely before him, and the open robe showed a shapely length of thigh below and a muscular bronze chest above. His face was smooth, the lines of his features clean and sharp. His forehead had been newly shaven that morning, but his glossy topknot was unusually awry.

Facing her was one of her two female friends. Rosamund was Matsudaira Konnosuke's prisoner. But she also ruled his inner chambers with undisputed control. Okiku enjoyed looking at the foreign girl whenever she could, which was fairly often. A mass of blonde curls spilled down, framing a beautiful face with regular features. Eyes of an unusual colour and shape — blue, and rounder than was natural — stared back at her. Rosamund was dressed in a rich brocade robe, tied rather carelessly. Her feet were tucked under her, and her hands rested on her lap. Okiku could not resist a quick glance at the blonde's neckline. She loved those large, pinkish white breasts, the tops of which she could see. They were so different from her own, and so beautiful. Hidden between the beautiful thighs, just kissing the golden-furred pink slit. Okiku knew of a tattooed red rose. No doubt it was now glistening with the couple's juices. She smiled at them and broke the silence.

'After all these years, and you *still* can't tie a kimono properly!'

Rosamund turned to Goemon and laughed. 'Not when I'm in a hurry!'

Okiku bowed. 'For me?' she asked. 'You could have stayed as you were. You know I love the sight.' Then her mood changed. 'Forgive me for disturbing you. I've had a message from Jiro. He has still not found Osatsuki, but he asks us to meet him at Koya-san. He is very cautious, and the message was by word of mouth, but there is something happening there. . . .'

Goemon chewed his lip thoughtfully. 'It is not like the big man to call for help. Should we take some men with us, I wonder?'

His response pleased Okiku. She knew that both her friends were as committed to Jiro as she was.

'No, I don't think so; otherwise, he would have indicated the need. Only the three of us . . .'

'It will take some doing.' Goemon warned. 'Fortunately it is after the court sessions for this week, and I can plead the need for some retreat from the heat . . . I'll go to Hiei-san again.' In the past few years, Matsudaira Konnosuke had become somewhat devout. He had taken to performing long retreats in a minor hall of Hiei-san, the temple that topped the mountain northeast of Miyako, the old imperial capital. The retreats coincided with the activities of a certain wandering doctor, Goemon by name.

'We will leave tomorrow at noon,' he decided. 'By then

I will be able to finish all my official duties. I have a suggestion, though. Let us take palanquins. The travel is swifter, and more secluded.'

Okiku nodded, but Rosamund frowned. She did not like to be reminded that her movements were circumscribed by law: officially she was a prisoner, and in any case, the Shogun, it had been said, was considering enforcing the anti-foreigner laws promulgated by his predecessors. Angrily, she bit her lip; then she bent forward to hide her emotion.

Chapter Four

During their forced march, Satsuki had a chance to observe her captors with greater attention. She was overwhelmed at first by their wildness. Their unbound hair waved in the air, their language was rough and uncouth, and their manners while eating or addressing her were vile. Then, as the day wore on she noted certain things. the wild manner was not natural with many of them. Some of her captors used words and concepts that seemed well above their station. One of them, passing a yellow blooming field of rape flowers, cited a short line she knew as a court poem.

They chatted among themselves, seemingly in no hurry once they had left the environs of the city. By choice they walked the ridges and kept to the forested places. Most peasants gave them a wide berth, some bowing deeply as they passed. The *yamabushi* took no notice except to shield her from sight with their bodies. The light bonds they had tied her with were hidden by her voluminous sleeves, which were becoming dirty. The heat of the day and the exercise began to take their toll. Satsuki's steps began to falter. Her feet hurt, and her tongue was dry. They urged her on, one with blows of his staff. She sobbed silently for a while, protestingly, then was taken up on the back of one of the *yamabushi* and rode there in relative comfort.

By late afternoon they were far from Miyako. They stopped for the night in the grove of an old shrine, seemingly abandoned. An old peasant saw the band entering the grove and hurried off. Later other peasants arrived bearing food. The leader of the band, a man Satsuki had heard being called Tsuneyoshi, wrote out charms for them in the light of a fire. She watched him bent over the travelling box he had carried all day, which served him as a desk. Smooth features and graceful fingers seemed to belie the image of wildness conjured by the masses of hair and the strange garb. He

45

watched her covertly from behind the screen of his locks while he wrote.

When the last of the peasants had left, he came and squatted by her side. She waited patiently, hands in her lap. It had not occurred to her to cry out for help to the peasants. He smiled at her in the dark. His eyes glittered in the firelight.

'You do not want to escape? I note you made no sign to the peasants. . . .'

'But my dear sir, what could they possibly do?'

'Nothing much,' he grunted. 'And you? Do you know why you are here?'

'Of course not. Though I assume you will tell me in due time.'

Her composure seemed to startle him. 'Most townswomen would be screaming the place down — unless they join us by choice, of course.'

She shook her head. 'Forgive me — I am sure it would be delightful, but I have commitments, customers. . . .'

He grinned. 'The only customers you've got are ours. And us, of course, though we are your family now. Old Uchibei is properly dead, and you do not owe his customers a thing.'

'Forgive me for contradicting you,' she said in a low voice while ducking her head. 'I was never a part of Uchibei's people. This morning his men kidnapped me and brought me to the house you found me in. I am so glad you let me out.'

He reared back in surprise. 'I am sorry,' he said formally in somewhat different tones. 'I had assumed you were one of his stable we missed. . . .'

'Stable?' she said coldly.

Discomfited by her tone more than by anything else he said vaguely, '. . . Well, you know . . . the women he owned.'

She bowed again. 'I am afraid not. I am Osatsuki of Gion. I would be delighted to entertain you there. Your men did not give me a chance to explain. I am sure some compensation could be arranged for you when you return me. . . .'

He rocked slightly on his heels and laughed. 'So sorry. We're on our way to the Festival of Summer Peak, to celebrate. You will have to come with us. It is dangerous for a woman, particularly one of your appearance, to be out on her own. Of course, you will have to work for your keep. You won't mind that, will you now?' His eyes glittered over her. 'After all, it is religious work that we do. I think we should see what you have to offer, at least until our own girls get here.' He grabbed her shoulders and bore her backwards onto the mat-covered ground.

Satsuki forebore resistance. He opened her robe; less violently now that he could feel that she was not about to resist. His henchmen gathered round, anticipating their turn and enjoying the spectacle. Tsuneyoshi trailed his fingers down her chest. The sensation was not unpleasant, she decided. His index finger lingered for a while in the dip of her navel. He bent forward, and the tip of his tongue emerged. She smiled at him encouragingly. With a reflexive motion he bent his head as if to use his tongue on her. One of the men, who had crouched down to see better, moved. The sound broke the spell. He looked at her relaxed face sharply. She sighed, a low sound, for his ears only. His finger left her navel and trailed to the top of her dark bush. He toyed with the gleaming dark hairs for a short while.

His other hand was fumbling with the bow knot in front of his baggy pants. She noticed his distraction.

'Oh, excuse me!' she exclaimed in a low voice. Her slim hand snaked out and released the tie. His fingers dipped between her plump nether lips, and a faint musky perfume rose between the locks of hair that framed his face. She released the trousers and pulled them down, then felt for his white loin-cloth. Within she could feel an iron bar, warm to touch through the cotton. His fingers slid into the warmth of her slit, and his rigid digit was moistened by her delicate juices. His prick sprang erect from its confinement. Looking over the mounds of her breasts, she admired its sinewy length and spread her legs to facilitate his entry. Both his hands were now free. One roamed over the mounds of her breasts, then descended to pinch and stroke her thighs and bottom. The other worked at her warm cavern, one finger, then two, then more inside her, the rest rapidly strumming her erect little clitoral nubbin. She raised her hips slightly, both to accommodate and to excite him. The deep breathing of the men beside them speeded up. He knelt between her legs. Her soft fist guided the plum-shaped head of his manroot into her waiting cunt.

He shoved forward with all his might, keeping the weight of his body on elbows and knees, looking into her face all the while. She smiled, and a small mewling sound came from her throat as their hairs met and meshed. He looked deeply into her eyes. She met his gaze frankly and unafraid. He withdrew slightly, and she let him go. The tip of his cock rested at the entrance to her cavern, and she slid her thighs caressingly over his. He started a swirling movement, dipping the tip of his member ever deeper into her waiting nether mouth. She smiled and responded with a counter-rotation of her thighs. He looked at her respectfully and started another sequence. This time he withdrew from her completely, then dipped the head only between her slickly waiting lips. He repeated the process seven times, and she sighed in proper appreciation and anticipation. Then he thrust fully into her, the entire weight of his hips descending onto her. She responded with a slight raising of her crotch and a squeezing of the base of his cock.

The other *yamabushi* crouched around them in a circle. From their impatient looks, Satsuki could tell they had no idea of what their chief was doing. Tsuneyoshi repeated his sequence of movements, and this time she responded a bit more. Again, and her hands began a roving motion on his back. Again, and the motion of her hands increased, stroking down to his bare buttocks, squeezing the muscles under the rough coat on his back, kneading his neck gently. He plunged in again, and this time she thrust up at him, meeting the power of his loins. He withdrew, and she let him go. Another repeat of the cycles, and her thighs entered the act. Again, and she began biting his exposed chest gently, licking the length of it as far as she could reach.

His moving maintained their pace for a long while. Sweat

48

beaded his forehead, and his eyes began staring out of his head with the effort. His control suddenly broke, and he plunged into her wildly and uncontrollably. She guided his weight with her thighs and arms. He rose over her in a bow. His eyes were screwed tight. Jets of sperm boiled out and splattered her waiting interior.

'Please, please!' he cried out from clenched jaws. Knowing what he wanted, Satsuki let herself go for one short, delicious moment. Her mouth opened and she gasped for air as tremours of delight shook her frame. A wave of pleasure ran through the soft tissues of her cunt, squeezing the last drops from Tsuneyoshi's manhood. He collapsed onto her, and they shuddered together for a long, delicious moment. He raised his head and stared at her for a long while.

'Would any of the other gentlemen care to indulge me?' she said respectfully as Tsuneyoshi rose from between her legs. 'I'm afraid I have not the necessities for ablutions,' she said with a sigh, aiming a glance, half-remonstrative, half-joking, at Tsuneyoshi. He cast a sharp glance in her direction, then retreated while another man took his place.

This one was far less elegant and considerate than Tsuneyoshi had been. Without pause, he aimed his rather thin cock at her overflowing cunt and lurched forward. His hands clawed at her breasts as he bucked into her like a rabbit. Though his grasping paws were unnecessarily rough, Satsuki bore it all cheerfully. The man's arse strained and drove at her. He licked, then bit at her prominent nipples. His movements got wilder and wilder. Hoarse calls came from his throat, and he bit her again, almost hard enough to draw blood.

She was about to remonstrate with him, when a shadow looked over them. A blow sent the man rolling off, still clutching at her in a violent grip. He drove at her unheedingly, his full prick driving into the skin at her thighs. The cock gushed thick white semen as Tsuneyoshi demanded furiously above them, 'Are you trying to ruin the merchandise, fool?'

Unable to answer, the man lay on his side as his seed

pumped out over her thighs and hips. Satsuki's lips compressed in shame. She would never be able to clean herself up for the next one, and that knowledge was beyond bearing. Tsuneyoshi squatted beside her and wordlessly handed her a handful of thick tissue paper.

She inclined her head gracefully, and said in a low voice, 'Thank you, sir. This will do very well,' and wiped her cunt and body, then lay back for the next one. She was saddened by their unimaginativeness, but then, perhaps that could be remedied later.

Chapter Five

They walked until noon the following day, following ridge lines whenever possible. The air was balmy and warm. Satsuki was tired from the previous day's efforts, though the walking was easier. Apparently there was less need for haste now. Tsuneyoshi walked beside her. He remained silent, except when giving orders to his men.

In the early afternoon they heard a trio of loud bangs in the distance, followed by two more. The *yamabushi*'s face brightened. One of them rushed ahead up the path and returned several minutes later.

'A festival!' he called while still running. 'In the village before us. The local shrine is having a festival!'

Their pace quickened, and they headed for the distant sounds of the drum that Satsuki now realised had been beating in her ears for some time.

'Well,' Tsuneyoshi said sardonically, 'you will have plenty of opportunity to exercise your talents.'

'Pardon me?' she replied, nonplussed.

'Lots of people at the festival,' he answered. 'We will sell your services. Usually there are several women with us. This time, until we meet our friends, you will be the only one to serve.'

'I'm not quite sure I understand — ' She broke off at the look of unbelief in his face, covered her mouth, and giggled while looking at his expression of incredulity.

'Oh, the professional part is no problem. I'm afraid I still don't know who and what you are. . . .'

He looked at her and threw his head back proudly.

'We are *yamabushi*!' he said in a deep voice.

She bowed gratefully.

He looked at her for a moment and explained. 'We study the Way. The true way of the Buddhas and Gods. We fast in the mountains, do pilgrimages, cure the sick, reach for

53

immortality. We are the followers of the sage En-no-Gyoja, who first taught the way. It is a narrow path, not for everyone. We travel from holy place to holy place, seeking for translation into the realms of the World Peak. When our rituals are performed correctly, any one of us is more powerful than an army, more pure than mountain waters. We walk on fire, to show our faith and to cure the afflicted. You will see. In a few days' time we will be in Yoshino, where you, a mere woman, may not go. There we assemble for the Summer Peak and meet with our leader, the great ascetic Daisangyoja, who will lead us in austerities and pilgrimage.' His eyes blazed at this last, and those of the group who were within hearing echoed his call.

She bowed humbly at his glory.

The village was relatively large as agricultural villages go, almost a town. There was a large house belonging to the landlord, a small tea-shop, several relatively prosperous houses, an ostler's, a community kiln, and the usual complement of common houses with neatly thatched roofs. Slightly outside the village, across a curving wood-and-stone bridge was a high gabled shrine nestled amidst a grove of ancient cryptomerias. Though the shrine was thatch roofed like all the other buildings, its thatch was new, its wooden walls well patched.

The grove, the shrine, the way from the gateless square arch to the shrine, the very village itself were thronged with people. The peasants in celebration were wearing straw sandals, and their clothes were clean. The more prosperous townsmen brought out their finest robes, most of dyed cotton, some of silk. Gaily decorated booths lined the way to the shrine. Delicious smells of grilling dried squid, dumplings, and warming sake floated in the air. Long vertical banners snapped on their bamboo poles, declaring the festival.

Satsuki looked on somewhat disapprovingly. There was little of the elegance she associated with festivals. Those of Miyako were very refined, exhibiting restraint and elegance. Here the festival goers shouted and danced, and the music was loud, with pipes and drums predominating. She followed Tsuneyoshi through the throng. People gave the *yamabushi* a wide berth. Their rough manners and haughtiness, as well as their magical powers, made them feared opponents, and few commoners cared to cross them.

They came to a clearing just outside the shrine. Some of the *yamabushi* who had hurried ahead had staked out a broad area, which was free of merrymakers. A screen of white cloth, higher than a man's head, enclosed a small area off to one corner. The cloth was printed with magical Sanskrit characters. The *yamabushi* scattered to various corners of the bare area. Some set up large chests and began a series of rituals; others dispensed medicines. Two older *yamabushi* in white sat facing one another. One held a small wand tipped with streamers of white paper. As Satsuki watched, the man holding the wand started to tremble violently. The other grasped him firmly by the knees. Mutterings came from the trembling man. The other called out, and a commoner hurried over from the sidelines, marked with straw rope, and knelt to hear the shaman's words.

Tsuneyoshi bowed her towards the enclosure. 'That is for you,' he said dryly.

'Oh, thank you,' she answered with a bright smile. 'That is most considerate.'

He grinned sardonically. 'I'm afraid you do not understand. You will entertain customers in there.' Behind the enclosure she could see a small group of young and older men looking at her anxiously licking their lips.

'But of course!' she said brightly. 'Of course I shall. So kind to ask me. I'm sure you have also arranged the necessities. . . .' Her voice trailed off, gently chiding.

'Necessities?' Tsuneyoshi gaped at her. 'There's a mat in there. Don't forget to roll it up and strap it to your back when we leave. It is yours to use from now on.'

'Certainly — how silly of me. But I've forgotten to bring any paper and of course water. . . . A brazier and tea makings would be so nice too. I'm sure you have supplied them,' she added ingenuously.

'I'll see to the supply,' he promised, surprised at himself. He gave her one lingering and doubtful look before rushing off to fulfill her commission.

She entered the enclosure. There was a grass mat spread on the ground. The space had been swept, but she was disappointed that no pains had been taken to at least rake the ground in a pleasing pattern, conducive to lovemaking. And some fresh sprigs or dried hollyhock leaves to indicate dalliance would do well too. She knelt on the mat.

The first customer slipped through the opening. He was a rather hefty townsman, perspiring freely. She smiled at him sweetly and bowed to the ground. He would simply have wrestled her to the ground while exposing himself, but she held him off with a laugh.

'Please, wouldn't you rather be comfortable? Please make yourself comfortable. Shall I loosen your robe?'

She worked that entire day. The men were exceedingly unimaginative, Satsuki found. Mostly they wanted her to lie on her back while their pricks − long and short, fat and thin, young and old − dipped into her cunt as fast as they could and spewed the contents of their balls. Then they left, not even waiting a polite period of time for her to wipe them properly. At first she tried to offer more. She moved her hips in the intricate motions she had practised as a girl, she whispered appropriate passages from classic poems in their ears, she admired their muscles and hair and skin with her hands. Few responded, and those who did, did so out of bemusement. As time went on she tried less and less, accepting them for what they were: poor peasants and townsmen out for a quick good time.

Tsuneyoshi, true to his word, brought a supply of soft paper and a small brazier for tea. Few of the men cared for either. Tsuneyoshi or one of the other *yamabushi* was always within earshot, protecting their woman if necessary. Only once did a *yamabushi* intervene.

The customer was thin faced, a deep scar across one side of his forehead. He limped into the enclosure. Satsuki had just brewed some tea. Her light gown was loose, falling off one shoulder, and her hair hung down, held only by a single ribbon. She glanced over her shoulder at him, presenting, as she knew, a charming vision of womanhood. He glanced at her and licked his lips. His eyes seemed to lose their focus, and he stared at her blindly, as if lost in thoughts of long ago. He dropped his robes feverishly, and his loincloth followed. she turned to rise and help him, but he leaped forward and bore her back. She made some slight resistance to increase his pleasure. Instead of responding appropriately, he pummeled her roughly to the ground. He knelt over her, her thighs under his shins, and stared wide eyed at her spread figure. With a sob he slapped her half-parted thighs, and she spread them further, trying to indulge the poor man. His breathing was heavy, and saliva collected on his lips.

He slapped her breasts again and again, muttering, 'I've got you, woman; now I've got you,' then plunged forward deeply into her. She stroked his shoulders as he began to move. He pulled out and looked at her, anger enlarging his eyes to frightening proportions. He grasped her hips roughly and forced her over on her belly. He pulled her back and entered her from behind. It was a pleasant variation on the monotony of the day, and Satsuki responded by moving her arse in a wide circle, something she knew was a good preliminary. He cried out something inarticulate, then slapped her buttocks. She knew some men preferred a bit of violence with their women and did her best to comply with his pleasure, ignoring the pain. He screamed at her this time, and withdrew from her again.

Suddenly she felt the sticky knob of his cock poised at her rear entrance. Although she had no overt objection to that way of entry, she felt she should stand on her right to some preparation. She turned her head and started to say, 'Dear sir, please – ' when he grinned savagely at her and lunged forward. A burning pain, unexpected and therefore unbearable, lanced up her bottom. Satsuki responded by trying to pull away. He yelled in triumph and his blows rained down on her buttocks. Suddenly terrified, she heard the slithering-clinking sound of steel being drawn. Her calm shattered, she tried to pull away from the hold on her neck.

There was a rough cry, the sound of a blow, and the

57

weight was gone from her back. She rolled over and away, conscious suddenly of the ridiculous figure she cut, stopped, and came to her knees. The scar-faced man was on all fours, one of the *yamabushi* standing over him. The *yamabushi* held his staff at the ready, while the man heaved with racking dry sobs and tried to crawl away. A short-sword lay on the mat.

'Please let him go,' Satsuki said in a low voice.

'He was about to kill you!' the *yamabushi* responded angrily. 'We do not allow this sort of treatment to a member of the band!'

'Nonetheless, I beg of you, please let him go.'

The *yamabushi* looked at her doubtfully, then at the blade. He bowed his head once, then gave the cowering man a kick in the ribs.

'Get out of here, animal! If you ever come round us again, that will be your end!' He took several threatening steps forward as the man scrambled away, rose to his feet, and hobbled off, bent over his hurting side.

It was an exhausting way to make a living, she decided that evening, but the rewards were pleasant. And of course, it was infinitely more interesting than her previous effete life as a *kuge* noblewoman in the old city of Miyako. The *yamabushi* feasted that night on a rich vegetable soup and white rice. Satsuki ate delicately, knowing that greed would impair her faculties. She was somewhat piqued to note that none of the *yamabushi* required her services that night. Consoling herself with the thought that with training they would improve, she composed herself for sleep. In the morning they would be moving on through the mountains.

Chapter Six

The inn was not sumptuous, but adequate rooms were provided for rich travellers and samurai, their retainers, and their women. It was common to see even high-class nobles travel on pilgrimages in the summer, and Matsudaira Konnosuke's retinue, travelling badgeless, aroused no comment. Goemon, Okiku, and Rosamund made themselves comfortable in a suite of rooms overlooking an interior garden.

Night fell. They dined on a stew of mountain vegetables, taro, and loach cooked in cheesy bean curd. A young maid served them. She was a small thing with an unusually large bust. As she bent over, the front of her robe would part, revealing enormous globes that almost, but not quite, rivalled Rosamund's own.

She left after asking them if there was anything else they needed. Rosamund followed Goemon's thoughtful gaze as the maid left the room, and her bare foot nudged Okiku. Okiku grinned in agreement and looked at Goemon maliciously. An idea took shape in her mind, and she smiled at her friend and raised an eyebrow. Then something else attracted her attention. Casually she gathered her feet under her and tapped her rice bowl with her chopsticks. Goemon shifted slightly on his seat, holding his bowl loosely in his left hand. Okiku's hand flipped back over her shoulder with a long dagger held ready. Goemon held the rice bowl for throwing as a quoit.

'Pardon me for disturbing you, Lord Matsudaira,' a polite voice said from the veranda. There was something familiar about it, but Goemon could not pin it down.

'May I?' asked the invisible owner of the voice.

Not to be outdone, Goemon first took another mouthful of rice. 'Please do,' he said.

There was a step and an armed figure, dressed in black

61

from head to foot, bowed to them on one knee from the veranda.

'Hanzo!' breathed Okiku.

Hattori Hanzo, the shogun's spymaster, bowed in acknowledgement. 'I have a message.'

There was only one possible source for that message. Matsudaira Konnesuke, in the usual course of things Governor of Miyako, when occasion demanded an *onmitsu*, a private agent of the Shogun, bowed in respect.

'There is a rumour of unrest among the people. The *yamabushi*, some of them at least, are following a new leader. He claims descent from En-no-Gyoja, or worse. Such could upset the current delicate situation.'

Goemon nodded thoughtfully. He knew what it meant. In the south, Christianity, fomented by Spain, was making headway notwithstanding edicts against it. In the centre of the country a populist religious movement such as that of En-no-Gyoja, founder of the *yamabushi* order several hundred years before, could have grave consequences for the peace of a country which had been riven by civil war for the preceding hundred years.

'You must investigate, if possible terminate, and report.'

'This may accord well with something we have heard. One of us is currently investigating. . . . Do you have any other information?' demanded Goemon.

'There is to be a great meeting of his followers in the Yoshino mountains. We hesitate to arrest him. It would definitely cause more unrest. The leaders of the Tozan-ha and the Hozan-ha, the two main divisions of the *yamabushi*, support us, and this new leader will not be permitted to go to the Summer Peak rituals with them, but he will be advancing on his own, perhaps from Mount Koya.' The black-clad man bowed in farewell, then in a less formal tone added, 'I am glad to see, Lord Matsudaira, that you are keeping a close eye on your prisoner.' He bowed again and was gone.

'Could Jiro be somehow aware of this? I wonder,' Goemon said thoughtfully. 'I wish the big man would let us know where he is. And what he is doing. In any case I should not be too late in my return.'

'To return to the matter at hand?' Okiku said, as if continuing an interrupted sentence.

'Yes, indeed,' said Rosamund. 'You were interested in that little big-boobed maid, weren't you, Goemon?'

He smiled. 'They were not a patch on yours, my dear, but quite adequate.'

'If we weren't here you'd bed her immediately, wouldn't you?' queried Okiku maliciously.

He entered into the spirit of the game. 'Of course I would. I'm entitled to such pleasures as are necessary to my well-being.'

'How would you do it? After all, you wouldn't beg such a chit, would you? Like you beg me sometimes?' Rosamund leaned forward, her eyes bright. She moved her shoulders suggestively, and her full breasts swayed under the light material of the robe she had put on after her bath.

'Of course not!' The very idea seemed to shock him, and both girls giggled lightly. 'I'd order her here and have my way with her!'

'Nonsense!' snorted Okiku. 'She'd lodge a complaint against you. You're not the lord of this demesne.'

'True,' Goemon winked, 'but I have influence . . . Besides,' he added in a serious tone, 'do you really believe a serving maid at a public inn would complain about being played with by a high-ranking samurai, even if she were not ready for it?'

Okiku nodded. 'It's true. Most commoners would fear to report or complain, even if the law were on their side. The richer a man is, the more the law is on his side.'

'That's not what I meant!' Goemon cried indignantly. 'The law is upheld for all regardless. I am a magistrate, and I tell you that. I meant she would be pleased nonetheless, because of the chance of favour. . . .'

'No matter,' Rosamund said, seeing the cynical look on Okiku's face. 'I want you to do it!'

'Do what?' Goemon had lost the thread of the argument.

'I want Matsudaira Konnosuke to call for the young maid with the fat tits, order her to lie on her back, and mount

63

her, you oaf. We, of course, will stay here to see that your comfort is provided for.'

Goemon looked at her doubtfully. He rubbed his shaven pate and looked at his mistress out of the corner of his eye. 'Pardon me for asking, Lady Rose, but what do you get out of it?' he asked suspiciously while bowing with exaggerated politeness. He knew that Rosamund was indefatigable in search of her pleasure, and though she was prepared to share him with her friends, that was on a reciprocal basis. In addition, Okiku seemed to be in cahoots with the blonde, and from experience he knew that the dark girl's manipulations could be painful at times.

Rosamund bowed just as politely. 'Why, master, to ensure your pleasure, what else?' she asked sweetly. At her side Okiku bowed politely too, though she could not hide the glint of a smile. 'You couldn't possibly fear such a suggestion?' Rosamund added.

Goemon made a face. He knew she was baiting him, hoping for a beating perhaps. Her indulgence in sex mixed with pain was a source of constant amazement to him, as well as a goad.

Goemon called for service impatiently. The sliding fusuma door, painted with a faint view of an island in the sea, slid open. The maid was kneeling in the anteroom. She bowed, and the nightingale floor sang under her as she moved her weight. The guard outside the door looked in and, satisfied that all was well, resumed his vigil with his back to the room. Goemon motioned the girl to enter.

'Close the door,' he added as an afterthought.

'Remember you are a samurai!' Okiku whispered his favourite exhortation to him as they watched the maid approach. She was short and rather plump. Her slightly crossed eyes gave her face a puzzled look. Her feet were bare and clean. Most impressive was the front of her dove-grey kimono, which bulged pleasingly forward. She stopped to kneel, but Goemon motioned her closer. She knelt and bowed, then asked, 'Is there something . . .?'

Goemon looked her up and down for a moment, making up his mind. There was a mild cough from Rosamund. His chin firmed, and he took a breath.

'Lie down and spread your legs!' he barked abruptly.

For a moment all four froze in a tableau. The maid's eyes swung from one to the other, the rich nobleman, his small concubine, and the other, the strange woman that looked like something out of a dream: yellow hair and round eyes. Her lips parted as if for a scream or a protest. But years of training and of service in the inn took over.

'Yes!' she coughed. She lay back and spread her legs, her eyes closed.

Goemon looked at her doubtfully for a moment, as if not ready to believe his eyes. He turned to look at Rosamund. The blonde smiled back at him, then flipped her skirts up, exposing her perfect, smooth-skinned legs. She stroked the length of her own thighs, ending with both hands in her lap, barely covering the golden cloud at the junction of her legs and belly. Goemon took a firmer grip on himself.

'Open your robe!' he commanded, more surely, almost more gently this time.

The maid obeyed. Some of the fear and surprise must have left her, because there was a hint of coquettishness in her motions as she flipped back the sides of her robe and uncovered first one and then another pale thigh. Her petticoat was a bright red. Okiku leaned forward, thinking how charming the combination of colours was. A small black triangle of hair was set at the angle formed by the pale tan legs, which in turn were framed by the blood-red of the spread petticoat. The red petticoat in turn was bordered with dove grey, the entire set out against the gold of the tatami mats.

Goemon seemed entranced with the view. He looked at her spread before him for a long time. His lips pinched in thought.

'Your sash . . .'

She twisted her arms to get at the knot under her back.

'No, do not move yet,' he commanded. He leaned forward and loosened her tie with a few quick, practised motions. She was breathing slightly faster now, and with languid motions pulled the sash from under and around her.

The material made a slithering sound as it came away.

'Open your robe completely!' He commanded.

She obeyed with alacrity, her eyes open. Disappointed, she saw he was not looking at her breasts.

'Now sit up!' She smiled at his order and rose, the better to show off her most promising feature. Her breasts were large, their brown nipples jutting cheekily upwards. The half globes were smooth and full. She lowered her lids and glanced at the tips of her breasts, then at the samurai before her. He was young and pleasant-looking, his hair newly oiled after bath, his skin shining with health. She smiled slightly. He might not turn out to be a perfect lover, but with his position it did not really matter. His handsome appearance only made things pleasanter.

Goemon ran his hands over her breasts. He pinched the nipples lightly for a moment, then squeezed a breast with each hand. Each globe was larger than his palm, the nipple brushing against his skin. Still holding both breasts he pushed her back. She did not resist but assumed the position she had lain in before. He let go one breast long enough to flip back his robe, then knelt between her spread legs.

'Guide me into you!' he commanded.

Her work-roughened hand found the erect pillar of his manhood. It was thick and warm to her touch. For a moment she wondered what it would taste like, but she pushed the perverse thought from her mind. She laid the blunt tip of his cock at the entrance to her cunt lips, teasing it up and down fractionally. But before she could rub it on her sensitising flesh, he was on her.

Goemon stretched out his full length on the girl beneath him. At the same time he pushed his cock deeply into her. She was still not wet enough. His thrust rubbed against the walls of her cunt, and she grunted a bit. Without pause he pushed forward until he could feel their hairs mingling. He let her bear all his weight for a moment. Then his powerful arse muscles went into action. He pulled out of her almost the entire length of his rampant cock, then pushed it back in again, slowly this time. Grinding his hips against hers, he brought a grunt from her again. This time there was more pleasure mixed with the discomfort.

He pulled out slowly and began a steady sliding drive. The walls of her channel filled rapidly with slick juices, the smell of which penetrated to his nostrils each time the air between their bodies was forced away. He nibbled at her full breasts occasionally, his hands roaming her body freely. Her legs came up involuntarily and clutched at his heaving back. Her eyes closed, the whites showing under the full lids. Her mouth opened, and soft cries came from it. His movements speeded up, and she added the oscillations of her own full arse to his.

Rosamund and Okiku looked on in fascination. This was not the first time they seen Goemon fuck, but it was a pleasure for both of them nonetheless. The man's muscular frame easily controlled his companion's plump figure. The skin on his back and arse bunched with his effort. His topknot bobbed over the actors, its almost metronomic movements indicating the closeness of the climactic moment. Under him the maid's soft curves made a perfect contrast, highlighted by the bright red backdrop of her petticoat. Her soft round arms, their skin paler than his, snaked over his form. She was obviously taking as much enjoyment from feeling him as he from her. Her fingers traversed the length of his back, dipped between the muscles of his buttocks, fondled his balls gingerly. Their motions speeded up. Goemon closed his eyes and jerked in and out with the speed of a dragonfly's wings.

Driblets of come, heralds of the flood soon to arrive, moistened her interior, and he ground his hips against her eager pelvis. She mewled with desire and uncontrollably arched her body under him, her knees clutching at his sides, her fingers digging into his buttocks. He clenched his teeth and eyes, and pumping streams of creamy come flooded her interior. She came at the same time, her head jerking from side to side, her frame quivering.

For a long moment Goemon lay on her as if dead, his eyes glazed. Then he raised his head and looked at Rosamund and Okiku. Two sets of breasts, fully erect, stared back. Both women had bared their torsos. The upper halves of their robes lay about their waists, held by brocade sashes. He looked carefully for a long minute, his eyes clicking from one set to another as the women sat erect, hands in their laps, eyes steady. Only Rosamund, the less restrained of the two, could not contain the twitch of a smile. Her breasts, she knew, were the finest Goemon had seen. Perfect round globes, they glowed with a pale white perfection tipped with pink aureolas and darker prominent nipples, Okiku's tits were smaller and flatter but still of perfect shape. Dark aureolas forming almost perfect circles were centered by prominent nipples as erect as small stubby fingers.

Goemon rose from the maid to his knees.

'Lie down!' he commanded harshly.

Rosamund, divining his intention, made as if to rise and flee. In a flash he was on her. The smack of his overheated body on hers sent her tumbling back. The air oofed out of her as his full weight bore down. He forced his knees roughly between hers. She struggled furiously, and he pinned her down with a clenched forearm. His other hand snapped down and gripped her hip painfully, then shifted between their bodies. His fingers found her lush cunt. It was dripping with her interior moisture. Without pause he shoved two fingers inside the lubricious channel. His palm served as a guide as his slick, hard cock made its way between the full lips of her cunt.

She ceased her struggling as soon as he was well seated. Goemon, however, was carried away by the violence of the moment. His full weight came down on her soft curves as his rigid penis made its hurried way up her vagina and lodged deep in her belly. He stayed deep inside her for a moment, wriggling his hips forcefully, making her take in another fraction of his body. She responded by raising her head and kissing him on his lips. Her mouth covered his. Her tongue slid into the warm masculine cavern and submissively explored within. He licked her probing tongue, then pushed his own almost down her throat. His lips sucked at hers, extracting the taste to the full. Then his hips began pounding at hers.

With long strokes at first, then more and more rapidly, his man-tower bore into her. She greeted such assault with a yelp of pleasure, each withdrawal with a sigh that was half enjoyment for the rapid friction, half regret. Their motions slowly grew to a climax. Goemon was still seized with the mood she had worked on him. He felt he could not pause for a moment. Rosamund was so turned on by the sight she had seen earlier that her own responses were as quick as his. They were soon both panting, her teeth nipping at his neck and shoulders, his fingers squeezing, pinching, scratching her at places he knew she liked. Her whole body started to tremble uncontrollably. Shudders ran down her skin. Her arms and thighs clutched at his pistoning frame in a frenzy.

'Goemon. . . . *Goemoooon!*' his assumed name burst from her lips as a torrent sluiced from her well-lubricated insides and made a sopping mass of their entwined hairs. His own climax was a pale thing compared to hers. Spurts of milky juice jerked weakly from the tip of his cock as he stiffened in her arms. He raised his head to see Okiku's hand between her legs. She looked at him and smiled broadly, three fingers making long, slow strokes at her clitoris. Her body too began shaking with the coming climax. His teeth clenched. She was laughing at him, he knew. In his present mood, he was not prepared to consider that she laughed with him, rather than against him. Rosamund, they all knew, had wrung him dry for some minutes to come. But he was a samurai. Sun Tzu's maxim about the use of many weapons came to his mind.

'Stop!' he ordered peremptorily. Normally nothing could be better calculated to cause Okiku to disobey. This time, caught in the enchantment of the moment, she paused. Still lying with his full weight on Rosamund, who observed his actions closely, he pulled Okiku's hand to him. He sniffed at her fingers, enjoying the warm, rich smell of her randy cunt.

'Lie down!' he commanded again. Okiku obeyed and spread her legs, raising her knees slightly. His flaccid, sopping cock emerged from Rosamund's cunt with a barely audible *plop*. He knelt between Okiku's legs and bent forward to study her lower lips. They were framed in a heart-shaped forest of soft black hairs. The lips were delicate, bisected by an almost invisible line. He opened them like a flower, uncovering the tiny nubbin and hole between. Then he lowered his head and began tonguing her cunt.

He started with long, slow strokes with a flattened tongue. The slightly rough surface brought goose bumps to Okiku's thighs. His pace grew more rapid and he moistened his tongue with saliva and the inner juices from the channel between her cunt lips. He changed pace and began sucking hungrily at the tiny clitoris, which lay like a pearl within an oyster's tissues. She sighed and clutched at his head, her own head thrashing from side to side. Again his pace changed, and his tongue, stiff as a finger, drove deeply into her hungry cunt. She arched her hips in response, and her clitoral nubin was crushed pleasingly between her pubis and his teeth, which he covered obligingly with his upper lip. The lingual fucking continued, and Okiku lost control. She gave herself up to the sensation. Waves of pleasure engulfed her, and her body spasmed into controllable tremors as a wash of salty juice flooded Goemon's mouth.

Goemon raised his head and rocked back to sit on his knees. The maid bowed before him and offered a sheet of pure white paper. He wiped his lips, and then she bowed before him and wiped his cock with another sheet, admiring the proportions of the member that had been in her. Goemon grinned at Rosamund, his composure returned.

'Well?' he said, and cocked his head.

Rosamund smiled broadly and, still smiling, bowed her face to the floor. The other two followed suit. Rosamund's tits, Goemon noticed, were the only ones to touch the tatami mat.

Chapter Seven

The high sound of the flute played with a manic energy came first to Jiro's consciousness. He slid down a muddy slope, pausing for a second to adjust the strap of a sandal, when he became aware of the deeper beat of the drum. Between the trees he could just about make out the sight of smoke. The wild skirling of the *fue* flute seemed to make the smoke dance.

The mountain trail was steep, and there were few travellers. He had been told at an earlier stop that the path would shorten his road considerably. In fact, the effort was hardly worth it, though he had enjoyed the quiet of the mountain air.

The village became visible. It was a substantial one, a stopping place for pilgrims on their way to the sites farther south. The drum and flute were both heard clearly now. Perhaps, thought Jiro, he would be able to receive some news here of Satsuki and her captors.

The main street of the town was crowded with merrymakers. The fair booths lined the sides of the main street and spilled over to some of the side alleys. Sellers of children's whirligigs, fried noodles, fish-shaped waffles stuffed with sweet bean jam, and sake competed for attention.

The shrine, where he called first, was decorated with long blue banners which hung limply in the heat. A steady crowd of visitors streamed into the shrine grounds. They rang the bell hanging from the front beam, clapped their hands and bowed to the kami inside, then received a drink from the attendant. Jiro rang the bell and contributed his copper to the offertory box, then prayed for the success of his venture.

The smell from the booths was irresistible. He bought a grilled dried squid, then a bowl of wheat noodles in soup.

Most of the townsmen gave the giant samurai a wide berth. Samurai were unpredictable and uncontrollable. For the commoner, it was best to steer clear of strange ones. Later, full and comfortable, he relaxed in the shade of one of the giant cryptomerias that shaded the grounds of the shrine. The wild music continued. The musicians ensconced in a wooden tower in a wide clearing before the shrine continued throughout the afternoon, fortified no doubt by the enormous quantities of rice wine they had been drinking.

The stream of visitors increased as the sun set and people finished their daily chores. A ripple of excitement ran through the crowd. Children and adults lined the entrance to the shrine, packed as close as they could get. The shouting came closer. A tightly packed wild mob of almost naked men came into view. They carried an ornate *mikoshi* — an elaborately carved wooden shrine, decorated with a towering copper phoenix. The structure swayed and swung on its bearers' shoulders. At times it seemed to go round in circles as men armed with fans tried to control its movement. They were the only sober men of the lot. The porters shouted, '*Washoi! Washoi!*' as they came, dressed in nothing but loincloths and headbands. The staggering edifice, towering over the heads of its porters, reached the shrine. Above the head of the mob, Jiro could see another coming. He smiled. He liked the sight of the *mikoshi*. He had helped carry one not many years before.

The second *mikoshi* was smaller than the first. It was also something of a surprise. In the flickering light of the lanterns that now lit the scene, Jiro could see that some of the porters were women. Unlike the near-naked men, they dressed in tight indigo-dyed trousers, aprons, and coats favoured by some workmen in winter. But they chanted and drank as lustily as their male counterparts.

The audience greeted the appearance of this *mikoshi* with cheers. Jiro gathered by eavesdropping that having women carry a *mikoshi* was a unique local custom. Crowded together under the thick carrying pole, they presented an unusual and piquant view. Jiro laughed with the other

74

spectators. His size allowed him to see over the heads of the crowd, and he could appreciate the sight of young women enjoying heavy labour and drinking. One of them caught his eye. She was smiling like the rest, sweat running down her brow. Her coat was open, displaying the bare tops of heavy breasts. Her body, sandwiched between those of two plumper girls, was full and ripe, and Jiro could imagine the feel of the thighs that now rubbed against heavy blue cloth. Something stirred between his legs as he looked on. The sweat on the high-cheeked faces reminded him of sweat brought on by other circumstances. He shrugged in annoyance. The women he knew were far off, he had not sufficient money to pay for companionship, and in any case, he was busy. The thickening of his prick subsided.

He strolled, vaguely dissatisfied, through the throngs of merrymakers. Lurid green or red glares, the product of small fireworks set off at intervals, lit the scene. Near a small outbuilding by the side of the main shrine building, he saw a laughing group of people. The young men who had carried the larger *mikoshi* were crouched or sprawled in a circle, drinking from large clay bottles and eating festival fare. Jiro turned away. More movement caught his eye. In the light of several lanterns, the carriers of the other *mikoshi* sprawled on the ground. Their high voices identified them as women. The one who had grinned earlier at Jiro was among them. He passed between them and the light with a deliberate tread. The shadow of his massive figure and erect topknot caused the girl to look up. Her hair was held by a twisted piece of cloth that fell almost to her eyes and rode high over the long hair she had tied behind. It gave her a rakish, almost piratical appearance. She grinned at him again, and he moved on into the dark.

The girl rose and stretched mightily. 'Well, me for a bath and bed.'

'So early, Osachi? There's still plenty to drink — and to look at,' her companions joshed her.

'Ha! Just like you,' one of the men said. 'You dance and sing all day, with nothing left for the evening. . . .'

Everyone laughed, and Osachi waved at them and walked

off into the dark. She watched dancers around the drum tower, pinched a piece of friend octopus from an acquaintance's booth, and made her way slowly through the crowd. She angled off to one side, casually noting the tall samurai who no doubt had headed in that direction to relieve himself. The passage between some tall cryptomerias was dark, but it was the shortest route to her home.

Suddenly a tall figure loomed out of the dark at her. She squeaked, then covered her mouth with a hand.

'Did I frighten you, miss? I hadn't intended to do so.'

The tall samurai stood before her. She looked him up and down carefully. Behind her the light of the fires and lanterns, etched his strong face. His hair was curiously soft, even worn in the unshaven pate of a masterless samurai. His hands were large and looked as if he had known physical labour — odd for a samurai.

'What do you intend to do with me?' Since he seemed to be standing there quite harmlessly, the question seemed odd.

He smiled at the meaning behind the words. 'There's a small building deeper in the shadows.' He turned and moved off into the dark. Slowly she followed him, her heart pounding and her hands clasped before her. He stood before the old shed, used formerly as a minor shrine. He bent and kissed her. For a moment her lips resisted and her body stiffened; then she melted into his arms. He raised her into the air and deposited her on the old soft tatami, then lay down beside her. His hands slipped into her coat and around her to untie the blue apron. Thick strong fingers found first one and then the other of her nipples, and she groaned slightly. Her own hands sought a way into his split *hakama* trousers, and she mewed her frustration. It was the first time she had tried a samurai, and the intricacies of his dress defeated her. Inside the rough cloth she could feel the iron-hard bar of an enormous cock.

He pushed her hands impatiently aside and rapidly slipped out of his trousers, robe, and loincloth. His cock jutted aggressively forward as he leaned over her to untie her tight trousers of rough indigo-dyed cloth. The massive tool swung before her face, and she captured it with her mouth. It was almost too big to fit into her mouth, but he jerked forward, and a length of his shaft scraped past her teeth. The tip tasted salty and musky on her tongue, and she sucked hungrily, her cheeks expanding with the effort. She was conscious of her pants being torn off her and of the samurai's face being thrust between her legs. His unshaven cheeks scraped the insides of her thighs, and she wondered momentarily how he could bear the sweaty smell.

Overtaken by his lust, Jiro sniffed at the rich, sweaty female smell of the girl. He pushed forward, his tongue reaching for the inviting hole. It brought back memories of his first time with Okiku, the first time with a woman. He could not remember who had raped whom, at that time, but the rich, earthy smells of a sweating woman in heat always brought out a slavering beast in him. He lapped at the fleshy lips for a long time. Her hips squirmed incessantly, as if trying coyly to reject his tongue's advances. His hands gripped the woman's buttocks, and he forced his tongue deeply into her. His nose did duty for both of them, rubbing silkily against the oiled pearl of her clitoris and raising a pleasurable haze in his brain as the musky, earthy smell hit his membranes.

Jiro's cock was being sucked inexpertly by the struggling girl, and he restrained himself, knowing that it took much practice to take his entire engine in. At last the needs of the moment overtook him. He withdrew from between her thighs and pulled back from her mouth. Her eyes gleamed in the dark, and he realised that she was as ready as he. He lay flat on her, uncaring of the floor. His cock; wet and hard as a sword from the sword-sharpener's pond, poised for a second before her dripping cunt; then he drove forward.

Osachi met the samurai's stabbing thrust with a clenching of her inner muscles and a shaking of her body. Well before he had sheathed himself fully in her, she had begun a movement of her hips. Her arse came up from the floor to meet the onslaught. The little wooden building creaked as their combined weight came down.

The floorboards were moistened by their juices. She extracted every bit of pleasure she could from the body covering her. He was a stranger, well built, and she would never see him again. She satisfied every curiosity and whim she could in the silent dark, something she could not do with the local lads for fear of being too forward. Her hands roved over his back and down to his buttocks. She slipped hands between his buns and fingered his hairy arsehole. Osachi squeezed his scrotum, feeling the two eggs inside as they slapped against her rump. They were wet with juice, the hair plastered against the silky skin. He slapped her breasts with breathless annoyance when her squeezes became too rough.

She laughed inwardly at men's fragility and continued her explorations, her mind almost detached from the volcano of pleasure that was churning her slit. She tested the length of his shaft as it emerged from her tight hole. The hairs meshed in a sopping mass, and she tightened her cunt once again. There was a tremour from the bag and a rapid contraction that she could feel with the back of her hand. The man's weight descended on her, stuck to the hollow of her thighs like a leech. She felt waves of pressure shoot up the fleshy hose and inundate her insides. Gratefully she surrendered to the sensation.

They writhed for a long moment, their hips joined, his tongue forcing its way into her willing mouth.

The sweat cooled on their bodies in the dark as they lay side by side. Osachi's rough hands stroked Jiro's massive chest, and she nibbled at the skin over his ribs.

'What are you doing here! We see very few samurai.'

'I'm looking for a friend, kidnapped by *yamabushi*. Have you seen any such?'

She laughed. 'Many, of course. This is the season for their mountain pilgrimages. Some of them come through all the time, but particularly now. Why, there was a group that came here just two days ago. They would have stayed for the festival, but they were hurrying to their meeting at Mount Yoshino. They gather there every year for a pilgrimage. Usually they have women with them, but this time there were only two. I must say the boys were disappointed.' She sniffed deprecatingly. 'It's not as if they were deprived here. Why, I've had two boys a night crawl into my bedding. . . . There's even one I'm going to wake up and scream for.'

'Wake up and scream for?' Jiro asked in puzzlement.

'Of course! The one I'm going to marry.' Osachi turned on her side and looked at him, then laughed. 'Why, how does a city girl choose a husband then, eh? The boys here come and visit at night, and if you like him, you wake your father and then . . . But until then, we can have a little fun, no?'

'Judging from how you perform, a lot of fun.'

She laughed in response and poked him in the ribs.

'He'd probably get away though, wouldn't he?'

'Mostly the father goes and arranges it with *his* father. But get away? From me? Ha! Goro will never get away from me.'

'How would you hold him?' Jiro teased.

'With my legs, of course. Like this.' Osachi swung herself onto his supine form. Her wet pussy smacked against his flaccid prick. She rubbed herself back and forth on his member. Her fingers stroked her tiny clitoris with each move and incidentally brought more pressure onto Jiro's manhood. Slowly the soft roll of flesh thickened and hardened. The slickness of the lips that bracketed the skin of his sensitive cock hardened his penis as few other things could. He raised his hands and lifted her in the air. His cock sprang free, and Jiro positioned her hungry opening over the tip, then let go. Gratefully she sank down, her nether mouth engulfing the thickness gratefully. He raised her again, then brought her down forcefully onto his body. She scratched his chest with strong fingers and grinned at him in the dark. She tried to rise and slide down his pole again, but he would have nothing of it. She struggled in his arms for a moment. He slipped his hands to her hips

79

and started a rotating movement of her hips.

'Like a *suribachi*,' she giggled, and started grinding her hips on him.

Jiro released his hold on her hips, and the girl ground herself into him, humming a song women used when grinding sesame into paste in a ribbed *suribachi* mortar. The young samurai laughed at her. His hands slid around her bottom. One finger poised for a moment, then slid deeply into her anus. Osachi's tongue peeped out of the corner of her mouth, and her eyes closed. The twirling motion of her hips continued, and Jiro felt waves of pleasure engulfing him. The fingers of his other hand felt along the shaft of his cock. He nipped her slick lips, which were unusually long, between thumb and forefinger and strummed the sweet flaps of flesh. She shivered, and he increased the speed of his motions. His stiff finger probed unceasingly into the tight ring of her anus while he arched his back slightly.

Oscachi trembled and sighed slightly, and from the sudden rush of moisture, Jiro knew that she had come. He was not yet ready, and his fingers continued their dance in her anus and along her liquid lips. Her eyes opened, as did her mouth, and she looked down at him for a long moment. Her hips stopped their churning, and before Jiro could do anything, she had risen from his probing cock without a word. He started to scowl and pull her toward him, but she poised herself for a long delicious moment above his cock. The full, muscular half moons of her buttocks were parted by the erect column of his rampant prick. She pulled at his hand, and his finger popped out of her nether hole. She moved her hips forward and the tip of his male sword barely nudged the tight ring of her anus. She looked down at him fiercely.

'Don't you dare move!' she whispered fiercely.

She lowered herself gradually onto the waiting prick, her thighs ridged with muscular effort. She raised her head in pain as the fleshy sword parted her lubricated bottom. The size was almost too much for her. She bit her lip and forced herself downwards. The flanges of the cock head passed the constraining ring of muscle, and she felt the long, slick shaft make its way up her. She let herself down farther until she could feel the stiff hairs of his crotch scratching against her soft bottom.

Osashi stopped, amazed at herself, at her temerity, her perversity, the very fact that there was a strong cock, full of lust, resting up her arsehole. She looked down at the man beneath her, but for the moment he was as remote as the *harigata* of wood she used on herself when she was particularly randy and no lover had come by. She raised herself and felt the long column pull reluctantly out of her depths. Before the head could extract itself, she had plunged down again. She repeated the process, and as it became easier, so did the pleasure increase. The man beneath her reached for her empty cunt, but she pulled his hand aside. She held her cunt lips open with four fingers on either side. The longest finger of each hand dipped into the waiting sweet hole, and her thumbs squeezed her prominent clitoris. Sliding her hands over the inner recesses of her cunt and moving her arse up and down the male shaft that impaled her, she masturbated to a climax.

Jiro lay beneath the girl and watched as she used their bodies. The tightness of her anus began reaching to him, and gradually, as she dreamily played with her cunt while riding his cock, he felt his own pleasure reach a climax. She shuttered on top of him, then again. Small climaxes grew on top of one another until her body was shivering in a continous Saint Vitus' dance. Mewling sounds came from her throat. Jiro noted all this through a haze. Pinned by her thighs he felt helpless, unable to employ his massive strength. At last the tightness of her anus was too much for him. The sound of her enjoyment, the juices and smells of her body brought on an explosive climax. Streams of come flooded her interior, and the straining of his hips collapsed her to his side.

They lay quietly together for a long while. He felt her over lazily, his fingers dipping into the pool of juices between her buttocks and along her thighs. She sighed with contentment, aftershocks of pleasure racking her body when

81

he touched particularly sensitive points. The tremours died down, and they lay quietly together while the drums played into the night.

Before she left he asked casually, 'Those *yamabushi* you saw — do you know where they are headed?'

'To the entrance to the Yoshino sanctuary. They are a closed-mouthed group, but their leader, the *daisendatsu*, is a man they call Daisangyoja.'

Jiro bowed his thanks as the *mikoshi* carrier slipped away, then curled up in the warm dark to sleep.

Chapter Eight

The hills the *yamabushi* group were walking through now were higher and much wilder-looking. They followed a highway traversed by crowds of pilgrims. Most were dressed in traditional white: gaiters, trousers, jackets, and hats. Some sported banners that proclaimed their destination. Most of them, Tsuneyoshi explained, were heading for the great monastery at Mount Koya, where the sage Kobo Daishi, founder of the Shingon sect of Buddhism, was buried. As they walked Tsuneyoshi expounded on Shingon lore and told Satsuki tales of magic and demons that made her head spin. He also explained something of their own objective. He and his band were followers of a *daisendatsu*, a master of the *yamabushi*. This master, Daisangyoja by name, a true holy man, was envied by other *yamabushi* leaders. Daisangyoja had called a meeting of his followers to perform a pilgrimage to the holiest of *yamabushi* sites, the mountains of Yoshino. There, he had promised his followers, he would perform a miracle that would reaffirm his claims, strengthen his powers, and overwhelm his opponents.

'All of that?' asked Satsuki innocently.

Tsuneyoshi peered at her suspiciously from between his hanging locks. She was not, as far as he could determine, laughing at him.

'Yes,' he said gruffly. 'The Master will reaffirm the principles of the universe with his ritual. He will cleanse himself and us, and at the end of the ritual of the Summer Peak, he will announce himself to the world. The millenium will then surely come to this bright land of ours.'

She bowed in respect for the miracle as they walked.

By evening they were at the outskirts of a substantial village, almost a town. There was drumming going on, and the unmistakable smell of a festival.

85

On a wooden hill outside the village nestled a large thatched-roofed shrine. Several vermillion-painted gateposts marked the entrances to subsidiary shrine buildings. the giant cryptomerias that shaded the shrine sighed in the wind, ignoring the bustling crowds below them. Visitors came to pay their respects, receiving their sip of wine and seaweed, a share of the kami's bounty, in return.

The *yamabushi* began looking around anxiously. Satsuki was beginning to feel apprehensive herself, when they were hailed. Greetings were exchanged, and the two bands of Daisangyoja's followers retired to a side clearing in the wood. Around them swirled a cloud of humanity, warned away as before by the paper-festooned ropes. The *yamabushi* prepared themselves for their various performances. Boxes were unpacked, the shamans and their assistants sought out corners of the forest. Tsuneyoshi and the leader of the other band headed off into the growing darkness, in the direction of the shrine.

Satsuki was conducted by one of the *yamabushi* to a secluded corner. There was no screened area prepared for her here. She knelt on her mat, waiting passively for her work to begin.

'Well, look what we 'ave 'ere.' The rough voice interrupted her thoughts. Satsuki turned her head slowly. In the gloom, which was slowly being lit by flambeaux and candles, she could see three female figures. They were dressed in bright, though stained travel clothes. All three wore their hair unbound. They sprawled gracelessly on the ground. One of them spoke again, her accents the rough village accents of Kyushu Island.

'Oo're you, lovey? So pretty and fine you look.' She laughed loudly. 'A proper lady, ain't cha?'

Satsuki bowed slightly from her seat. 'Osatsuki of Miyako, at your service.'

'Wot a luverly snotty accent she've got.' The second slattern's tones were if anything rougher than the first's.

'Leave her alone!' said the third figure. Her speech was as rough as the two others', but she spoke in a kindly tone. 'I am Midori. Please do not worry. I understand from some of our men that you are new to the band. However, we will take care of you. . . .'

'Sure, sure,' sneered one of the others. 'We'll 'ave to tyke you down a peg too, Midori love. . . .'

The one called Midori rounded on her companions in fury. 'Shut up!' she hissed at them. 'Or I'll brain you.' Either the tone of her voice or the rock she held in one fist convinced them, because the two women cowered and muttered among themselves.

'Really, this is quite unnecesary. I do hope we can be friends,' said Satsuki ingenuously.

The others chuckled out of the darkness. 'Well, at least we'll have to work together, so we might as well be friends.'

They chatted idly for a while, waiting for the screened area to be erected. All three girls had been living with their band for some time. They travelled the breadth and length of the country, from one pilgrimage centre to another, servicing, the pilgrims and the townsmen alike. They had been from Mount Haguro in the north to the eighty-eight pilgrimage sites of Shikoku to the south. They were from similar backgrounds. Midori, the third daughter of a poor craftsman, had run away from home and joined the *yamabushi*. The other two came from poor farm families and had run away as well.

'Ah, there is Hachibei.' One of the three women raised her head expectantly.

Satsuki saw Tsuneyoshi approaching through the crowds, accompanied by a *yamabushi* she assumed was Hachibei. Both men seemed very excited. They stopped and spoke to the men in the compound, and messengers raced off into the darkness. Eventually the two approached the kneeling women.

'This is the one I mentioned to you, Elder Brother.' Tsuneyoshi indicated Satsuki. The other looked her over carefully, and his breath hissed from his teeth. He laughed and shook his head. 'It is a shame we must refrain from sex for the next day, as the firewalking ritual requires. Otherwise I would like to receive your permission to try her.'

87

Satsuki bent her head and murmured, 'I am honoured.' But her formal greeting was eclipsed by the other women's exclamations of surprise.

'A firewalking? How wonderful!' There was an excited feminine babble.

'Yes, I am afraid you will not be able to work tonight. We must prepare the ground anyway. The shrine priest is of the Shogun sect, and he has given permission to perform the ritual. The portents have been rather bad for the region, and he is anxious to perform a prophylaxis.' The two men moved off while the women relaxed and chatted.

The firewalking grounds were surrounded by a rice-straw rope decorated with straw wisps and paper streamers. Expectant spectators, hoping for the benefit of the ritual, surrounded the flimsy yet powerful barrier. In the middle of the rectangle was a pile of wood and brush. Additional wood was piled nearby. The *yamabushi* were dressed in their best, and they had stationed themselves self-importantly in the various appropriate positions. The ritual was long and complicated. Prayers were said. A large conch trumpet was blown. One *yamabushi* shot arrows at the four directions. Others blew water and waved sprigs of an evergreen bush.

The pile of brush was lit, and bright flames leaped forth. The *yamabushi* chant rose in volume. The pillar of flame grew and then gradually died down. Eventually only a pile of glowing coals remained. Some of the *yamabushi* spread the coals more evenly using long green branches.

Hachibei rose and stepped out of his wooden pattens. Satsuki, kneeling on her grass mat in the crowd of other *yamabushi*, could see only his broad back. From the set of his shoulders she could see that he was calm, unconcerned. Before him the coals glowed with a ruddy light, a twinkling field some thirty feet long. He stepped forward unhurriedly, placing his feet deliberately. Without pause he strode out on to the coals and across them. Satsuki could not see his face, but there was no indication that he even felt the glowing heat under the soles of his feet. Tsuneyoshi rose next. He spared a single glance at Satsuki, whether out of concern for her or for the ritual she could not tell. He strode quickly across the orange sea, and another rose to follow him. A drum was playing all the while, and the beat entered Satsuki's blood, bringing an almost painful feel of expectation.

'Do not be afraid!' Midori whispered beside her. 'Trust in Amidanyorai and no harm will come to you.'

Satsuki looked at the brown-haired girl in surprise 'Afraid?' she repeated wonderingly. 'No, of course I'm not afraid. I am concerned, of course. . . .'

Midori patted her knee reassuringly.

'It is a serious problem,' continued Satsuki. 'I have no idea how to act, and that is most distressing. Perhaps you could give me some advice, as I see you have gone through all this before?'

Midori nodded. The other two women craned their heads as they noticed the whispered conversation.

'It's this robe. It's hardly the correct colour for the flames, and what is worse, our feet will undoubtedly be blackened from the ash. How then can we avoid exposing our shins unseemingly while protecting the hems of our gowns?'

Midori's brows creased in thought, while the other two trollops giggled at the inanity of the city girl's question. It was a holy thing they were to do — what matter if their shins were seen?

'Osatsuki, I am afraid it does not matter,' Midori said gently. 'In case you don't know, many men will see more than our shins after the ritual is over. . . .'

'Of course. I realise that,' countered Satsuki. 'However, it is so inelegant and vulgar to be exposed in this fashion. I cannot recall a single poem or precept from the past that could help us.'

'You can read!' gasped one of the other girls.

'Of course, my dear. Can't everyone?' Satsuki asked in surprise.

Midori shook her head 'Truly you are different than us. I am afraid I have no suggestion for your important question' — a smile curved her lips momentarily — 'other than to hold up your skirts.'

Satsuki considered the suggestion gravely for a moment, then pursed her lips. There must be *some* solution to the problem, she knew, but unfortunately, she could not think of a single precedent.

Midori rose and urged her to her feet. It was time for them to cross the sea of redly glowing coals. She had little time to consider elegance but would have to act forthrightly. One of the girls before her reached the coals and started walking. She hopped a little as the heat touched her. Satsuki waited for the signal to start, not wishing to crowd those before her. She watched Midori step onto the fire. Her eyes were almost closed, her face composed, and there was no sign that she was walking across glowing coals.

Satsuki stepped forward. Fingers of one hand unconsciously looped a fold of her robe and raised it slightly. With her other hand she lowered the collar down her back so as to provide some coolness and also, she admitted ruefully to herself, to distract the onlookers. With stately steps she trod across the red expanse, taking great care to lift and drop her skirts in rhythm with her walking. Her progress took on some of the aspects of a stately dance. In consequence of her actions her walk took twice as long as anyone else's. She glided across the expanse, taking great pains to maintain her posture. She was conscious of the eyes upon her, of the fact that she was alone on the expanse of coals, but her attention was wholly focused on taking the proper steps, on preserving her essential dignity and propriety.

Midori and Tsuneyoshi were waiting at the other side. 'You took twice as much time as anyone else.' Tsuneyoshi said gruffly. He looked at her feet. Only the soles were blackened by charcoal. The arch and toes were perfectly clean. He touched his lips with a moist tongue, but his face was inscrutable as he turned away.

'You were wonderful!' Midori stroked her arm lightly. 'Such a stately walk! Such elegance!' Admiration shone in her eyes.

Satsuki bowed deeply in gratitude. 'Really, it was nothing,' she said.

A stout man dressed in a grey silk kimono, a short sword thrust through his sash, was watching the two women closely. At the other end of the enclosure an opening was made, and penitents streamed through, controlled by a *yamabushi* elder, to pass over the dark ashy bridge of coals.

Midori looked at them. 'They will purify their sins and be ready for Amida,' she said in response to Satsuki's unasked question. 'We go first — we are *yamabushi* and can show them the way. But it is our duty to bring them closer to Amida.' They turned to leave. 'Well, back to work. My feet do hurt a bit — don't yours?' Midori asked ingenuously.

'No — should they?' responded Satsuki. 'I would have thought that with your experience . . .'

'It always hurts a bit, at least, sometimes one gets burned seriously. I think my faith is not all it should be. . . .'

'Oh, no, my dear. I am sure it is quite adequate. However, you really should maintain greater decorum. After all, we *are* on display, and propriety must be observed.'

Satsuki and Midori collected their *goza* mats from the pile of their belongings and headed for their enclosures. A small line of men, mostly young, had gathered there in anticipation.

'Well, at least we don't have to work on our feet,' commented Midori.

Satsuki turned to her, shocked. 'But of course you sometimes have to stand. How otherwise will your men get their full pleasure?'

Midori was still digesting this surprising bit of information, when they were stopped by Tsuneyoshi. He was accompanied by the stout, richly clad gentleman who had observed them earlier.

'This is the head of the festival committee, Yamamura Jichisai. He has observed you throughout the ceremony. He will engage your services until we leave.' He bowed to Yamamura and strode rapidly away.

Yamamura bowed to the two girls. They studied him gravely from lowered eyes. He was not an ill-favoured man. He looked bulky and prosperous. His topknot was tinged

91

with grey. His robe was plain but of silk, not cotton.

'I wish to have a small party to thank the other two members of the committee for their help in the successful completion of the festival. I would be grateful for your assistance. Please follow me.'

Midori giggled as they followed Yamamura and said in a low voice, 'I do believe your *sendatsu* cares for you. In the secular world he would no doubt keep you for himself.'

Satsuki considered the remark gravely. It was true that Tsuneyoshi seemed preoccupied with some problem whenever he came up to her, but she was not sure it was her person that concerned him so.

They came to an elaborate house set in a formal garden. He conveyed them into a set of rooms near a bath.

'Please make yourselves comfortable. The men will be here soon, but there is time to prepare.'

He left them, and the two women started making themselves ready for the party. There was a table of expensive cosmetics, which Satsuki used after her quick bath. Midori was at a loss in her new surroundings. Swiftly, Satsuki took charge and helped her friend prepare her face and hair. When Midori could at last look into the polished silver mirror, she gasped with delight. Her face had been powdered lightly, her eyebrows darkened and straightened, her lips painted a bright rose. Her hair rose above her head in the newly fahionable style of Miyako, only slightly less elaborate than Satsuki's own.

Satsuki looked on her handiwork critically. 'I am sorry my work is so poor. I am afraid I am terrible at it. Please accept this – it will compensate for my clumsiness.' She tucked an elaborate hairpin enamelled with azaleas in varying colours into Midori's hair. It complemented the glossy brown hair magnificently.

Midori was speechless. She looked from her own image to Satsuki, then back again. 'Oh, no, Lady Osatsuki,' she said spontaneously. 'No one has ever made this of me. I am ever so grateful to you.' She knelt at Satsuki's feet with tears in her eyes.

Satsuki raised her and patted her arms. 'No, dear Midori.

You have been extremely kind to me, showing me how to behave among the *yamabushi*. You should not address me formally. We should be sisters to each other.'

Midori nodded fiercely and embraced Satsuki. 'You shall be elder then. I will take instruction from you.'

Satsuki kissed her lips lightly. 'When we get back to Miyako, it will be most wonderful. This wandering life is interesting, but I so much want to show you real elegance.'

The banquet room had been well set by servants. Considering the rustic environment, Satsuki thought they had done rather well. The flower arrangement she decided was rather vulgar and overblown, and the matting underfoot was coarse, but the dishes had a charming simplicity about them that catered to senses jaded by capital overrefinement. She remembered some of her erstwhile peers, noble *kuge* who would benefit from these surroundings. She herself, when she had lived her life as the second wife of an imperial courtier in the enclosed *kuge* quarter of Miyako, had had no idea that esthetic pleasure could be derived from anything so countrified.

She and Midori entertained the guests, poured their wine, offered them food. Yamamura looked well pleased at the success of his party. Satsuki rose and sang, and Midori displayed a heretofore hidden talent on the *fue* side flute. Satsuki studied the men covertly as she engaged them brightly in conversation, sprinkling her talk with fascinating anecdotes from Miyako, a place none of them had been to. Ando, a tall, cadaverous farmer, would be pleased with the simplest of pleasures. Batto, apparently called that because of his long horsey nose, seemed like one who would be open to elaborations. He was a minor merchant, selling agricultural produce to middlemen from the city. He had some pretentions to being a doctor, having descended from an impoverished samurai family (or so he told her), and thus considered himself a man of culture.

As the men drank more, they began to feel freer with Satsuki's and Midori's persons. Controlling the flow of the party, Satsuki at first discouraged intimacies and signalled Midori to do the same. She slapped Ando's hands away when he slid them up her leg, and delicately extricated herself when Batto slipped a hand into the neckline of her robe.

With deliberate indifference she teased the men more and more, gradually allowing them more liberties. Confused at first, later enjoying the game, Midori followed her lead.

They played a finger game, and Satsuki purposely lost a forfeit. When she giggled and refused to pay — she did not care to sing a song designed for the male voice — Yamamura caught her wrist. This time she did not resist as he bore her back onto the seating cushions. His hand slipped into the bosom of her robe. Thick fingers rolled her sensitive nipples and pressed them into the full flesh of her tits. She smiled at his face to encourage him, and he bent forward and nuzzled her neck. She shivered with the feel, and her hand stroked his newly shaven pate as the tip of his tongue travelled down her shoulder, pushing off her loosely held robe. She peered over his shoulder as his mouth finally fastened on one of her prominent nipples.

Midori was well occupied, she could see. Batto had opened her robe, and her pear-shaped breasts were being subjected to a greedy sucking. He would squeeze one while sucking ravenously at the other, then reverse the positions of his hand and mouth. Ando, as Satsuki had expected, was less of a lover. His robe was open, and he squatted between Midori's parted legs. Her knees were slightly raised to afford him a delicious view of her pink slit. But he was holding his stiff prick before him and was in the process of shaking it erect. Without further ado he pushed forward, forcing it between her lips and rubbing his pole on her soft tongue.

Resigned, Midori closed her eyes, merely encouraging Batto by scratching at his back and arms.

Satsuki returned to her own affairs. She slowly guided Yamamura down the length of her body. His lips slipped down the pleasantly padded length of her ribcage. Her wide obi sash was in the way of her pleasure and rather than have him take it off in discomfort, she guided him back up again until his lips whispered at her ear. She twisted her torso skillfully aside, then raised herself slightly to afford him a better view. Bending forward from the hips she loosened the intricate knot at her back, then leaned aside. Knowingly he loosened the sash with one arm.

Satsuki found the sound of silk slithering as it opened to his access stimulating. She shivered involuntarily, and he chuckled in a low voice. The knot was untied, and he pulled at the fabric. She aided the movement unobtrusively, and again the sound of silk slithering off her body brought great pleasure to both. She twisted back and leaned forward so that her nipples peeked out of the robe. He admired them for a while, and just at the right moment, before he became satiated by the view, she lay back on the cushion, one knee artfully raised. He moistened his mouth with sake, then leaned forward and laved her nipple with the liquid. The liquor stung pleasantly, and she arched her body. His fingers wandered downwards until they encountered her perfumed bush. He dug deeply into her cunt; then another finger wandered to the tiny starfish of her anus. She poured some sake into her palm and wet the bush, which he sniffed appreciatively. At the same time she began opening his robe.

Now the stimulation of Satsuki's movements had become too much for Yamamura. He rolled over her and shoved his prick deep into the waiting cunt. Though surprised at his sudden boorishness, Satsuki knew that it was her duty to please him as well as she could. She raised her hips in perfect counterpoint to his. He breathed heavily now, his face screwed into an expression almost of pain. He bit her neck, her nipples, her mouth. His hands went around her buttocks, squeezing her to him. She helped him with measured pressure from her cunt and thighs. As his climax approached, she raised her knees and pummelled the backs of his calves with her heels.

She glanced again at Midori. Batto had replaced Ando, who was sitting cross-legged watching his friend at work. The horsey-faced man was bucking over Midori in a lively manner. Unlike his predecessor, he was aware of his companion. He would stop every once in a while to regard his handiwork, admiring Midori's pointed breasts or withdrawing completely to examine the fine brown hair of her pussy, now streaked with the froth of his movement.

Midori appeared to be enjoying him, as well. Audible gasps came from her mouth as he moved deeply into her. Her eyes were closed, and a bead of sweat (inelegant but appropriate, Satsuki thought) lay on her upper lip.

The two men climaxed simultaneously. Yamamura gave a low growl and stiffened, and his thick tube hosed Satsuki's insides with a flood of sticky come. Batto wriggled on Midori like an eel, muttered something incomprehensible, and collapsed on her breasts.

After lying there for a while to allow the men to get their breath back, Satsuki sat up. Discreetly she wiped the insides of her thighs with the tissue paper in her sleeve. She frowned at Midori, who was about to cover herself up inelegantly with the hem of her robe. Smiling, Satsuki poured cups of sake for the men and withdrew to repair her toilet, motioning Midori to follow. They would return to perform some more once Satsuki thought them presentable.

'We could have had them again,' Midori protested when they were alone.

'Darling Midori, of course we could have. But what elegance could there be in that? They can have village girls any time they like and futter them like pigs in the gutter to their hearts' content. No. You and I, we present them with elegance. We play on their senses, we tease them while not appearing to do so. We must never wear out their desire for us, never offer them enough. I would not do it this way for a city gentleman, of course. But each type of man must have what he is least familiar with. In a while we will return again, offer them some drink, talk some more, entertain them, and before they know it, they'll be in us again. Darling, you must trust me.'

'Of course, Elder Sister.' Midori smiled in acquiescence. 'Though I do wish Mr Batto had not finished so soon. I was just about to . . .'

'Yes, I know, dear. I was watching you. I am sure we can get them to have you again. And if not . . .' Satsuki smiled and then leaned forward mischievously. Before Midori could react, she found her skirts raised and Satsuki's skillful mouth applied to her newly washed lips. There was flick of a knowing and loving tongue — Satsuki withdrew.

'You do have the softest and most beautiful lower hair I have known,' she said conversationally. They checked their appearance for the last time.

Chapter Nine

It was a stiff walk, even for Jiro's tough frame. The rumour he had heard in the festival was subsequently confirmed at other places. Satsuki was somewhere ahead of him, probably on the way to Yoshino. Towards evening he came to a village with a post house on the road. The village boasted a large inn. Jiro smiled grimly. More than food or lodging, he craved a bath. He felt at his sleeve: quite empty. A thought occurred to him and he entered the prosperous- (and expensive-) looking establishment.

No, the proprietor explained. No, he had no need for wood. Look, he said, and showed Jiro the bath house. A natural hot spring gushed from the rocks, filling a large bath in which bathers sat and steamed themselves. Jiro shrugged and turned to leave. Behind his back, the innkeeper wore a broad smile. Few samurai would descend to the level of begging for work, and it was a minor pleasure to be refusing one. Most of them just took.

'Why are you smiling at my friend's departing back?' a hoarse voice interrupted him. He turned and bowed defferentially to his most illustrious guest, while Jiro paused in midstride.

'Miura-san!' the hoarse voice called out. 'Would you leave without having a drink with me?'

Jiro turned to see the sumo wrestler Tatsunoyama beaming at him. They exchanged greetings, and within minutes Jiro was ensconced in a large room occupied by the wrestler's bulk. A slightly smaller, younger, slimmer version of Tatsunoyama was arranging luggage and laying out a robe.

'That good-for-nothing is my student and valet,' Tatsunoyama indicated. 'He'll get us some food and drink.'

The youth hurriedly disappeared, and soon Jiro and his host were inundated with food and drink.

'I had no idea sumotori lived so well!' exclaimed Jiro as he dug into a rich stew of fish, taro, pounded rice cakes, and vegetables. Though a large man and a hearty eater, he found it impossible to keep up with the wrestler, who ate as if he had not eaten for a week.

'You think I pay for this?' Tatsunoyama laughed. He was in a jovial mood. 'No, the landlord is only too honoured to have me. His rooms will be full tonight as men come to catch a glimpse of me.' He made a face and slurped at his bowl, then reached for the wine. Jiro reached the bottle first and looked for a cup to pour for his host. Tatsunoyama looked about him, saw the tiny sake cup, sneered, and held out his rice bowl. Jiro filled it and held out his own in a spirit of sharing Tatsunoyama's hardships.

Their bellies full, both men relaxed on their seating cushions, chatting easily. Their sizes and consequent temperaments created a natural sympathy between them. The velvet night covered the wooded hillsides, and still they talked. A maid came in to light the candles.

'Is there anything interesting to see in this town?'

The maid giggled behind her hand at the wrestler and said excitedly, 'Actually, there is a small troupe performing plays down in the old shed. Perhaps the honoured guests would care to attend?'

Both men rose and agreed that a stroll would do them good. The old shed turned out to be an unused rice depot. The sides were open now, and a crude stage had been erected at one end. Jiro looked at it critically. It was like a parody of a formal stage. A passageway was left for the appearance of the players, but there was no pine-tree prop, as all real stages should have. Instead someone had painted a backdrop of a city scene in garish colours. The players were on stage. Rather than proper players' masks, they wore simple makeup. Instead of a formal elegant presentation of the classics, they were singing a popular song that Jiro had been vaguely aware of in Miyako. And both actors were girls. The audience — farmers, youths, some of the inn guests, a merchant or two — were enthralled. They laughed at the jokes and innuendos, cried at the pathetic songs. Some called out encouragement to the actresses who posed before them, changing costumes and props swiftly before the audience's eyes. Most of the show consisted of dances and songs with short skits interspersed between musical sections. Jiro found that he recognised some of the pieces from the formal No theatre he had been exposed to in samurai society. But the changes made on the originals were delightful and witty, and he found himself enjoying the skits more and more.

Occasionally one of the players would strike an attitude, emphasising a mood or emotion. This was new to the audience, and they expressed their appreciation noisily. One of the actresses struck a particularly effective pose before Jiro and Tatsunoyama. Jiro looked at her critically. Her costume was sewn together of bits and pieces of material, mended many times. Some of the pieces must have come from rich robes, he decided. He looked at the actress' face, and a shadow crossed his brow. He had seen the face before, but he could not recall when. He looked at the other actress, and the shock of recognition almost brought him to his feet. The second actress' face was a mirror image of the first. The make-up they wore was not heavy enough to hide the fact. Jiro also recalled now where he had seen the two before. They were Lady One and Lady Two, the twin mistresses of a Lord Matsudaira, whom he had helped kill some time before. Satsuki's husband had been another one of those killed, when Jiro and his friends had foiled a planned coup d'etat. The play rolled on, and Jiro cautiously relaxed.

'We shall have to kill him!' The girl's voice was harsh and strained.

The other one nodded in agreement but voiced an objection: 'We will need to plan it well. I think he is staying at the Matsubaya Inn. . . .'

'Tonight. He came with the sumo wrestler. That should be easy to find. Those big men attract plenty of attention.'

'The samurai? He killed our master!'

'No, of course not. The other — the wrestler. I'd love

103

to have him inside me. We haven't had a decent man for months.'

'For several months. Ever since our Lord died.' There were tears in the girl's eyes and a catch in her voice.

'Ever since he was killed,' the other spat harshly. 'Well, tonight his shade will rest well!'

Jiro and Tatsunoyama had drunk deeply, enjoying one another's company. Jiro found the wrestler odd. He combined a formal mien with an assumption of equality that roused the samurai in Jiro's makeup. At the same time that he was a humorous and considerate companion, he could be entirely oblivious to admiring glances and the outstretched hands of wrestling fans. He responded only rarely to any of the messages that the room maid brought from time to time. When he did respond, it was usually by scrawling his name on a plaque presented for the purpose by some admirer, or more rarely by pressing his hand into an ink stone loaded with red ink and imprinting his palm on a sheet of paper. His apprentice would take the paper reverently and rush off to present it to the delighted follower of the sport.

At length they went off to the bath. The bathroom was spacious, with a cedar-lined tub and well-appointed fittings. They talked leisurely while Tatsunoyama's apprentice scrubbed their backs and they rinsed with the sulphury-smelling waters. They watched the crowd of humanity that had come for a late-night soak. Some of the women, Jiro decided, were quite pleasantly shaped. None, of course, like his own Okiku and Rosamund, but pleasing nonetheless. There was a group of several women pilgrims who had monopolised one corner of the huge sunken tub. In another corner an elderly samurai dozed, cold towel folded on his head. Two men, local farmers by their accents and hairdos, talked of crops. A father and two young sons scrubbed themselves in another corner. Someone sang softly in the candlelit steamy gloom.

They lowered themselves into the tub, each covertly examining the other. The wrestler saw a large, heavily muscled samurai with peculiarly sallow skin and light, almost greyish eyes. Jiro was taller than the wrestler. His wrists were thicker than a samurai's should be. Jiro's father, Tatsunoyama knew, had been a foreigner. As the Shogun's admiral and shipwright, he had trained his second son in his own craft, owning it no shame for his younger son, who could never inherit his position, to learn a trade. Miura Anjin's son Jiro had not, however, become a shipwright like his English father. Instead, he taught letters to young children and foreign knowledge to whoever would hear.

Jiro saw a massive mountain of fat descending into the steaming pool beside him. Under the fat, however, his warrior's eye saw layers of muscle and brawn. And the wrestler's hands, he knew from report, could crush a man's head like a melon. Both massive bodies subsided beneath the hot waters with a sigh, causing a small tidal wave in the crowded pool. Some of the pilgrims in the far corner who had been chatting animatedly glanced at the two massive bodies, whose maleness was inadequately hidden by tiny towels, then returned to their conversations.

Jiro awoke with the sensation of a threat. He oriented himself in the dark, opening his eyes to mere slits. Closer to the window he could make out the massive snoring bulk that was his host. Another, slightly higher sound intruded on his senses. Slowly and silently he drew the short sword that rested beneath his pillow. A mat frame creaked. A figure loomed over him. Twisting to one side, he threw his quilt over the assailant and rolled away. His foot struck a wooden pillar, and he rolled toward the attacker. The figure gave a muffled cry and fell back, crashing over the wrestler's massive form.

The snoring stopped abruptly. Another muffled scream and a figure seemed to launch itself in the air, over Tatsunoyama's recumbent bulk, to the area where Jiro had been before. There was a resounding slap, and the leaping figure crashed to the ground. There was the sound of continuing struggle for a short while from Tatsunoymama's bedding, then silence. Jiro, his senses alert, probed for any more attackers. Tatsunoyama lay sensibly still, one of the bundles beside him inert, the other struggling feebly. Jiro's acute senses, trained by Okiku, who had been a professional assassin, told him of no other threat. Leisurely he lit a lamp.

'Let us examine your prizes, Tatsunoyama-zeki.' He had a feeling that he knew who the prizes were.

Lady One was lying at full length on the matting. There was a growing purple bruise on one temple. She was dressed in tight-fitting black clothes, black turban, and a black gauze mask. Beside her outstretched hand lay a long stiletto-like pin. Its tip glittered stickily. Jiro moved it carefully aside. He did not know the type, but the sticky substance on the blade seemed to indicate poison. He examined the girl with caution. She seemed stunned, not dead.

'Well, not too badly damaged, I imagine,' Jiro said conversationally while he bound her with his sword cord, released from the scabbard.

'Let's look at the other one,' Tatsunoyama said with the same tone of indifference. 'I suppose they were for you? I can't imagine them as supporters of mine on a surprise visit.'

'I am terribly sorry for the inconvenience. They were indeed aiming at me.' He explained the circumstances while they removed Lady Two's weapon − a straight-edged dagger − and uncovered her. She glared at Jiro and made a move to leap at him with bared teeth.

'Stop that!' Tatsunoyama ordered, shaking her. Her teeth rattled in her head as her neck snapped back and forth with the power of his movement. She looked at his face and seemed to recognise him for the first time.

'You're the wrestler. We deeply apologise for this intrusion. It is a matter of revenge, you see. You must let us go.'

The fat man laughed. 'What do I care for your revenges? You disturbed my sleep! I hate that!' He emphasised each statement with a shake. Her head shook back and forth like a puppet's. 'You must never do that again! Do you understand?'

She nodded in agreement. Her twin moaned and stirred.

'Besides, you disturbed my guest. That is not done. If you want to challenge him, do it outside!' She nodded again, and he released her. She shot forward liked a striking snake, snatching for the dagger that Jiro held negligently before him.

Fast as she was, the fat man was faster. There was a meaty slap, and his massive palm smacked into her back. His other hand swept her legs from under her, and he pinned her to the ground.

Impassively he said, 'You apparently were not listening. I said not to do that!' This time he emphasised each word with a slap on her squirming buttocks. She cried out but continued to struggle. His impassivity did not change, nor did the tempo of his hand coming down on her roughly clothed bum.

'Stop that!' Lady One had recovered from her blow and was writhing in her bonds. 'Leave my sister alone!'

'When she learns to obey me,' Tatsunoyama said impertubably.

'Never! I'll kill him!' came the muffled retort. Lady One increased her struggles, but Jiro knew his knots too well. He looked on with interest as she tried to extricate herself.

Tatsunoyama hauled himself to a sitting position. He groped behind him and found a small *raku*-ware sake container, which he drained. His other hand kept Lady Two pinned on the floor. She still struggled furiously. 'Might as well be comfortable,' said the wrestler. He hauled Lady Two onto his crossed knees. 'You will do what I say. You will refrain from misbehaving. Until then I will punish you.' He raised his meaty hand again and brought it down on the girl's inflamed buttocks. She struggled furiously for a while as his blows rained down steadily.

Jiro looked down at her. She glared back. 'Do you enjoy being beaten?' he asked. 'I know a woman who does,' he added for Tatsunoyama's benefit. 'She gets excited that way.' He refrained from describing Rosamund's other talents and attributes.

'Is that so?' wondered Tatsunoyama, surprised for once. 'I find that very odd. Pain is not after all pleasant — though

107

sometimes it is necessary.' His hand did not pause for a moment.

'No, I don't!'

'You don't what?' Tatsunoyama inquired.

'Enjoy being beaten. Stop, please — oh stop, please!'

Tatsunoyama stayed his hand. 'You will obey? Stop fighting?'

'Yes, yes, of course, I will have to kill him another time.'

He released his hand, but again she tried to lunge forward at Jiro. Tatsunoyama's hands clamped on her body.

'You are forcing me to exercise when I should be asleep. Now I must relax again. I assure you, you will obey me in the end. I was an apprentice for many years before I fought my way through the curtain into the ranks of the champions. I have trained as an apprentice, and that is hard, and as a champion, and that is harder. I assure you I can train you. But first I must relax. I do not like to be annoyed.' His moon face was suffused with a frown.

He pulled at the rough fabric of her blue-dyed workman's trousers. There was a ripping sound, and the fabric parted. Her buttocks glowed rose with the force of his blows. She shivered involuntarily as the cold night air met her overheated sensitive skin. Holding her down with one hand, Tatsunoyama shrugged out of his light sleeping *yukata* robe. The enormous dome of his belly overshadowed the stout, fat prick that banged against the overhang. His balls hung down from a forest of curls between his legs, though the insides of his thighs were rubbed bald from the rough hemp loincloth he wore while fighting. He slapped apart her legs after ripping the leggings down, and knelt between them. She looked behind her fearfully.

'Have no fear. I will not let my weight down on you — unless you struggle and provided you say, "I will obey," by the time I am ready to finish with you.'

She squirmed around fearfully, but he held her down by neck and hip. He squatted down between her thighs and lowered himself. Jiro marvelled at the man's flexibility. His joints, notwithstanding their massiveness, were as flexible as a baby's. The tip of the cock massaged the back of the girl's buttocks for a moment. He pushed forward slowly. She felt the mass of his belly on her overheated bottom and shied away. He probed remorselessly, and the tip of his pole found the tiny button of her anus. Not knowing the size of his tool but knowing that his entry was inevitable. She raised her buttocks to facilitate entry into her cunt.

Her heated mound touched the arch of his belly, and she quivered again. Fear of being smothered under the mound of flesh and muscle, rather than of the coming act, made her frame tremble. He eased forward again, saying, 'You will obey me! Do not try to escape.' She nodded wordlessly as the tip of his machine probed the outer fringes of her cunt. To his surprise, he found it moist. Enjoying and using the slickness, he eased forward, parting the fat lips of her sex. They both let out their breaths in an audible sigh as he slid his length up her slick channel.

To her surprise the pressure of his belly on her bottom was not unbearable. The skin still stung, but she was not crushed. She elevated her buttocks to facilitate his entry, and he moved obligingly back and down. Then he pulled out of her entirely. She aided his movements by a bucking motion of her hips, and again he drove forward. He released her nape, but she made no move to escape as his cock shuttled in and out of her.

Jiro observed with delight and amazement as Tatsunoyama's massive frame hovered over the girl's slight body with the lightness of thistledown. With amazing agility the fat man moved his hips in wide circles and plunged himself deeply into the woman before him. She responded with a dreamy smile and an occasional grunt, more of pleasure than from the feel of Tatsunoyama's weight.

Their climax approached. Tatsunoyama moved faster, and the girl moved with him. She rose to her elbows now. One of her hands moulded her dangling breasts. With the other she reached beneath her and lightly supported Tatsunoyama's dangling scrotum. Fearful for his friend, Jiro readied the dagger to stop any suspicious move, but the girl seemed sincerely intent on protecting the man's jewels.

'Will you obey me?' Tatsunoyama asked in his hoarse voice.

As if in a faraway dream, Lady Two answered, 'Yes, Yes, I will.'

'You'll do what I say,' emphasized Tatsunoyama. 'You will leave Master Jiro alone!'

'Yes, yes, of course,' she answered dreamily. Then she turned her face to him and made a bowing motion to the floor. Tatsunoyama surged up behind her. He pulled her to him and ground her buttocks into the hollow under his belly. His buttock muscles pumped, and she squealed as wave after wave of pleasure overtook her. His massive arse muscles pumped his own liquid into her at the same time, spraying her insides and overflowing onto the sleeping pad. Lady One looked on from her bonds, her eyes glaring fearfully.

Tatsunoyama released Lady Two and let her gently down onto the mat.

'And you?' he asked Lady One conversationally. His dripping prick seemed to threaten her from under its protecting ledge. It had lost much of its stiffness but appeared still serviceable.

'Sister! Do what he says!' Lady Two hissed from the floor.

'But our master!' agonised the other.

'We are masterless now, don't you see? How can two strolling players have a master? No one can expect us to be masterless for long. . . .'

'I will bring you under my wing,' croaked Tatsunoyama. 'After all,' he smiled, 'In some ways we are alike. We both display to the crowds as a living. In years to come sumo will become more of a spectacle, now that the old masters are gone and we rarely kill in the ring. And this thing that you do, these performances, no doubt they, too will become popular as entertainment even in the cities. What do you call this acting without masks?'

'I don't know,' answered Lady One while licking her lips. 'It has no name, but it is more popular than the No plays or the *sarugaku*. . . .'

110

'Sister . . .!' pleaded the other twin.

'Very well. We will do your will.' She smiled at him. 'I rather liked you from the movement I saw you. But you have to prove yourself to me,' she added fiercely. 'The master could.' She rolled over on her back and spread her legs.

Jiro, excluded from the conversation by the twin's enmity, bit his lips. He remembered that he had deflowered both twins almost simultaneously when he was a captive of their deceased lord. His balls ached from the desire to stab himself again into that sweet cleft he knew was hidden under the rough fabric.

'No,' Tatsunoyama smiled in his turn. 'That is not the way I care to do it. You will do it my way.' He laid himself comfortably on his back. 'Release her!' he ordered Lady Two.

She divested herself of the remains of her pants and moved to obey. She squatted with her back to him, and Jiro could see the length of the crack between her rosy buttocks and the tangled, spermy end of the beard hanging below. He would have liked to step forward and introduce himself into the inviting opening, but a warning glance from Tatsunoyama restrained him. His massive fists clenched painfully. Lady Two untied her sister and rubbed her limbs briskly to restore circulation. With several swift motions she removed her sister's clothing as well. The two were perfect twins, differing now only in that one was slightly wetter and rosier than the other. They rose and stood side by side for a moment.

Tatsunoyama admired their stance and composure, then motioned to his prick, hidden from his eyes by the mound of his belly. Lady Two knelt swiftly by his side. Her pink tongue slipped out and licked the semi-hard rod with a quick flip. Another followed, and another, until she was laving the length of the rod with her tongue. She sucked and nibbled at the member until it stiffened anew. Holding it with her fist, she turned to her sister. The slim figure of Lady One straddled the mound of muscle. She poised there for a moment, like a child riding a tortoise, then slid down until her open crack hovered over the waiting impaler. Lady Two

111

bent behind her, and her tongue licked out. The hairy crack was moistened rapidly, and Lady One struck herself gradually onto the waiting tool. Tatsunoyama looked on approvingly as she began rapidly bobbing up and down his stiff pole. The slick coated length appeared and disappeared, now hidden by her bush, now pulling at the lips that let it go reluctantly.

Jiro eased himself out of the room into the dimly lit corridor. It was obvious he was not invited to the party. The only thing to do, he decided, was to take a bath. He would have the bathhouse to himself, and the heat would at least soothe his tension. He walked through the silent corridors and down to the steaming room. Stripping off his *yukata*, he could not help but think of the scene he had abandoned above. His massive cock reared its head futilely for the second time that night. He tried to ignore the pressure and marched determinedly to the pool's edge, pausing while he decided whether to be polite and wash or whether to simply plunge in.

'*Saaa . . .!*'

The drawn-out sound startled him out of his contemplation. He turned his head. Six pairs of eyes looked him over thoughtfully. In his confusion, he fell more than slid into the bath, almost babbling apologies before he remembered his rank and status. The six women pilgrims he had seen before resumed a low-voiced conversation. He tried to relax and ignore them. In the heat, his painful erection would not go away. Neither would the women. He could not masturbate, considering the circumstances. He examined them out of the corner of his eyes. They were not young, but not, he noticed, particularly old either. Two of them were out of the tub, and their chunky, muscular bodies gleamed with water and health. A farmwife pilgrim association, he surmised. The government had inveighed against the pilgrimage practice, because it took time away from the serious business of work, but it was the people's sole relaxation sometimes, and many indulged in it when they could. Times were peaceful now that the Age of Wars was over, and people tried to relax more.

112

One of the women got out of the tub and passed behind Jiro. She splashed herself with cold water from a barrel near the wall, then dipped the bucket again. This time the bucket slipped, and Jiro felt the splash of cold water send currents down his back.

'Oh, I'm terribly sorry! I really wasn't careful. . . . Allow me to apologise.' The female voice was very near.

Jiro turned his head. She was standing near him, bending over solicitously. Her breasts, with a pair of tiny nipples, swung suggestively before his face. She had a pleasant, flat face, and there was a hint of mischief in her tone.

'Are you all right, mister?'

He nodded, and she took that as an invitation to sit beside him on the tub rim. She was quite unselfconscious, and he noticed that her legs were spread comfortably. Tiny outer lips barely covered long inner folds in her cunt, he saw.

'We're from Nara and on our way to visit the sites near Mount Koya', she said. 'Are you a pilgrim too?'

'No,' he answered, struggling to maintain his composure. 'I am looking for someone, a friend.' He described Satsuki.

'We haven't seen anyone of that description,' she cooed. 'Girls, this gentleman is looking for a friend.' She repeated Jiro's story. There was a general agreement to her denial, and some sentences Jiro could not hear clearly. One thing he thought he did hear was, 'She's a lucky girl, though, if that's the way he's looking for her!' The words were drowned in a burst of laughter. Jiro did not know how to react. He was about to rise and stalk off, when the woman beside him leaned forward again.

'You must be very sore from your journey,' she said solicitously. 'Please let me rub it for you.' She rubbed the muscles in his neck slowly. While doing so she had to lean forward, and Jiro was conscious of two tiny glowing spots that dragged along the skin of his back. She rubbed harder, and his shoulders relaxed, though the relaxation was not apparent underwater.

Suddenly he was conscious of another figure near him. A voice sounded by his left ear. 'I see you need help, Mitsuko.' A pair of plump, work-strengthened hands were

113

added to the first. Another figure splashed to join them. He opened his eyes to find himself surrounded by expectant female faces. Before he could recover, they seemed to have reached a decision, based on nothing more than a brief exchange of glances. Two firm hands dived underneath and grasped his prick.

'It's lovely!'

'Such a big one!'

Six pairs of hands hauled him gently to his feet and laid him on a nearby wooden bench. His cock stood erect along his belly, ready for action. The pilgrims admired their catch for a moment. Jiro's cock was indeed impressive, and they relished the sight.

'Looks like there's enough for all,' Mitsuko breathed. 'Now don't disappoint us, lovey. There's six of us, you know!' She swung a strong leg over him and settled herself on top of his erection. She posed there for a moment, then let herself down with a deep breath of satisfaction.

'Good, in't?' asked one of the others. Mitsuko's only answer was a beatific smile as she began bouncing up and down the length of the magnificent maleness lodged in her juicy hole.

Jiro supported her with his hands, enjoying the sensation he knew would lead to his release. He was not worried about the other five. He needed release *now*, and he intended to get it. He arched his back and plunged up to meet her downthrust. He was barely conscious of a whispered conversation beside them. Only a fragment reached his ears '. . . but men don't do *that*! . . . well, *I've* never tried it. My old man won't do it to me.'

'He'll do it. He's ours.'

'I've got to.'

'Nonsense, no man would!'

The dim light in the bathroom was suddenly blotted out. Jiro, lost in his approaching pleasure, was barely conscious of it when a warm, moist, earth-smelling cushion fringed with hair enveloped his face. Instinctively, recognising the smell and textures, he sent his tongue out and into the proffered hole. There was a faintly heard squeal of delight.

114

'Sweet, Jizo! He's doing it, he's doing it! How wonderful!' The redolent cunt was mashed against his lips as he contined tonguing it, running his tongue the length of the slit, nipping delicately at the prominent clitoris. The pressure in his balls grew and grew, and he shoved up with all his strength.

A fountain of creamy sperm shot out from his balls just as the two women on top of him forced themselves down in a last frantic attempt to move before they also came. The three thrased on the bench like a tangle of eels, the woman on Jiro's face almost falling off in the intensity of her pleasure. At length Mitsuko and her partner rose from his recumbent form.

'Oh, no,' said one disappointed woman, a plump figure with full breasts and a pleasantly curved belly. 'He's done for. Look at him, Mitsuko. You've milked him dry.'

'Milked him, but not dry. Look at his lovely tool.'

The object in question was as stiff as ever, though coated thickly with a frothy residue.

'It's my turn now!' announced one woman uncere-moniously. She threw a leg over Jiro's hips and drew him into her. He thrust up deeply, intent on her pleasure as well as his own.

'I'll follow Omurasaki!' announced the plump one. Before Jiro could react, he found himself imprisoned between two plump thighs. Full, clean cunt with fat lips pressed against his mouth. He moved his head in meek protest, but the movement of his nose brought on pleasurable squealings, and he renewed his tongue work again. He raised his hands to feel her plump buttocks, but apparently others had a different idea. He found his hands seized and straddled. The callused sides of his palms were rubbed roughly against hungry lips, readying them and pacifying them until the real thing were to arrive.

The juice in his balls rose again. This time, before he could explode he found a soft yet firm hand squeezing hard at the base of his cock. He tried to protest, but the force of two bodies on his hand and one on his face limited his opposition. The slick sensation on his prick continued. He was conscious of a clenching and rocking as his rider finished, and a new, slightly tighter cunt was on him, and a lighter body was riding him. His tongue tired, but not before his rider rocked to completion. His face was wiped with a cool towel, and a new rider replaced the one on his face.

Several times he almost reached a climax, only to be frustrated by the firm grip at the base of his cock. At last, barely conscious, dipping into a dream of sensation, he felt himself elevated beyond the caress of flesh. He was a tower of strength, set to serve the demanding mouths about him. His power bore him through cavern after cavern until he felt a blaze explode within him. He knew this time that the holding hand would not suffice, and the hand knew it as well. Massive grunting sounds emerged from his mouth and translated themselves into sawing motions of his tongue, which could no longer feel the weariness of the hour. The power grew and grew. He was vaguely conscious of his hips arching high, of a body riding his, their only connecting point the strength of his maleness and the complimentary female cavern.

The explosion came. It rushed from the base of his spine, gathering power as it swept everything before it. He poised at the top of his arch, his body supported by shoulders and heels alone, his cock high in the air. Soft, irresistible, wet pressure pounded on him from above as his juices spurted from him in an unending jet, forced out by his internal power, all visible muscles motionless.

He collapsed back on the bench.

Coming to, he found himself alone in the bathroom. The candles had guttered down. His head was pillowed on a towel. Folded neatly in it were six amulets. He shook himself and rinsed off slowly in the hot water, then in cold, then in the pool again. Wearily he headed back to Tatsunoyama's suite. The wrestler was on his back again, snoring. On each side of him snuggled a smaller bundle. One of the twins opened an eye. She saw Jiro's face by the light of the candle, ignored him, and snuggled up again to her massive lover. Ignoring her in turn, Jiro fell into an exhausted sleep.

Chapter Ten

Two groups stood in a clearing on the bank of the cool Yoshino River. A tall, thin man with a strong hawk nose and brooding eyes looked on as the men argued. In the background, women with unbound hair stood watch over the quarrel. Satsuki knelt by a small camellia bush, watching its buds, then raised her eyes with a wistful look to Yoshino Hill, which rose above them. Midori, kneeling beside her on her *goza* mat, rested a hand on Sastsuki's arm.

'Please do not worry, Elder Sister. Our leader, Daisangyoja, will not bow down to these. . . .' She indicated the opposing group, far smaller than their own, by a toss of her shapely chin.

Satsuki turned her head curiously. 'Oh, of course,' she said indifferently. 'I was actually sighing because of our loss.'

Midori looked at her with troubled eyes. 'Loss?'

'Yes. We will not get to see the hundred thousand cherry trees bloom.' She indicated the wooded hillside with a sweep of her full sleeve.

Midori was perplexed. 'The argument does not concern you?'

'Of course not, my dear. The men will settle it among themselves, and we will do whatever is necessary. Come, we must think of this camellia. Will its blossoms complement the scene, do you think?'

Midori bit her lip. Osatsuki was so strange; her actions were incomprehensible. Undoubtedly though, the men would settle the affair, and she knew she could trust Daisangyoja, their leader.

The two groups of men were fingering their swords hilts nervously. Tsuneyoshi, who was slightly to the rear, dried his hands on the deerskin that hung behind him and served him as a seat in the wilds. He did not care to fight other

119

yamabushi, but Master Daisangyoja was right. He had led them here, and his awe-inspiring words brought proof that salvation was near at hand. The poor, deluded fools of the Tozan-ha sect who opposed him here would see their error when the time came for him to perform his miraculous prayers. In the meantime though, lesser leaders shouted and argued precedence on the route to the holy mountains. The Tozan-ha could not stop them, nor could any priest, nor warrior, nor any man. Daisangyoja was the heir of En-no-Gyoja, founder of the *yamabushi* and initiator of mountain pilgrimage. Daisangyoja's spells were so powerful that all demons fled before them. He was capable of the most awesome austerities and his prowess as a leader was unquestionable. Why then did the misled ascentics of the Tozan-ha refuse to accept his innovations and his leadership? It was a puzzle to Tsuneyoshi.

The hawk-faced man, who had stood silently while the argument waxed, stamped his ring-topped stave on the ground once. The dispute ended as if cut by a knife. Even the Tozan-ha opponents, impressed by Daisangyoja's mien, stood waiting. He strode forward.

'I am Daisangyoja, the Supreme Vision of *all* ascetics. I am before you. Please see me as I am now. In days to come I will be transformed. Before your very eyes.' His voice was melodious, powerful, almost hypnotic. Men and women listened to him. Even though his words were arrogant, his tone was such that no one could doubt his power or sincerity.

'I and my people will go up to the mountains. We will prepare ourselves by the usual methods. In addition I will perform another magic — one not performed since the olden days. Doing so I will be transformed, and so will those with me. I will eat pine needles and I will be reborn in this life. Come with me into the mountains.' He turned and strode to the river, shedding his clothing as he walked. His own people followed unhesitatingly. A small number of the Tozan-ha members followed hesitant suit. Some of the Tozan-ha hurried off, possibly to inform their fellows. The vast majority stood its ground.

Midori tugged at Satsuki's sleeve. 'Come, we must bathe,'

she said. 'We are not permitted on the mountain, but even those of us who are left behind must be cleansed.' The *yamabushi* and their few women, the men in their white loincloths, the women in red petticoats, marched into the chilled waters. Satsuki felt her nipples pucker with the cold. The water was not freezing, merely colder than she liked. She dipped the ritual three times, the rocks in the river bed making her footing uneven and threatening her poise. She looked at her broodingly for a long time. She bowed gracefully. Beside her Midori drew in an audible breath, but the master ignored her. His hooded eyes seemed to look deep into Satsuki's soul. There was something inhuman about his gaze. She felt he was not interested in her, in her sex, in anything she had to offer. He was examining her for some quality she might possibly have, but he had no interest in her as a person.

They emerged dripping from the water into the hot afternoon sun. Tsuneyoshi was at her elbow. He bowed and approached Daisangyoja.

'This is your new woman? The one you told me about?' asked the master.

Tsuneyoshi indicated assent.

Daisangyoja looked at her one last time. 'I will try her and see. Perhaps she is the one we are waiting for. If not . . . we will have to wait again.' He strode off without another word.

The small outbuilding she had been called to was floored with fresh tatami mats. They smelled of clean, sweet grass and rice straw. The master sat in the middle of the tiny structure. Beneath him was a thin cotton pad. Beside him rested a dipper with water and a large travelling box of the type carried by many *yamabushi*.

Satsuki bowed at the doorway, her hands properly together, then sat awaiting his command.

'Approach!' he said.

She swivelled slightly on her heels and delicately closed the sliding door, rose, took three steps, and knelt again, her hands on her lap. He examined her for a while. She had the flat face and high forehead of the true aristocrat. Her lips were full but small, her carriage erect. Only the browning of her face indicated that she had spent several days in the sun. Her eyes were modestly downcast, and her long hair hung down her back, held by a simple ribbon. She waited with perfect patience and acceptance for whatever he would deign to give her.

'Strip!' he commanded, his face immobile.

She raised her hands gracefully to the small of her back and quietly slid the intricate knot of her sash free. With an elegant motion she moved her shoulders, and the fabric of her robe pooled about her hips. She restored her hands to her hips and arched her neck to one side, affording him a glance at her perfect neck. Her eyes were downcast, and a faint ghost of a smile played about her full red lips.

He raised his hands before his face, and his fingers curled intricately in a mudra of power. 'Undo me!' he commanded. Satsuki leaned forward, her breasts swaying with the motion. Her deft fingers undid the ribbons of his pantaloons, then delved between his legs to loosen his loincloth. His cock lay in a bed of black hair. She sat back again, her hands once again in her lap. He had, she noted, almost perfect control. She wondered what would be the best way to please him. Obviously he expected no initiatives, at least overt ones, from her, but even so, there were possibilities.

He waited for a long time, his glittering eyes never wavering from her face. She sat quietly as a porcelain doll, only the slight rise and fall of her pale breast, tipped with pink, betraying the fact that she was a living thing.

'I am male!' His voice was deeper and even more powerful. His right fingers pursed into the shape of closed flower bud pointing up. His cock, like a soldier called to duty, swelled at the words and came erect out of its bed. The plum-coloured knob stared at Satsuki's downcast eyes with its single blind eye.

'You are female!' His left hand, held low, opened into the cupping shape of an open flower. She bowed slightly and readied herself appropriately. With the suddenness of a tiger he leaped upon her and bore her back. Her hands cushioned their fall. His cock pushed between her legs, and with one thrust he was carried the length of her sopping quim. Their hairs meshed with a squishy sound. He stared at her with some surprise and a trace of respect. Satsuki felt as if a glowing coal filled her channel. His pole was a warm, strong core that warmed her cool being. She held him lightly with her thighs, warmed by the pressure of his presence. He jogged his rump once, then again, allowing her to feel the full length of his masculinity. His mouth sought her, and he filled the cavern with the warmth of his tongue. She met the probing oral digit with a surrender of her own, lightly licking the surface as he probed her insides.

Suddenly he started moving his cock furiously into her. His balls banged against the mounds of her bottom. She smoothed the muscular thighs with her own, her face as remote and quiet as before. He raised his head and looked at her face. The calm acceptance he found there seemed to please him, as did the tiny beads of sweat that lightly dusted her forehead.

He changed his plunging thrusts to a circular motion, and she fitted her own movements to his. Her tiny clitoris was ground under the power of his muscles and bone, and she felt the delight well up inside her, though nothing of her internal sensations showed on her face or in her movements. He brought the tip of his member to the lips of her cunt and twiddled it there for a while, then plunged in anew, bearing down on Satsuki's beautiful body with his full weight. Her breathing quickened as he repeated the treatment.

At last he withdrew altogether, then knelt before her. She lay there, a picture of female joy. Her eyes were slightly closed, her face lightly touched by sweat. Pink nipples, erect and glowing, peered at the ceiling atop faintly flushed mounds. Her smooth belly curved down to a mass of sopping black curls in which trickles of moisture could be clearly seen. The hair barely hid the sweet red gash, slick with her moisture. Her thighs were slightly raised, framing her damp pussy, waiting for his bidding.

His cock started to twitch and pulse. 'Do not let it go to waste!' he ordered.

She opened her eyes and focused on his crotch. Without a second's hesitation, she came to her knees and bowed before him. As the first spurts of milky fluid emerged from the open mouth of the hole, she caught them in her waiting lips and swallowed. So skilful was her mouth that he could feel the faint stir of her breath on the sensitive tip while the tremors of his orgasm shook his frame. Not a drop was lost.

He folded his arms and looked at her while she knelt before him.

'You might be the one,' he said thoughtfully. 'We must check fully.'

'I am honoured, sir, at your confidence in my poor self,' she murmured.

'Come, we will try again.'

This time his procedure was straightforward. He lay back and helped her mount him. She slid down his waiting pole, which had not lost any of its hardness, until their hairs meshed. He guided her with his hands, then indicated that she should move herself. With growing confidence she rocked over his body. She clenched her cunt sometimes, enough to increase the urgency of his sensations, yet not sufficiently to hurry him. Occasionally she varied her movements, swaying gracefully over the tip of his maleness or grinding her soft lips hard into the base of his cock. He regarded her unmovingly for a while; then, as if he were unable to control himself, his hips started to gyrate wildly on the floor. She followed his movements with her own as her passion grew. His hands stroked her flanks and insinuated themselves between their bodies, where he pinched her labia. She sighed with pleasure, and her movements increased their tempo. He was now arching himself clear off the floor, and she rode him like a bucking horse, her own movements becoming as uncontrolled. Her mouth opened, and deep breaths emerged from her labouring throat. Her eyes closed to slits as she enjoyed the masterful use of his hands on her breasts, genitalia and buttocks.

Behind the ecstatic mask she carefully noted the control in his movements. As Satsuki matched her actions to his, it was clear to her that Daisangyoja's pleasure must precede her own. She controlled the reactions of her body, holding much in reserve, adding to her own pleasure in measured amounts. He reached beside him, and there was suddenly a hard pressure at her rear entrance. She smiled at him and leaned forward to bite his chest in gratitude and to allow the *harigata* easier entrance. The ivory prick slid easily up her waiting anus, and she leaned back again to enjoy the entire benefit of the two cocks, one real, the other artificial, that filled her.

It took a long time before Daisangyoja would admit defeat. The female principle would outwait the male, being passive. But its passivity could be checked another way. He removed the *harigata* from between Satsuki's moon cheeks and raised her powerfully on his extended arms. She was bent like a moon bridge now, her face and feet close to his, her hips arched high in the air.

'You must let down your dew now!' he commanded and Satsuki obeyed.

She trembled like a leaf, and her insides contracted in a powerful orgasm. She gasped for air at the power of her feelings as wave after wave of pleasure soaked her entire frame. The world came to an end, a pinprick of time surrounded by the sensations of her orgasm. Her liquids overflowed and ran down the insides of her thighs. Her only contact with reality was the grip of his fingers on her hips. As the waves of pleasure subsided he brought her down to rest on his chest, and felt the final tremours of her pleasure fade away. She closed her eyes and looked at him blindly for a long time, then smiled slightly and raised herself to kneel at his side.

He rose to his feet and stood facing the wall for a long time, then turned back to her.

'You are the one, undoubtedly. I can now proceed. The New Age of the Law is come. We can go into the mountains for the last time in this age. When I return, power will return with me.' He was looking at her face but seeing infinity. She did not know what the meaning of his words was, but she responded with great propriety to his pronouncements. Bowing, she said, 'Yes, master.'

'Hasegae! Tsuneyoshi!' he called.

The two subleaders slid the doors aside and crouched at the entrance.

'She is the one! We will proceed at dawn. Before that we must accustom her fully to her role. We will perform the purification now.'

They bowed in response and entered the hut. Outside, the *yamabushi* crouched in wonder as the first steps were taken in their salvation.

A fire was lit, and samples of the pure grains were burned. Charms were read over Satsuki's supine body, and mystic signs were traced on her skin in sanctified ink. The droning of the chants, the conch blasts, and the jangle of instruments lulled Satsuki into a trance. As the fire died down in its brass bowl, Hasegae drew Satsuki's legs apart. He inserted himself slowly and smoothly into her moist channel while chanting the appropriate verses. He rolled them onto their sides. His hands loosely caressed her breasts and back, then dipped lower to her bottom, spreading her cheeks like the two halves of a peach.

Chanting too, Tsuneyoshi laid himself behind her. He inserted his prick into the flexible ring of her anus. Slowly, still chanting, he eased his way into her. She felt the hardness of the two pricks in her as they nestled into the channels of her flesh. Gently, softly, she enclosed them within herself, squeezing them as lightly as she could.

Two pairs of hands now stroked her body. Rising higher, they found her throat and lightly fingered her mouth. She opened her soft lips, and Daisangyoja's prick was gently inserted into the warm waiting cavern. It slid forward, resting on her relaxed tongue. She breathed easily through her nose while laving the full morsel of flesh with the moisture of her mouth. Daisangyoja touched the top of her head approvingly.

The doors were closed, and they lay that way dreamily through the night, Satsuki slowly urging her men towards a climax by tiny motions of her body, by minute shiftings and clenchings of herself. As the rooster crowed the dawn she was inundated by streams of come from all three men, who were shaken in turn by her climax.

126

Chapter Eleven

Osatsuki cast one last look down the trail, through the square *torii* arch, at the face of her friend and apprentice. Midori looked back at her elder sister, unable to erase the worry from her face. No women had gone through the arch in living or recorded memory. Osatsuki was the first, and Midori feared for her. Vague tales of the magic doings on the mountains rose persistently into her mind. She banished them forcefully, reminding herself of the master's power and righteousness, but they returned again unbidden.

The last of the white-clad novices, trailed by a brightly dressed vanguard of senior men, disappeared past a curve in the trail. Midori still stood and stared, confusion and unhappiness on her face.

'Well, come on, love. Let's get a move on. Can't stand there all day.'

'Lost a lover, dearie?' another of the *yamabushi* women laughed.

'Yow, but she don't have a cock neither,' a third giggled.

'Oh, shut up!' demanded Midori fiercely as they turned down the trail. She hoisted up her *goza* mat and the small bag of her possessions. She was still worried, but there was money to be made before the men returned. Just in case . . . just in case the master was wrong and the millenium, with gold coins showering from the skies and rice bales for the asking, did *not* come.

The group of *yamabushi* women paused at one of the larger temples down the trail. They turned in to the temple courtyard, to rest under the eaves and drink from the spring that bubbled near the entrance. Some prayed before the temple doors; the rest sat and chattered.

A tall, massively built samurai entered the compound. He was filthy and stained from travel, his clothes plain. His unshaven pate marked him as a lordless man: a ronin. He drank thirstily, then looked around. Seeing the women, he drifted casually towards them. Noticing his arrival, some of the younger women eyed him sideways. The older ones, knowing that ronin were penniless more often than not, ignored the man. He looked the women over casually as he approached the steps to the temple, fumbling in his sleeve for a coin to throw into the offertory box.

The memory of a conversation floated into Midori's thoughts. The ronin was very big, and his hands were enormous. Also, his features were slightly strange. There was something Elder Sister Osatsuki had said about one of her friends. . . . Yes, that he was the son of a southern barbarian father. If so, perhaps help, or at least a way to calm her fears, was near. She looked to either side at her companions. If there were only some way to attract his attention without drawing theirs . . . The massive figure bulked before her.

'Excuse me, lovely lady. Could I entice you to indulge me?'

The group of women sitting on the temple steps had attracted Jiro's attention from the start. He had climbed the path up Yoshino Hill, stopping at each concentration of *yamabushi* he passed to examine the women. So far he had seen no trace of Osatsuki, though it appeared that many of the *yamabushi* were in a frenzy of excitement over something. That was their affair, however, and Jiro continued on, merely becoming more alert than before. Among the women sitting on the stairs was one who momentarily drew his attention. Her features were more regular than the others', the hair a fine soft brown. Unusual for a common woman and whore. For a moment, while she sat still under the shade of the porch, he thought it was Osaksuki. The brown haired woman's movements were very much like the Miyako courtesan's. As he moved closer, however, the similarity vanished. It was merely a similarity of gesture.

He walked to the porch, and the woman stared at him thoughtfully, then looked at her companions to either side. Something caught Jiro's eye. It was a hairpin worn by Brown

Hair. The visible end was decorated by an enamelled polychrome of azalea leaves. Jiro knew that the part stuck in her hair was a blade of the finest steel. He had seen Okiku make it herself, as a gift for her friend Satsuki — Azalea — and he himself had taken the blade to be enamelled.

For a moment he wondered how he could find a way to talk to the woman; then he laughed inwardly. The mat tied in a roll to her back was the obvious clue. He bowed slightly to her and indicated his desires.

The couple walked into the grove, staying within sight of the women, who observed them casually from the stairs.

'Are you perhaps from Miyako?' The girl's voice was pleasant and polite, in contrast to the other whores' chattering behind him.

'Yes,' he grunted shortly, trying to work out a way to inquire about the pin.

'Perhaps you are acquainted with the Gion area?'

He turned and frowned at her, then nodded shortly.

'Then perhaps you have heard of a certain woman, Osatsuki by name?'

'What do you know of her!' he asked, gripping her shoulders roughly.

She laughed lightly, and her friends, keeping an eye out for her protection relaxed. 'Not so roughly, please, Mr Samurai. Are you perhaps acquainted, too, with a woman named Okiku?'

He nodded again, his brows contracting. 'I am Miura Jiro of Miyako. I know Osatsuki, and Miura Okiku is my wife. You will tell me what you know of them!'

She knelt down and spread her mat. 'You must make love to me now.'

'Here? In full sight?'

'They are merely seeing to my well-being. They will follow if we are completely out of sight. Here we are slightly hidden, and no one will suspect us or fear for me. Come, join me. There is a message for you.' She lay down and spread her thighs. He lay down beside her, and she loosened the ties of his trousers expertly. She delved inside his pants, and his flaccid cock rose to the challenge. She laughed softly. He pulled aside the hems of her robe and exposed the length of her legs. They were smooth and rather pale for a country woman. The pads of his fingers travelled their way up the soft inner parts of her thighs until he reached the juncture of her spread legs. He touched the first of her pussy hairs, and his cock stiffened at the challenge. The hairs were unusually soft, softer even than Rosamund's, he noted.

Jiro bent forward and kissed her on the lips. She looked at him in surprise, unaccustomed perhaps to such practices from her customers. He grinned at her, admiring the smooth lines of her face, then bent to kiss her again. Midori responded this time. Her tongue, trained in a different mouth by her elder sister, snaked out and licked delicately at his. The young samurai pressed his mouth onto hers, and his fingers penetrated her lower lips, precipitating a plentiful flood of dew there.

They loosened one another's clothing. Jiro's large hands roved over Midori's slim body. Her nipples were taut, and he pressed the rubbery nubs into the buttery softness of her breasts. Her tongue licked out and laved his ear while her hands dug into his back urging him on. Jiro rolled onto her, and she spread her legs and raised her knees for him. He guided his stiff prick into her opening. The thick, warm shaft parted the slick lips of her cunt, and he pushed himself forward. Her channel was elastic and very deep for a small woman. The head of his pillar sought the depths until its penetration was blocked by the merging of their hairs at its root.

He pulled back, and Midori dug her strong fingers into the muscles of his arse. She enjoyed the feel of those muscles, knowing they would soon bring her pleasure, and her fingers applied more pressure than was really needful. He grunted and pushed forward again. Her tiny clitoris was mashed beneath the power of his pubis, and she wriggled her hips to show her appreciation. Jiro started to pull back again, but the brown haired girl stopped him.

'Now we must talk!' she said firmly.

'Now?' the young man, sunk in her juicy interior to the hilt, was obviously surprised. His tone hardened. 'I've been without a woman for a long time now. You must not get me into this state and then. . . .'

'And I without a man,' she said calmly. 'But we must not allow our preferences to interfere with our duty to our friend. We must avert suspicion this way. If we were to stand and talk, my companions would be suspicious and perhaps come to see what we are doing.' She clenched her thighs around his back. To the outside world, her smooth face wore no particular expression. Inwardly, however, she was grinning happily. Most men finished too soon to suit her. Having this large samurai lend his prick for her pleasure was a comfort. By the time she allowed him to move again, she would be ready too.

'I will move slightly,' she added sweetly, 'so that we will not arouse suspicion.'

'Tell me about Osatsuki!' he commanded.

'She and I travelled together for some time. . . .' She described the circumstances, and then her fears for her friend. 'You must go after them. Taking a woman into the mountain is most unusual. And I have a bad feeling that she may not come out again.'

'Why do you fear that?'

'I don't know,' she said, 'but the whole thing is very strange.'

He contemplated her face for a while, as she jogged her hips in place to keep him pleasantly hard. He rubbed his loins in a circular motion against her and grinned conspiratorially.

'Can you get away from your companions?' he asked suddenly.

'Perhaps.' She shrugged. Divining his meaning she asked, 'Will it help Elder Sister?'

'I have sent a message to Miyako, and I hope it will be answered. Some friends of mine are waiting at Koya-san, in one of the pilgrim inns below the monastery. Seek them out. Tell them what is happening and have them head back in this direction. I will follow the *yamabushi* up the mountain. But if I find Osatsuki and manage to escape with her from their clutches, I might need help.' He described his friends to her.

'I will do it,' Midori said. 'But hurry — please hurry. I am so afraid for Elder Sister Osatsuki.' She shivered in fear.

The tremour of her frame returned Jiro from contemplation of his duty to the needs of the here and now. He clutched Midori's backside to him and raised himself slightly on his knees, then set to in earnest. The brunette responded fiercely. Her arms clutched at him, roving over his body, tickling his balls, and then rubbing the length of her creamy lips as far as she could reach. Her body arched, and she threw her head back as Jiro plowed into her. His movements became more rapid until at last he stiffened. She bit his shoulder, and a stream of thick seed hosed into her interior, pulsing the length of her gluey channel. She grunted quietly at his weight, and then forgot the familiar discomfort as the tremors in her own body grew into a wild climax.

They rested thus for a while until Midori, with an expert and well-practiced twitch of her body, rolled the young man off her. He lay on his back and contemplated the dappling of the leaves high above them.

'You must pay me something,' grinned Midori, her eyes on her companions who waited on the temple steps.

Jiro's eyes opened wide. 'I am sorry. I have absolutely nothing to pay you with. When you find my friends, they will be able to repay you for all you have done. . . .'

'Oh, just like a samurai!' she said in exaspiration. She smiled then. 'I should be used to it by now. slide your hand into my sash. There is a string of cash there.' He did as he was told and palmed the small string of copper cash. The square-holed coins, threaded on a string, clinked dully. He passed the money to her ostentatiously, and she laughed in bitter amusement.

By midday, Satsuki's fortitude and good humour had become ragged at the edges. They walked at first up a relatively easy slope through an open wood of pine, pawlonia, and other trees Satsuki could not identify. Gradually the path became more difficult and the forest closed in. The mountain trail wound before and behind

134

them, fleecy white clouds rose above, and in between marched the *yamabushi*, chanting their liturgy.

They paused at midday for some rest, food, and the inevitable ritual. Towards later afternoon they paused beside a mountain hut in a large clearing. Satsuki sat beside a mass of wild rhododendrons in full bloom, idly plaiting a wreath while the *yamabushi* went through the by-now-familiar motions of clearing and marking a sacred site for a ritual. Prayers were said, a fire was lit, swords and axes cut into the air while sacred formulas were recited. The purity and power of those assembled grew with each moment. Satsuki was not called upon to participate in the ritual, nor was she approached throughout the night. They set off the following dawn.

They passed the statue of the Fudo of Greeting and rested for a while. The path climbed, following a tortuous ridge. Rituals and observances were kept. They climbed certain rocks that lay off their path, avoided certain others while reciting appropriate verses. Then they started climbing in earnest. Satsuki trudged on, concerned about her bedraggled appearance. Suddenly the column broke into sunlight.

They were standing in a clearing on the lip of a cliff. Behind them the forest spread away on three sides. Before them was nothing but the empty sky. She crept closer to the ledge. Below her the ground fell away for hundreds of feet to a carpet of green moss. Suddenly the picture came into focus. The 'moss' was the tops of trees that lay below. Bare rocks, some white, some black, crowded the base of the cliff like hungry fangs. Inwardly shaken though outwardly composed, Satsuki crawled back to her place in line. Daisangyoja stood facing them, waiting for the last of the *yamabushi* to reach the clearing.

'We are now on the Cliff of Judgement. It is here that the real purification will take place. Are you all of pure mind?' He asked forcefully.

'Yes!' responded the *yamabushi* with a shout.

'Are you pure of body?'

'Yes!' they responded as before.

'Let all those who are not depart this place!'

None of the *yamabushi* moved.

Two of the senior ascetics approached the cliff and knelt facing one another. The first of the men in line, one who had been on the pilgrimage before, lay down on his belly before them, then crawled over the cliff's edge. The two held on to his ankles, lowering him until only his hips and legs were visible.

Daisangyoja stood between the man's legs and commanded, 'Confess!'

'I will confess,' responded the ascetic. 'I have been uncaring of my parents, abandoning them in their old age for a life of banditry, before I began following the way. I did not respect the buddhas or the shrines. . . .' His litany was a long one. At long last the *yamabushi* leader stood aside.

'Let him be tested!' Daisangyoja called out in a terrible voice. The men holding the penitent's ankles released their grip.

As the *yamabushi* slid helplessly into the void, the two assistants renewed their hold on his ankles. An almost silent sigh came from the congregation. The two assistants hauled the man up, and he was replaced by another. Satsuki shivered inwardly, trying not to think of the result of a slip by the assistants. Daisangyoja positioned himself between the man's legs again, and the ritual was repeated.

Sunk in her own thoughts, admiring the scenery, Satsuki did not follow the ritual closely. The man suspended over the cliff, the fifth or sixth in line — Satsuki could not tell — had just finished his confession.

'Let him be tested!' said Daisangyoja. The assistants released their hold, and the man started sliding down. They snatched at his heels, but his slide continued. There was one sharp cry, and then silence. The two assistants looked at one another in impassive silence. Groans came from the assembly. Daisangyoja faced them 'A man is not always fully penitent. The Judgement Cliff can always tell. He will be reborn again, to start on the Way once more.'

The ritual resumed. The only sign of the missing man was the trembling of the novices as they approached the cliff.

Finally it was Satsuki's turn. Her mind had been revolving around the question of how to maintain decorum while suspended head down over a cliff. She knelt elegantly at the cliff's edge between the two assistants, bowed at Daisangyoja, bowed to the assistants, then slipped forward over the cliff. Strong hands gripped her ankles and spread her against the cliff. Daisangyoja stood between her legs and demanded her repentance. She recited her sins: she had not been able to present herself properly for the use of the *yamabushi* band because of lack of proper materials; she had not been able to restore customers to proper sartorial condition before they left her; she had rejected and not dealt properly with the poor man who had so enjoyed inflicting violence with his lovemaking. . . .

The litany was not long, and at last it ended. She waited calmly for the final act. There was a change in the order of things, however. Daisangyoja stood between her legs without moving. 'The In and the On must be purified together,' he said, refering to the universal male and female principles. He knelt between her legs, and she felt him raise the hem of her robe. His chest slithered over her taut buttocks, and then the tip of his prick probed at the crack of her anus. His palms were on either side of her body, and he dug about for a while until he found the proper entrance. Charmed by the sentiment, she waited patiently for what was to come. The wide head of his member found her soft lips, and his pole lodged itself in the hungry mouth. His weight pushed him down slowly but inevitably until he was sunk fully in the depths of her cunt. He let his weight down onto her back, and then she saw him raise his hands and clasp them before him, over her head.

'Now!' she heard him say softly, and the assistants let go of her ankles. For one moment she was free. All earthly cares fell away from her as their twined bodies, his supported only by the cock lodged in her belly, slid towards the sky before them. Illusion fell away, and she was borne, exhilarated, through layers of her illusion to the final reality. Her senses disappeared, and she was conscious only of the now, and of the point of joining of herself and the other.

The cruel grip on her ankles brought her back to mundane reality. For one moment that seemed like eternity she was ready to fight to be free again, and then the illusion of good manners and breeding took over again, and once again she was Osatsuki, a lady of Miyako. The sudden thrust of Daisangyoja's body into her precipitated an orgasm that shook her body into shards of feeling. As she was pulled back, she lay passively allowing the waves of pleasure to finally subside. Daisangyoja rose from between her thighs and the assistants returned her to her place.

The ritual continued. The *yamabushi* prayed on the cliff. The novices confessed fearfully over the drop, their fears making them truthful.

Daisangyoja had been peering down the cliff, a puzzled look on his face. As the *yamabushi* file left the Cliff of Judgement, he called two of the senior men to him for a whispered consultation. They bowed and hurried back down the trail while the rest of the group proceeded on their way.

The sylvan atmosphere and the lengthy climb made Jiro less cautions than was his wont. He had not drunk any water in some hours. His breakfast had been bracken shoots, some wild berries, and a single delicious pine mushroom. The sound of a stream penetrated his consciousness. A ridge of rocks barred the path, and he started to clamber over it.

His attackers, fortunately, were less cautious than they should have been. The first *yamabushi* leapt with a yell from the heights of a rock that bordered the path. Jiro pulled back from the sword blade that stabbed at his side. He twisted desperately, and a stone rolled out from under his foot. He slipped to the ground, and the sword hissed over his head. His rolling body tripped the second *yamabushi*, and they both slid down the path.

Jiro recovered first. He rose to his feet, and his great sword arced from its scabbard. He paused to collect his wits, his head still ringing from its contact with the stones of the path. He cut down, but the *yamabushi* managed to roll away. The other man advanced from above, his sword ready. Jiro slid forward and thrust with both hands. The *yamabushi* parried effortlessly, but Jiros move was a feint. He slipped sideways, reversed his sword, and thrust under his left armpit. The second *yamabushi*, who had silently rushed him from behind, grunted as the long blade stuck into his abdomen. Jiro released the long sword and drew the short blade from his sash. The *yamabushi* yelled and charged, expecting his longer blade to give him an advantage. The other *yamabushi* grunted in agony and slid forward onto the sword, which hit the ground and drove itself further into his body.

The charging *yamabushi*'s blade whistled down. Jiro's hand, held stiff and flat, rose parallel to the blade and deflected it. He cut at the *yamabushi*'s torso, and his blade stuck into the man's hip. The mountain man checked his charge. He made a convulsive leap backwards and rose through the air, to land on a jutting rock. Well out of reach he panted heavily as Jiro retrieved his long *katana* blade. His panting changed to a scream of agony as Jiro's short blade grew from his belly. The *yamabushi* looked down in horror at the hilt of the short sword protruding from his belly and toppled forward off the rock. The last sound he heard was the whistle of Jiro's long sword as it cleaved the air.

Chapter Twelve

The morning dawned bright and clear. Before the *yamabushi* rose the peak of a massive mountain. Around them rose other peaks, as massive and imposing. They started through the mists of the morning. Satsuki bore up well with early rising, something that was not her habit. She wondered what she, a lone woman, was supposed to be doing here. From the comments she overheard she realised that the younger *yamabushi* were as puzzled. The older ones kept their counsel, but she managed to note many a searching glance sent in her direction.

Now the route became difficult. They clambered over and between massive rocks and through brush where the path seemed to disappear and only the knowledge of the more experienced *yamabushi* allowed them to proceed.

Their path led up, switching back and forth across the steep face of a cliff. Near the summit the climb necessitated handholds. Then the ledge widened somewhat. Satsuki peered over the shoulders of the men before her. Daisangyoja stood before a wide crack that bisected their path. There was no way around, and no way down, considering the difficulties of the climb. He turned to his followers and called, 'Believe!' then turned and leapt the chasm. The rest of the *yamabushi* followed.

When Satsuki's turn came, she looked down curiously at the cleft. Between the lips of the ledge was a fall of several score feet. Below it lay jagged rocks. Seeing her hesitation, Tsuneyoshi turned and called out, 'Believe!' Startled at the call she jumped and landed handily on the other side.

More cliffs, more rocks to be traversed. Again they climbed a cliff, inching painfully up a narrow path, the chasm below them yawning deeper. The ledge beneath their feet narrowed, then widened to a clearing that could take most of the group. Daisangyoja stood before them again.

'Here is the final test,' he said. 'To pass here you must think of the Eternal Nothing, you must banish the world from your thoughts. There is but one way to pass here, by purifying your minds.' On a more prosaic note he added, 'The only way to pass here is by sliding up the ledge with your back to the wall. When you reach the Rock of Nothing, you must pause. Thinking of the Great Nothing, you swing your body into the void. For those who are without desire there is a hold on the other side. For those who are still attached to the world, there is nothing but a long fall. . . .'

He turned and proceeded along the path, which narrowed as before. Inching down the ledge with their backs to the rough wall, the party progressed. Before her Satsuki could see far down and away into a verdant valley. The peaks rose in majesty around her. The sky was clear, and she was lost in its azure depths. Her outstretched left hand found a smooth, well-worn handhold, a rock sticking out of the cliff face. She held it firmly. Her left foot encountered emptiness, and a smooth bulge of rock impeded further progress. 'Now!' came a faint voice to her bemused mind. She swung away from the cliff. For a dizzying moment that seemed to last forever she was suspended between heaven and earth, supported only by a grip on a knob of rock. She had the momentary urge to let go, to sever all ties with this world of woe. All too soon her body dragged her back to earth. Her right foot completed its swing and found purchase on the other side of the rock. Her hand was held by Tsuneyoshi's, and she was hauled to mundane safety.

'Thank you so much!' she said with great propriety.

They travelled the steep wooded mountains the rest of the day, penetrating deeper into the wilds. At last they came to the thin thread of a small stream. They passed through a tangle of bush after reciting a magical formula imparted to them by Daisangyoja in a whisper. Satsuki was not vouchsafed a formula. She parted the bushes and bowed to the fierce-faced figure behind it.

'It's only a statue,' laughed Hachibei, who had been right before her.

'True,' she answered softly, 'but a statue of the venerable

Shakamuni.' And she bowed again.

A cliff barred their way. Daisangyoja stood before it, unmoving. The file of *yamabushi* clustered silently at his feet.

'We are now approaching the climax of our pilgrimage,' said the master in his hypnotic voice. 'The Tozan-ha and the Honzan-ha have perverted the way of En-no-Gyoja, our founder. Here is the site where the true letter of the law will be reborn. From here the brightness will be reestablished. You must go forward without fear or doubt. I will open the way for you into the precincts of the Western Paradise. Later, through my magic, I will open the New Age and reestablish through austerities that only I know, the New Age of blessings.' He turned and faced the cliff face and bowed deeply.

'Open!' he called in a terrible voice.

'Hear and obey!' called the senior *yamabushi*. The novices took up the call.

'Open!' he called again.

'Hear and obey!'

He raised his beringed staff in his left hand, then lowered it slowly until the butt touched the ground. He turned again and motioned Satsuki to his side.

'When the mountain opens,' he said quietly, for her ears only, 'you will crawl through the buddha womb. When you come out, straddle the exit and wait!'

He turned again and bowed to the mountain. 'I, the complete being, demand you open!'

He raised his right hand above his head and then in a flick of an eyelash slammed his palm against the rock face. There was a shattering sound, the part of the rock face crumbled to reveal a narrow opening in the cliff. Daisangyoja moved to one side, turned, and motioned to Satsuki with his eyes. She bobbed her head at him, climbed into the hole, and disappeared inside.

It was dark but reasonably smooth. The floor was rough rock, and the tunnel seemed to wander on forever in the dark. She could only crawl along on all fours, hoping for an end and wondering about her appearance. She tried to see behind her, but the small circle of light quickly vanished behind a turn in the tunnel. She wondered desperately how she could maintain her appearance after climbing through the dirt. She narrowly avoided hitting her head on the ceiling, turned with the tunnel, and saw daylight. She crawled out, to find herself on a small grass-floor glen between two rocks. She lay there panting for a moment, then recalled that others were to follow her. Hastily she checked her appearance. Her gaiters were filthy, she noted, though her robe had been protected somewhat by her travelling pantaloons. Her hair was a mess, but a few strokes of her comb made it at least manageable. Fortunately she had worn a kerchief, so the damage was not irreparable. Hastily she set herself to rights, then, following instructions, stood braced against the cliff wall, her legs straddling the cavern exit. She dreaded the ordeal, knowing that nothing in her appearance — neither her underclothes, her smell, nor her toilet — would bear close inspection. She vowed that the humiliation of having to present herself in this fashion, without the minimal amenities, would not soon be forgotten.

The first of the *yamabushi* poked his head out of the cavern, noted Satsuki straddling the exit, and crawled through between her legs. Another followed, then more. Daisangyoja was the last to emerge. He bowed to her without a word.

They were standing in a small fan-shaped meadow. The two sides were bound by cliffs that towered above them. The third side gave a magnificent view of the mountains, rolling away from them for mile after mile. The meadow sloped down, terminating abruptly in a fall of hundreds of feet. A perfect hideout. At the apex of the meadow was a shallow cave. The cliffs appeared unclimbable, but for some scraggly pines that clung grimly to the rock.

The *yamabushi* dispersed and began setting up a ritual enclosure. The paper-festooned rope was stretched to encompass the entire space. An altar was prepared on nine layers of nine sticks each. Brass implements, drums, conchs, and other paraphernalia were produced from the *yamabushi*'s bags. She wandered around, peeped into the

146

cave, which was nothing more than a small person high depression in the cliff extending two feet into the rock. Then she waited patiently, standing near the cliff's edge, enjoying the view of the mountains and the sky unfolding before her.

The rituals took up the rest of the day. Throughout, Satsuki sat where she was told and followed the intricate moves of the ritual with only half her mind. She could not help wondering what would become of her, what her place was in the scheme of things. And beneath it rose tiny streams of resentment. She had so much to offer, and it was all wasted on these wild men.

The ritual was over. At last she had her own role to play. Nude, she entered the cave as she had been bidden. Daisangyoja stood before her, his head touching the roof, his face shadowed. His magnetic eyes bore into her own, and he pressed his warm flesh against her cool curves. His mouth opened. She parted her own red lips expecting an exploring by his tongue. Instead of a warm oral digit, however, only a single syllable came out, a sound to end all sounds. With the mantra still echoing continuously from his mouth he sank down to a lotus position. His skin stroked smoothly over her own. The emitted breath of the magic syllable stirred her unbound hair, then caressed her face. He descended lower, sinking from her sight in the gloom. The power of his breath puckered the valley between her breasts. Her nipples, erect from the cold, felt the passage of the sound until it passed and penetrated the recess of her nave. There it stopped. As if in a trance she felt his hands urge her downwards. She complied, her thighs curving naturally around his body. She was not surprised to find herself being impaled on his massively erect member. The blunt head of the instrument parted her soft nether lips. She sighed in accompaniment to the magic syllable he uttered. The hot sword penetrated her willing flesh without pause until she rested comfortably on his thighs. Her heels clenched behind his hard buttocks, and her arms curled around his neck. She jobbed up and down to increase their pleasure, but Daisangyoja's firm hand stayed her.

There were sounds from the entrance. Past her shoulder

147

Satsuki could see hands coming and going as willing helpers blocked up the entrance to the cave with rocks and clay. The pale entrance grew darker and darker, the pale sky becoming a blot, a spot; then it was gone.

'How long will we have to stay here?' she asked tremulously.

'Forever!' he answered, and his sword of flesh stabbed up into her vitals.

Moving slowly, his hand began a sensuous movement over her back. In the narrow space, enclosed by masses of earth and rock, she could not move. He stroked the skin of her back, touching all the sensitive planes of her torso. Gradually the tempo of his moving hands quickened. She saw her former lovers in her mind's eye. Her deceased husband, the many men she had pleased in her professional career. She tried to move and support his thrusts into her willing body, but the binding earth stopped her motions.

Her breathing quickened with the tempo of his moves, and she was suddenly conscious of two things: his cock was barely moving in her, all sensation being caused by his hands, and her climax was rapidly approaching. She tried to resist the latter. She forced her thoughts onto mundane things, but the insidious motion of his hands on her back and arse brought forth the reality of her body. She whimpered in the dark, hungering for more pleasure; then the orgasm shook her, and she let down a shower of juices that moistened their joined hairs.

He commenced his movements again, his mouth sought hers, and he locked her firmly to him while his maleness plundered her soft insides. They remained joined until Satsuki lost all track of time; only her repeated orgasms served as a metronome, tolling away the hours.

With time, thought ceased. Her climaxes continued, but they detached her body from herself. She floated somewhere on a hazy cloud, approaching *satori*; the death within life, the unity with her lover, the cessation of her being. Not thinking any more, her limbs disobedient, she waited for death to come. Suddenly she felt cool air on her back. Painfully she managed to turn her neck. A small point of light came into being. It widened, and she could see moonlight illuminating the niche. Daisangyoja's face was unnaturally calm, his eyes open to mere slits, a slight smile on his lips. *He is beautiful*, she thought, and abandoned herself to the delicious pleasure of his erect member still distending her soft cunt.

She turned again as a crash of rocks and hard breathing broke into her reverie. A wild face, barely seen, glared at her. It glistened and stank of male sweat and a sweet stink that hinted of something worse. The wild eyes saw her in the moonlight, and a grin split the dirt-smeared face. More rocks flew aside until the opening was wide enough for the figure to insert massive shoulders.

'At last!' the face croaked, and a horny, filthy, massive paw grasped her naked shoulder and pulled her back. she looked at Daisangyoja's calmly smiling face and screamed as she was dragged into the moonlight.

Chapter Thirteen

The trail was not easy to follow. Jiro's city senses had been sharpened, however, by Okiku's training. She had grown up in mountains similar to these and had taught him the woodsman's craft. Occasionally he would make a mistake and follow a false trail, but somehow he always managed to recover.

He followed the *yamabushi* band across cliffs and rocks, through rough patches and over chasms they had leaped. Once when the trail seemed to be completely lost on the rocky slopes of a lowering cloud-drenching mountain, he found that a massive rock has fallen across what seemed to be the right path. At the time he had cursed and sought a way across the obstacle, only to find the true trail in his efforts. In another instance he found a mark — a deep scratch in a clay bank — probably left by Satsuki.

Towards evening, Jiro heard motion on the trail before him. Brush was being crushed under the passage of many feet. He hid himself among some loose rocks, sheltered by a large *sakaki* bush. A file of *yamabushi* passed him by, heading down the mountain. He looked on in puzzlement. There was an air of excitement about the group. The young samurai looked at them carefully from between the broad green leaves. Satsuki was not among them. He puzzled at the problem for a while as they moved out of sight. His thoughts brought about a renewed spurt of energy. He dashed up the trail, almost heedless of any ambush. At the head of the trail was a large bush. Behind it rose a massive cliff wall. There was no one about. He looked carefully at whatever footprints there were to be seen in the hard earth and rocks, puzzling out their message. There were no handholds up the cliff face, and no trail led off in either direction. Suddenly his craftsman's eye caught sight of the bare cliff face. He remembered his father's expertise as a shipwright and the pride he took in making wood joints invisible. Jiro examined the rocks behind the bush. They had been cleverly put together to hide a cave. Fear for Satsuki bit into him again. He set to work removing the barrier, dark thoughts of revenge turning in his brain.

A dark tunnel, marked by the passage of many bodies, met his graze. He considered the passage doubtfully. It *seemed* to lead somewhere, but to what purpose? Mentally he shrugged. No one was about to explain the mystery to him, so he had better explain it to himself.

Long sword held before him, Jiro crawled along the pitch-dark passage. His massive frame was barely able to penetrate the hole. He was about to give up, when he caught a slight greying before him. Jiro cautiously crept on. The smell of crushed verdure met his nostrils. He ached to pull himself out of the hole as rapidly as possible, but caution held him back. Lucky that it did, for within the greyness he saw some dark object move before the exit of the tunnel.

Jiro inched cautiously forward. A *yamabushi* dressed in white faced him, talking. Jiro froze, then realised that the guard was talking to another perched above the exit to the cavern. Jiro lay in the musty dark and considered his position. The guards faced one another, and the one above the cave entrance was particularly dangerous. There was no way of reaching him. Defeated for the moment, he rested on his elbows.

'Eh, Sunekichi, she's a good-looking woman,' the voice above Jiro said coarsely.

'Too good for you, Crook Face,' laughed the other.

'Think they're still fuckin' in there?'

'Watcha mean? The master's gonna screw her to death. . . .'

'Whaa? Such a fine piece of woman?'

'Don't you listen? The master's gonna combine his yang with her yin. Think she can stand it?'

'Hey, she don't have to *stand* it!' The voice above Jiro's head laughed.

'Well, anyway, they're goin' to be in the cave for a long time. Said your prayer yet?'

'Aw, hell. Is it time already? Surely the buddhas will forgive one miss. . . .'

'Say your prayer, animal. You're not likely to get any of that warm softness inside. The master will emerge alone in two weeks. Until then you and I and those who'll replace us in the morning gotta say our prayers and help repel the demons.'

Their discussion was replaced by the mumbling drone of a magic spell. Jiro crept backwards through the cavern, swearing softly in English as he negotiated blind corners. Japanese, he had long known, was not a good language to swear in. His father, an English seaman, had taught him that.

He sat in the dark contemplating the blank cliff face. His mind worked furiously, yet could find no solution to the dilemma. Under ordinary circumstances two guards would be easy to dispose of. Unfortunately they occupied an unassailable position. If he could pull one of them to him now — the one over the cavern . . . Or if they were to fall asleep . . . But any attack would entail delay in getting out of the narrow wormhole, and such a delay would be fatal.

In the end he had no choice. Selecting a stout branch, he tied a series of prongs to it from the branches of a thorny mountain lime. It would have to do duty as a sleeve tangler. He must thrust it at the cavern mouth guard and draw him down to killing distance, hoping he was quick enough to get out or at least hold the other at bay. . . .

Before he could crawl into the hole his eye was caught by an object glimmering in the moonlight above his head. It was too regular to be a rock. He looked at it carefully, then dismissed it from his mind. Someone had lost or inserted a *geta*, a wooden patten with wooden uprights for soles, into a crack in the rock above his head. Travellers were always losing their footwear. He was kneeling to crawl into the cavern again, when the idea struck him. What would a patten be doing there? He stood and regarded it for some time. The sandal was stuck into a horizontal crack in the rock face. As far as he could see the crack slanted upward. If it could be followed . . .

He reached upward and felt the rock with his fingertips. Hidden from view from below, there appeared to be a small ledge. He traced it with his fingers. It led higher than he could reach — perhaps to the top of the cliff? There was nothing to do but try. He tied his loose clothes tightly to him and strapped his long sword to his back. His straw sandals were useless for climbing.

Jiro stuck his fingers deep into the crack and took a deep breath. With sheer force of shoulders and forearms he hauled himself up. Aided by scrabbling toes, he managed to raise himself to some support, two feet off the ground. His toes found a hole, and he shifted his grip. At last he found himself standing on the narrow crack. Tiny, imperceptible cracks provided handholds. The patten was at the height of his nose now but several feet away. He inched towards it, and the crack raised him higher and higher up the cliff face. He reached the wooden sandal and passed it, noticing, as he did, that it had only one wooden upright instead of the customary two. There were more cracks, even ledges, the higher he climbed, but the way was never more than a sketch on the rock. He glanced down once and was glad of the dark. The silvery surface seemed far below him. He put all his energies into the climb, searching out the best handholds, thankful for his youth working on ships, grateful to Okiku for having taught him how to climb.

There were several unpleasant bulges, beetlings of the rock, which he knew he would be unable to contemplate in the full light of day. He overcame them and the climb eased. At last he found himself on a narrow ridge of rock. On either side the rock fell away sheerly into darkness. He collapsed gratefully on the hard rock, drawing in large gulps of air. The moon came out from behind an errant cloud and shone down into the two chasms.

There was a lighter glimmer below, and suddenly. Jiro realised where he was. He stilled his panting with an effort. Directly below him stood one of the *yamabushi* guards, his back to the cliff face. The bowl he was in was fan shaped, and the *yamabushi* and his hidden observer looked out over ridges of forested mountain, silvered by moonlight. Jiro looked down carefully. Finally he managed to locate the other man, standing below Jiro and to his left. His legs straddled a dark splash Jiro knew to be the cavern exit. This time the samurai smiled. He considered the cliff face minutely. The way down seemed to be easier. The slope was more gradual and covered by scrub that offered some shelter. He started the descent just as the breeze that blew over the mountains freshened.

There was a rumble of rock and a clatter of stones. The *yamabushi* below him jumped and turned around. The other laughed. Their voices came clearly to Jiro above them.

'Someone's coming!'

'From these cliffs, Crook Face? Never been in the mountains, have you? City boy, eh? It's only the mountains talking.'

'Come on, Sunekichi. Mountains don't talk.'

'Fat lot you know, city feller. Rocks crumble all the time. Me an' my dad was hunters in Ugo. Out in the mountains all day and night. Oh, they fall, all right. Every time the wind blows or there's a thaw.' Another slide of rock punctuated his words, and Jiro took advantage of the noise to descend several more feet.

Slowly he got closer and closer to his quarry. At last he found himself poised directly above Sunekichi. He was about to leap, when he heard the sound of a snore. Looking around carefully, he cursed himself for a fool. Four more figures were lying huddled near the cliff face. He leaned over and peeped down. The *yamabushi*'s head presented too small a target, and a slight overhang prevented him from dropping a rock directly on target. He touched his sword tentatively. The other guard was out of sight from where he stood, perhaps answering a call of nature.

Jiro dropped, and his sword whispered overarm from its scabbard. The startled guard had time to draw one breath at the massive figure that blocked his sight before the blade cleaved him from pate to sternum. Jiro was struggling to extricate the curved steel, when he heard a cry behind him. He spun and threw his short sword in one movement. The

157

blade thunked into the second guard's chest, but not before the man let out a cry.

'What is it? What's happening?' The other *yamabushi* surged to their feet and stared about. Jiro, unarmed, ploughed into them. A massive fist split the nose of the closest man, still dreamy from sleep. The others, more alert than their companion, had leaped to either side as waves part before a ship. Jiro spun around weaponless. The *yamabushi* considered the bloody giant before them for a moment, then leaped to the attack. Jiro fell.

He rolled over against their knees. Two of the mountain warriors leaped high; the third was knocked off his feet. Jiro rolled upright while the *yamabushi* writhed and screamed in pain, curled around the throwing knife Jiro had planted in his belly. The young samurai stood panting, and the other two *yamabushi* charged. He parried both attacks with the short sword he had taken from the knifed yamabushi. The sword was poorly made and had a bad balance, but it was the best he had.

They screamed and charged again. Jiro's sash snapped into the face of one, and the man parried the cloth, which slipped from his blade. A quick skip forward and a stop thrust to the face for the other one, who jerked back. Jiro slashed down and cut through muscle and flesh, exposing a length of intestine to the moonlight. The man grunted. Jiro snapped the sash again and entangled the last man's sword arm, then stepped forward and sank his blade into the hilt.

The click of the blade saved his life. He twisted and fell to one side as a short dagger wielded by the disemboweled mountain man ripped skin and some flesh off his hip. Jiro's hand chopped down viciously at the charging figure, and the *yamabushi* fell for the last time.

Jiro secured his weapons and took stock. The small valley was silent. The *yamabushi* were all dead, but there was no sign of Satsuki. On one side of the tiny valley near the cliff wall he found signs of a recent ritual: the remains of an altar, straw rope marking holy precincts, the remains of a *goma* fire with some missed seeds scattered about. He looked at the cliff with interest. There was a depression there, freshly sealed with stones and clay. Midori's warning came into mind, and he tore hurriedly at the wall, his heart sinking.

The moonlight was full upon him as he worked. Rocks fell away, and he paused to wipe sweat from his face, marking it with blood that still covered him. He grinned. The blood was not his, at least most of it. A stone fell away, leaving a tiny dark opening. He pulled more rocks, then a whole pile. Moonlight flooded into a shallow cave, and Jiro paused in shock. Before him the moonlight illuminated a tiny niche. In it were a man and woman, both nude. The man was seated in the lotus position, his hand gracefully supporting her back. Her long black hair fell down in waves. She rode his loins, her feet circling his back. Neither was breathing. For a moment Jiro was convinced that he had failed.

The woman's head turned as if unwillingly and looked at his face. Jiro was suddenly conscious of the image he must present. As if to confirm his thoughts, she screamed high and sharp as he reached for her to help her out of the cave.

Jiro paused in his ablutions. The morning sun shone through the trees.

'I still think I should have killed him.'

'He treated me well, in his way.'

Jiro grunted. He had no patience for religious fanatics or for those of any other kind. Besides, the man had insulted a friend and deserved to die. Privately he resolved that should the opportunity present itself again, he would not hesitate.

Satsuki smiled at him. 'You look so much better now. I was convinced you were a demon from hell when you opened the cave.'

He grinned and breathed deeply. Water ran down his cheeks and his massive chest. The brook chuckled down a mountainside between moss-covered boulders. The sound was so pure and clear, Jiro could almost hear the music of a flute in the notes of the rocks and water. Huge tree trunks obscured vision to all sides. Colourful flowers peeped coyly from between green bushes and ferns. It seemed as if they were alone in the world. There was no sign of pursuit, nor did they expect any. They were lost and, for the while at least, content to stay so.

'How did you find me?' she asked.

'It was rather peculiar. I lost your trail several times but was helped by your very clever device of the azalea wreaths.' She bowed in thanks to the compliment. 'Then at the worm hole I was stumped, but found a crack in the cliff face and managed to crawl up that.'

'What was so peculiar?'

'There was a pilgrim's sandal there, hanging on the cliff. I wonder how it got there. You were there during the day; you must have seen it. . . .'

She shook her head, puzzled. 'No, forgive me for my inobservance, but I am sure there was nothing there of the sort. It would have been rather obvious, would it not?'

He sucked in air through his teeth in puzzlement. There was something odd about the whole affair, now that he could think of it. The rock slides, for instance. There were none when he was climbing the cliff face, nor had he heard any during the preceding nights. His line of thought was broken by Osatsuki.

'Shall I rub your back?' she asked impishly. 'You must be very tired.'

He was suddenly conscious of her body beneath her rather tattered robe. He knelt on the bank of the stream, and she knelt behind him. Her soft hands stroked his sore shoulders gently. The soothing motion soon aroused other thoughts, and he turned, still seated on his knees. He was not surprised to find Satsuki naked to the waist. Her small breasts pouted fully, waiting for his kisses and his hands. There was a smile on her lips, encouraging him. He took full advantage of the opportunity, playing long with her breasts and torso. Then he bore her gently back onto the moss. His manhood stood forward from his belly for a short moment before it was plunged into her depths. For a short time he waited, looking deeply into her eyes, enjoying the fullness of the scene. Then his hips began pistoning, slowly at first, then, as the crisis overcame him, with greater rapidity.

She shook with passion along with him, her insides adding their copious moisture to his sprays of heavy cream. In the final moment she covered his mouth with hers and her eyes filled with tears.

They lay for a long time, teasing one another's skin with their fingers and tongues, gently kissing.

'That was nice and uncomplicated,' remarked Satsuki.

Jiro looked at her in consternation. 'You had a hard time then, Mistress Osatsuki?'

She laughed pleasantly. 'No, not too bad. Please do not concern yourself. And it was *most* educational. I hardly had any idea there were people who lived like that. It was edifying, but I am glad it is over. And please, do not be formal. Under the circumstances it would be ridiculous, and I do so want to get to know you better. Okiku and I have discussed you many times. . . .' She hid her smile with the palm of his hand, and Jiro laughed quietly.

'Very well,' he said. 'I will call you Satsuki, as is proper. We are practically blood siblings, after all, sharing so many secrets and adventures.'

Nonetheless, he could not help wondering what Okiku and Satsuki had talked about when his name was mentioned. They lay together, enjoying the peace of nature and pleasurable companionship, unwilling to go on travelling towards the rest of humankind. He turned to her again, his penis ready, and she opened herself to him.

The denizens of the mountain forest appeared from between the trees, dancing across the boulders like a troop of spirits. One softly played the drone of a *hichiriki*, producing eldritch music. Their music was in rhythm with the wind that blew between the trees and peculiarly in rhythm too with the movements of Jiro and Satsuki's bodies. Unseeing of the two, uncaring almost, they danced across moss-covered rocks teetering for seconds on fallen logs, shooting off in all directions. The speed of their movements grew with the speed of Jiro's thrust. Satsuki closed her eyes, and he laved her lips with his tongue.

The signs of her approaching pleasure were near. Her cunt

161

tightened on his driving machine. Her breath came in tight little gasps. Her nipples hardened to stiff points between his pinching fingers. At last she gave a gentle sigh, and her body trembled throughout its entire length. She tightened convulsively, and then Jiro felt her grip slacken. She opened her eyes in time to watch him come too. His massive frame reared above her body like a wave. A tide of seed sprayed out from his massive member as he sought to bury it deeper into her. He cried out in triumph, crushing a handful of earth, the only contact between their bodies being the length of his male member. He sank down gratefully onto her soft body.

They both raised their heads slightly and considered their visitors, who regarded them gravely in return.

All five seemed ancient. Their hair was full and white. It flowed over their shoulders in snowy masses. They wore the colourful clothes of the *yamabushi* but with a difference. Silk and gold thread predominated. The breeches were of the finest material, the robes tucked into them of silk. On second look, Jiro was not so sure of their antiquity. Faces were smooth and unlined, hands did not display the usual veins of age. Only the eyes contrived to look ancient and infantile at once.

'You did that very well.' It was the sole woman of the five who spoke. She was distinguishable from the men only in her lack of beard.

'We are the Goki, dwellers in the mountain,' another said, forestalling Jiro's question.

'Are you *yamabushi*?' Satsuki asked.

Jiro was nervously conscious of his nakedness and the fact that his swords were not close enough to hand.

One of the men laughed and looked at Jiro with amusement. 'You did not return my *geta*,' he answered Jiro's unasked question.

'So it was you?' he said. 'The rock slides too?'

They bowed from their seats on rocks and branches.

'Why?'

This time the speaker's face was serious. 'We do not care for what Master Daisangyoja was attempting. Long have

162

we dwelt in these mountains, ministering to true *yamabushi*. Master Daisangyoja wishes to disturb the natural order of things. Whether his magic succeeds or not does not matter. It is the results of his actions, his turning people against themselves, that we dislike. So we opposed him.'

'Come,' the woman smiled at them. 'We know the ways of the mountains. You wish to go to Mount Koya. We will show you the way. We are glad you have not killed Master Daisangyoja. But beware. He is a great *yamabushi*, but he is not likely to forget you.'

'I will take care of him, and not with my fist, should we meet again,' Jiro stated forcefully.

Chapter Fourteen

'Are you sure he said we must wait here for him?' Matsudaira Konnosuke asked the slight young girl before him. Obviously awed by the company, she bowed low to the ground while mumbling her replies. 'It will go hard for you if you are lying!' he warned, and she shivered as she looked at his severe face.

He was dressed in brocade silks. His topknot was black and straight as a sword slash. Though Midori knew him to be a stern man, administrator of life and death for the imperial city of Miyako, still she thought she saw a hint of sensuousness in the narrow lips and classical profile. He continued looking at her speculatively. Midori, experienced in the ways of men, still could not tell about this sample of the upper classes. She had simply had no experience with such high-class persons before. She looked around her nervously. The middle-rank guesting house was luxuriously appointed. Monks were supposed to be abstemious, as were pilgrims, but the Shogun's government demanded a minimum of comfort for its minions, at least the important ones.

The smooth, bare wooden pillars and beams of the room were clean and well made, exuding the faint fragrance of *hinoki* wood. The painted *fusuma* panels had been decorated by an artist, and the finger holes for the sliding *fusuma* doors were made of lacquered copper, each cover a different play on the shape of a crane. Peculiarly, the lord before whom she sat was unaccompanied by any attendants except the two women for whom she had searched, and so far neither had said a word. She had been several days on the way, searching for traces of Lord Matsudaira, and had then spent several days more searching for his resting place. All that time, fear for Elder Sister Osatsuki had driven her on.

There was an altercation outside, followed by a low voice calling for Matsudaira's attention.

167

'Forgive the intrusion?'

'Yes?' answered Matsudaira.

'A message from the ronin Miura Jiro, my lord.' The retainer slid the *fusuma* door open, stepped in, knelt, and slid it closed. He was a young samurai, plainly dressed in black overcoat. He bowed and handed a folded slip of paper to Matsudaira with both his hands, then turned and left.

Matsudaira read the short note and smiled. 'Jiro is at the nearby teahouse —'

He had barely finished speaking before there was a rush of movement. The slim woman Midori identified as Okiku rose quickly to her feet. She bowed (rather perfunctorily) in Matsudaira Konnesuke's direction and slipped out the door, not before flashing a brief smile at Midori. The other cowled figure stirred impatiently but did not move.

Govenor Matsudaira looked at Midori. He smiled at her for the first time. 'It seemed you were telling the truth, girl. Mr Miura says he has Osatsuki with him.'

'Wonderful! Oh, wonderful!' Tears of happiness coursed down Midori's cheeks, and she bowed gratefully.

Rosamund looked on curiously. The *yamabushi* girl was attractive in a common sort of way. Her most impressive feature was a mass of soft brown hair, unusual amongst the denizens of the Japans, whose hair was usually a course black. Rosamund longed to touch those soft tresses. She wondered if Goemon felt the same, hiding his feelings behind the stern exterior of his official persona. It was exciting to have Jiro back, and she was getting bored sitting in the guest house. She could not move around freely, since in her guise as Matsudaira Konnosuke's concubine she was restricted to her quarters or palanquin. She had wanted to visit the great monastery of Mount Koya but found the entrance forbidden to women. She wished they could all resume their former guises — Goemon as an itinerant doctor, Jiro as masterless samurai, a ronin, Okiku as pilgrim — and go travelling once again. The enforced inactivity of life in the House of Women, bound about by formal rules and the restrictions of her own uniqueness in this society, had palled long since.

168

'Goemon . . .' She started to ask for some respite from boredom, when she was interrupted by noises from the outside.

Okiku, Jiro, and Osatsuki bowed their way into the room.

'Elder Sister!' Midori squealed, her position and all decorum forgotten.

'It is regrettable you were not able to kill that person,' Goemon said thoughtfully. 'It will undoubtedly cause more trouble, and the Presence wanted the matter dealt with before any coal of discontent could turn into a full-blown religious fire.'

Jiro moved uncomfortably in his seat, his hands folded in his sleeves. 'Had I known we had a commission, nothing would have stayed my hand.'

'Oh, stop your bemoaning, you two!' Okiku demanded sharply. 'We can always take care of him later. I am glad we are united. What do we do now?'

Goemon raised an eyebrow. 'Return to Miyako, of course. There are official duties waiting for me.'

'Nonsense!' scoffed Rosamund. Jiro always wondered at her bluff ways, something no other woman displayed, at least publicly. 'I'm tired of being cooped up in that mansion all day. Let's have a holiday.'

'A holiday?' asked Goemon, scandalised. 'It is necessary to work hard. If a superior man minds his ways, his family will prosper. If the family prospers and attends to its business, the government prospers. If the government attends to its business, the country prospers. How then can a superior man engage in frivolities?' The sententious Confucian phrases rang readily from his lips. His face was held in humourless lines, black brows contracted under his shaven pate.

'Oh, foof?' declared his blonde paramour, accurately if inelegantly. 'If you don't take me,' she pouted, 'I'll get Okiku and Jiro to take me on a pilgrimage of Shikoku Island. That'll show you. You'll have to go without me for months!'

He grinned. 'I'll just have to lay Osatsuki. Or Oko, your delectable little maid.'

169

'Hmf,' sniffed Rosamund. 'You'll never hear the end of it.'

Okiku intervened before the argument could get more serious. 'You can't return to Miyako yet, Goemon. You are supposed to be on pilgrimage. Breaking it off in the middle would be considered a bad omen. In any case, we cannot return to Miyako before the matter of Master Daisangyoja is settled.'

'Very well. We shall have to go to Yoshino to wait.'

'There is another possibility,' Okiku continued. 'Let us go down to Kumano, by the coast. There might be some news of Daisangyoja and his men. The *yamabushi* normally exit the mountains at the southern end, and we will hear news of them there.'

'We will go to Nachi,' Jiro rumbled quietly from his seat.

'Nachi? Why Nachi?'

'I have always wanted to pray at the famous falls shrine there. Also, the Goki cast my fortune, and it was said I need visit the shrine. We are going to Nachi.'

Goemon shrugged. Jiro was always easy tempered, but there was a streak of stubbornness in him. Once his mind was made up, it was impossible to make him see reason. In any case, Goemon also felt the need to travel. Living the regimented life of a city governor with all it entailed was more than a bit tiresome. 'Very well. Nachi Falls it is, then.'

'And *no* retainers,' added Rosamund sharply. 'I'm tired of the palanquin.'

'I have an idea,' Goemon said thoughtfully. 'We can go to Wakayama, on the coast. My retainers will wait there while I cloister myself in one of the temples. Goemon and his friends can then travel by boat to Kumano.'

Okiku clapped her hands joyfully. 'Oh, yes! That's a wonderful idea. There are boats there for rent. And the time is just right.'

'Osatsuki can return to Miyako or wait for us in Wakayama.'

'She is afraid to travel alone,' cautioned Okiku.

'Besides,' added Rosamund sweetly, 'you do so want to

lay her. . . . Why, my love, you're blushing!' She laughed maliciously.

'And wherever Satsuki goes, Midori is sure to come too,' Okiku added. 'They have sworn sisterhood, and Midori acts as Satsuki's apprentice.'

'Okiku, my dear, it seems we two are superfluous. We should let these four travel by themselves, and you and I shall find some pretty boys and have fun by ourselves.' Rosamund was goading Goemon deliberately. He knew that; nonetheless his fist clenched on his thigh.

'I see you are anticipating an entertaining time,' Okiku laughed at her friend.

The boat they had hired at Wakayama was provided with a small cabin furnished with a single tatami-floored room and a clay-lined hearth. During the day the paper shoji windows and wooden shutters were removed, providing a view of the magnificent shores of the Seto inland sea. When they anchored for the night the shutters were raised and the six, tired by the excitement of travel, composed themselves for sleep.

They were rowing slowly down the coast, when their attention was drawn to the sound of fireworks announcing a festival.

'Do let us put in there,' asked Satsuki prettily.

'Oh, yes,' seconded Rosamund.

The two men, in nominal control of the party, looked at one another and smiled ruefully. The boatman was given his orders, and soon they found themselves on a small beach. Crowds of villagers of all ages were rushing about. Gay banners fluttered in the air. The village's newly painted fishing vessels, high prowed and low sterned, rested in a row while a formally clad priest in white robes and black gauze hat blessed them with an evergreen branch dipped in water. Children ran about everywhere. There were booths selling delicacies and small gewgaws for housewives and the young. A barrel of sake had been broached, and the liquor was being offered to all and sundry.

The headman approached the boat. He was responsible

171

for order in the village, and strangers were his concern. When he saw the odd composition of the party — a masterless samurai and his youthful page, the latter's face heavily made up as if going to war, a wandering doctor, a cowled nun, and a respectable-looking city matron — his suspicions were aroused. He was quelled, however, by the writ of passage signed by the lord of Wakayama himself, allowing these strange visitors free movement through the domain. Goemon, knowing the need for papers, had thoughtfully prevailed on the Wakayama lord, a distant cousin, to provide them. Like any true bureaucrat, the Wakayama lord was careful not to be too interested in the disguised activities of the Miyako governor.

They wandered about the village, admiring the festival decorations. A drumbeat started near one of the larger houses. A procession emerged, headed by several youths holding the flags of the village shrine. They were followed by men bearing offerings of rice, fruit, and wine. A young man, his face as heavily made up as Okiku's though in white rather than pink, and dressed in woman's clothing, followed. Behind him came a crowd of people: older men in formal garb, near naked younger ones carrying two objects on carrying poles. More people marched behind, some practising dance steps, others carrying boxes of beans and persimmons.

The procession reached the party of visitors from Miyako. Okiku, in her disguise as a young man, looked at the female impersonator. Under his guise and mincing walk she could see a handsome youth. He glanced casually in her direction, and their looks crossed. He seemed to smile, and she thought he had penetrated her guise.

When the carrying pole party reached their vantage point, Rosamund found it hard not to laugh. One of the objects being carried was a large, straw-stuffed fish. Though dried, its smell seemed to reach out and grab her by the nose, and its hollow eyes stared at her accusingly. To stifle her laughter she looked over the crop of young men. They reminded her of a different crop of porters she had met soon after arrival in the Japans. That band had raped her and then had the image of a red rose tattooed inside her thigh. The sight of these happy young men, and the memories they raised, brought a curious warmth to the juncture of her legs, and she watched their cadenced walk appreciatively.

The procession reached the gateless square arch of the *torii* that marked the entrance to the shrine precincts. It seemed that an altercation was developing. Some of the barrel guardians wanted to proceed directly through the arch, the porters were trying to bolt. The pushing and shoving developed apace. Men cried out, and bodies sweated with effort. The parties charged at one another, grabbing at opponents and the objects of their desire impartially. Occasionally one of the combatants would break off to drink sake out of one of the open barrels that had been left thoughtlessly by the roadside. Refreshed, he would plunge into the melee with a yell of delight. Onlookers – the elders, women, and children of the community – cheered both parties on impartially. Faces reddened. An occasional ear was mashed or eye was blackened as the struggle continued.

'What is going on? What are they fighting about?' Rosamund nudged Jiro, who was standing at her side. He repeated her question aloud to a village elder who was standing and chuckling at their side.

The man bowed respectfully. 'It is our custom, Mr Samurai. The young men try to prolong the festival and are reluctant to enter the shrine where their wildness will be tamed. Other men try to force them to enter. Eventually they will, but a long struggle indicates a good year, and so we prolong it.'

'So it's just a fake battle then?' asked Jiro, vaguely disappointed.

The old man cackled again. 'Not likely. There are bets riding on the outcome, and since this is an affair of the gods, everyone takes it seriously.'

'May anyone join in?' There was a strange light in Jiro's eyes as he regarded the screaming, scuffling mob.

'Of course, of course. Sometimes strangers to the village get carried away and join in. The gods are quite happy with the arrangement. Naturally, since they have no friends to help them, they tend to be more battered, but since this is a god affair, that is not too bad.' He was talking to an inattentive audience. Jiro looked long and hard at the scramble of naked bodies before him. It was obvious, an amused Okiku noted, that there was a struggle going on in his mind between the gravity of his position as a samurai and his youthful exuberance. Youthfulness won out. He handed his swords to Okiku and stripped to his loincloth in a trice. Midori giggled, bowed, and offered him a large earthenware bottle of sake someone had just handed her. He took a giant drink appropriate to his massive frame, shook his head, and plunged joyfully into the fray. He emerged a few seconds later, one hand pushing at a stocky fisher-boy, the other clutching a sake bottle. 'Goemon!' he called, then again, 'Goemon, come on!'

It took Goemon longer to shed his dignity, but soon he too was stripped to his loincloth, aiding one of the two groups.

The struggle lasted for several hours until darkness fell. The fish was almost torn to pieces, and the barrel had been rolled in the mud but miraculously had not been broken. The fight had taken the combatants, most of whom changed sides several times during the day, down to the beach, where both fish and barrel were washed in the brine. At length the village officials managed to restore order, and the two sacred objects were brought to the shrine and offered before the kami.

Jiro and Goemon returned after dark to the boat. They were greeted with derision by Rosamund and Okiku, and respectful bows from Satsuki and Midori.

'Go and wash in the sea!' commanded Okiku.

'You both stink of sake and puke!' said Rosamund, turning up her nose.

Abashed, both men turned to do as they were bidden.

'Oh Master Jiro, please allow me to offer you a towel.' Osatsuki hurried after them. 'And Master Goemon, please let me tend to your wound.' Goemon bore a large purple bruise on one shoulder, but he was well content to have it called a wound. They laughed uproariously, splashing water

174

in all directions as they bathed. They returned to the boat, and Rosamund looked at them critically.

'Both drunk as the poet Li Po. I don't think I will be able to stand it.' Rosamund rose to her feet.

Okiku rose too. 'I think we shall go for a long walk. Drunkenness in gentlemen is not to be tolerated.'

Osatsuki bowed at them. 'Pray allow me to stay and care for the poor gentlemen. Their hurts need attention.'

'My dear, you need not attend to these drunken sots,' Okiku answered. 'They'll soon sleep it off.'

'No, please allow me . . .'

They bowed to one another, though Rosamund could not forbear a slight chuckle as she and Okiku made their way off the boat. 'Shall we sneak back and watch?' she asked Okiku.

'Don't be silly,' her dark friend answered. 'I think it was very clever of you to suggest this way of allowing Satsuki to thank Jiro, but don't be too obtuse. I've something in mind too. Lets go along the shore for a while.' She set off, a definite objective in mind.

Back on the boat, with Midori in attendance, Osatsuki set about her work. She and Midori gently tended to the men's cuts and bruises. She then suggested a rub, which was accepted gratefully by both men. Her hands softened the tense muscles one by one. Only one stubborn part remained hard, and she took care not discourage the tendency, while affecting to ignore it. Midori helped as much as she could, observing her elder sister's actions with wide eyes.

They served dinner. Globefish soup, prepared expertly by Satsuki's own hands, was followed by slices of raw globefish, abalone, and vinegared seaweed. Tiny shrimp and large crayfish competed for the men's attention and their palates. They finished with freshly harvested rice, over which Osatsuki had poured tea spiced with pickled plums and sesame seeds: a specific against overindulgence in sake.

Later she danced, while Midori, who had practised several simple tunes on a flute, accompanied her. Jiro and Goemon were both entranced by the performance and by Satsuki's elegance. They made no effort to enjoy either of the women, knowing by now that Satsuki would lead up to that at the right time and fashion. She did so in the most unexpected fashion, by blowing out the candles that illuminated the cabin.

Ghostly touches were soon felt on both men's skins — the faintest touches of lips, hands, nipples, thighs on the most unexpected places. Their cocks unfurled and rose proudly erect, and the caresses did not ignore the noble members. There was a slither of cloth in the dark, and both men knew that the women had slipped out of their sashes. The touches continued unabated. Now their own robes were loosened. They sat pefectly still. A hungrily sucking mouth was suddenly applied to Goemon's turgid prick. The feeling was in such intense contrast to the previous light touches that he jumped. The mouth — Satsuki's or Midori's, he could not tell — warmed his cock to a pulsating readiness. Smooth, slim buttocks slid against his chest, then moved, downwards towards his belly. He sat perfectly still, knowing that Satsuki could be counted on to orchestrate the matter to perfection.

Gentle hands stroked his shoulders, his belly, grasped his cock. The smooth, full bottom before him continued to descend until it was poised directly over his waiting pole. Sure hands guided the tip until it poised at the dry, tight entrance to the nether hole. The woman before him continued her descent. The firm, tight muscular ring parted before his penetration. A feeling of pleasurable pressure surrounded his cock. The muscles reluctantly parted before his insertion. He stroked smooth breasts and two erect, rubbery nipples and was rewarded by the feel of two female hands covering his and urging him on. He squeezed the breasts roughly and buried his lips in the soft nape before him.

The mounds nestled comfortably on his thighs. His hairs tickled her arse, and she luxuriated in the feeling for a while. Then, using only the power of her thighs, she began riding up and down the long shaft. The pain of the insertion rapidly gave way to pleasure, and she barely managed to restrain herself from vocally noting her enjoyment. She leaned backwards, and Goemon relaxed back to the mat, supported by her helper. He played with the now flattened breasts and stroked the damp and ready lips of the pussy, while she squeezed her arse to increase his pleasure.

The touches of Jiro's skin soon gave way to the power of a single sensation. An expert mouth was applied to his cock and began sucking greedily. His magnificent prick expanded even more than it had before, and he helplessly thrust forward with his hips. After a while the mouth was withdrawn and a new one took its place, laving the length of his shaft, kissing the single eye at its head and sipping at the transparent fluid that gathered there. That sucking too came to an end. He was urged to his feet and knelt between outstretched legs.

The woman was ready, her cunt wet . . . and occupied by Goemon's fingers. Jiro explored some more and found Goemon's long, slim prick stabbing into her anus. He knew what was to be done. Aiming higher than usual, he inserted his shaft slowly into the waiting cunt.

The soft, slick lips parted quickly before his entry. He moved forward until her hairs mingled in a wet mass. Carefully he began a back-and-forth motion. His head lowered to suck at an available nipple, then sought the woman's demanding mouth.

Satsuki listened to the growing sounds of pleasure as both men fucked her apprentice. Midori was rather louder than she should be, she considered critically, but many men, she had noticed, rather enjoyed the sounds of a woman's pleasure. She stopped the action momentarily. Without allowing them to separate, she raised both men to their feet. The difference in sizes had been anticipated, and Goemon's feet rested on a pile of seating cushions.

Satsuki relit a candle. The sight was charmingly vulgar. Midori's slim, wide-hipped figure was suspended between the brawny figures of both men. Her legs were twined around Jiro's hips, her arse exposed to Goemon's ministrations. She sucked desperately at Jiro's lips, while Goemon bit and nibbled at her shoulders. Both pricks were inserted well into Midori's body. Their balls stuck together.

The long shafts, shiny with her juices, appeared and disappeared as Midori climbed up and down using Jiro's hips as a fulcrum. Satsuki looked on. There was much to criticise in Midori's performance, but for now it was satisfactory. There was much yet to be done this evening. She stepped forth with alacrity, dropping her robe.

Chapter Fifteen

'Where are we going?' asked Rosamund.

'I saw you looking at some of those men,' Okiku said irrelevantly. Her eyes moved as if she were searching for something in the dark.

'Yes,' said Rosamund thoughtfully. 'They were rather pretty, weren't they?'

'Don't you think we deserve some entertainment?'

'If you're thinking what I think you are . . . How would I choose one anyway? There were so many of them!'

'Why choose?' laughed Okiku. 'Can't we take them all on?' She hugged her friend, who smiled and arched her back. Her big breasts jiggled suggestively, their nipples erect.

'I imagine I could service them all, and that might just satisfy me. But still . . .'

'I'll help you. I'll choose the best ones for you. Ah, I hear something. This must be the place I was looking for.'

They turned in to a narrow lane, at the end of which was a large, rather dilapidated old barn. Sounds of laughter and music came from between the cracks in the walls.

'We must find a place for you,' Okiku added. They wandered about for a few minutes before finding a tiny building that was used to store grass for thatching. At Okiku's direction, Rosamund made herself comfortable on the soft, sweet-smelling pile. She spread her outer robe, released her sash, and lay back. Okiku could see Rosamund's teeth flash and her perfect white body glimmer in the dark, barely shadowed at her crotch by her golden bush. Okiku knelt quickly and kissed the blonde between her legs. She tasted pleasantly salty, and Okiku could not forbear a quick lick.

'They must not see you, so it will be all in the dark. I'll send them out one by one and caution them against showing a light. Have fun, my dear.'

'What about you?' Rosamund asked softly.

'I have something I want too. Don't worry, I'll be around. If there are any problems, call out. You have your chain and dagger at hand? Good.' Okiku was gone like a shadow.

The festivities in the barn were at full tilt. The young men who had battled so valiantly for the village's prosperity were being repaid for their efforts in wine, food, and an evening's respite from their daily labours. In one corner a group of young men were gambling, their faces flushed with drink and excitement. The largest group was sprawled on piles of rice straw in a rough circle. A man wearing the mask of an old peasant had just finished acting a comic skit. The punch line was rather obvious from the jerking of his hips, and his audience were helpless with laughter. The young man in woman's clothes was making ready to dance. His make-up had run and he was reapplying it, and his neckline was rather more open than a respectable matron's should be. Other young men lay about the barn, telling stories, drinking, or talking quietly. Some had passed out. In one corner a drinking contest was in progress.

No one paid much attention to Okiku's entrance. One or two of the revellers called out to her, offering a drink, recognising a visitor to their festival. She was still dressed in her page's outfit, the heavy reddish male makeup obscuring her features just as the loose sark and pantaloons obscured her figure.

Encouraged by cries of 'Kichibei! Kichibei!' the young man in woman's clothing began to dance. For a man he danced a woman's role quite well, and his audience displayed its appreciation. Gradually the tempo of the dance changed. It became more languid, then faster and faster as the dancer, helping himself with his fan, displayed the stages of a woman's passion. The music changed and the dance became a burlesque, with the fan portraying a reluctant lover and Kichibei an amorous old courtesan. The audience rolled on the ground with laughter, tears streaming down their cheeks.

A heavyset, well-muscled man sat near Okiku. He had been drinking rather less than most, and his eyes, full of laughter, were on the dancer. His loin-cloth bulged pleasingly. Okiku leaned over to him and whispered, 'Excuse me, but you must earn some merit. The nun Sister Bara has ordered me to call you to her. She awaits in the small hut where the grass is stored. Please be punctual and, of course, discreet.'

The young man looked at Okiku in puzzlement. She met his gaze squarely, and he lowered his eyes. She noted he had fine cheekbones, notwithstanding the coarseness of his life. He rose and left the barn. The sky was bright with the light of the moon. He oriented himself and stretched. Loosening his loincloth, he pissed against a convenient tree, then shook himself dry. He approached the small hut cautiously. There was someone in there. He sweated somewhat nervously. Ghosts were about in the night.

'Do not fear. Come here — there is a gift you can give me.' The voice was definitely female, if oddly accented. He crawled inside. In the dark he could barely make out the outstretched thighs of a young woman. His courage rose in him. Drink was fine, but this was better. He slid a hand up each long and tapering thigh. The legs were smooth and perfectly shaped, not the muscular, stocky thighs of the village girls into whose matting he had crept several times before. His face was near the soft bush at the juncture of her thighs, and he sniffed appreciatively.

Rosamund shivered in delight as the dark bulk of the man knelt between her legs. She raised her knees slightly to allow him his moment of quiet contemplation; then suddenly his weight was upon her. She sighed in satisfaction as his thick cock found the gluey entrance and drove up her channel. He was rough and uncaring, and she was grateful. His hard hands, callused from net and oar, squeezed her full breasts. He drove himself into her rapidly, while his mouth was busy about her neck, and shoulders. She felt the pleasure of his hands on her full breasts and the weight of him on her frame. 'Harder!' she whispered, and his movements became frantic and his hands tore at her full mounds.

'This . . . is . . . so . . . good!' he gasped. 'I have never felt such full tits.' He bit a nipple in emphasis, and she moved delightedly under him.

'Yes, yes, bite them, squeeze them! *Don't stop!*' she pleaded.

Sensing her mood, he left all restraint behind. His cock bore into her, the bones of his pubis mashing her beneath him. He bit at her full breasts and followed each bite with a twist of the nipple. She ran her hands the length of his back and buttocks; marvelling at the frantic bulging of his muscles. One finger teased his anus, and his buttocks tightened, driving his prick yet deeper into her. She scratched hard at the soft portion of his inner thighs, and he jerked in agony. The first faint drops of emission emerged from the tip of his prick, and then his sperm burst from him in full thick sprays that soaked her interior. Spent, he lay on her soft belly, his body still undulating slowly as the last of his sperm dribbled from his softening cock. Suddenly she stiffened under him, her teeth bit into his salty-tasting shoulder, and she moaned. Knowing she was coming, he squeezed her breasts as hard as he could and was rewarded with the flash of a smile and a mad dancing of her pelvis. Her spasms died down, and she stroked his back.

'You must go now,' she said softly. 'Return later if you will, but many more must earn merit this evening.'

He climbed off her and while still between her legs, bowed deeply. The night air was cool on his sweaty skin as he walked back to the barn. The party was still going on at full blast when he walked in the door and helped himself to some sake. The young samurai servant caught his eye, nodded, then leaned over and spoke to another youth. . . .

Okiku finally decided it was her turn. Young men were leaving quietly on schedule for rendezvous in the grass shed. Kichibei ended his dance to the delight of his audience and scampered off. She spoke to three young men who had just finished a long and serious talk, and watched them troop off into the dark doubtfully. They would occupy Rosamund for some time. Then Okiku slipped off into the night after Kichibei, who had no doubt gone off to change.

He was standing by a well, about to draw water for himself, when Okiku approached.

'Let me do that for you,' she said in a soft voice.

184

He stared at her warily. There was something about this young samurai lad that stirred his blood. He had no objection to the sort of relationship he thought was being proposed to him, but there was something decidedly odd here. Okiku ran her hands down Kichibei's chest. It was muscular but not too bulky. She leaned forward and bit a pectoral.

'I am sweaty and stink,' he objected.

'You smell just fine to me,' the figure before him countered coolly. 'I like sweaty bodies, my dear.'

Suddenly Kichibei felt he knew what was expected of him. He turned his shoulders coyly and glanced down. The samurai lad laid a hand gently on his shoulder and tilted his shy chin, then kissed him deeply on his painted mouth. They shuddered together, and the samurai youth's arms went around Kichibei's hips.

'I am ashamed,' he whispered.

'Nothing to be ashamed of,' countered the youth, leading Kichibei to a nearby patch of grass. They knelt together, and Okiku's firm hands slowly explored Kichibei's body. She stroked his chest and his sides then loosened his sash while he sat passively on his knees, hands fluttering on the silk sleeves.

'You look so fierce with your short sword,' Kichibei murmured as the hard pommel dug into his hips.

The samurai youth laughed and loosened the scabbard, laying it and the sash aside. A hand descended lower and touched Kichbei's sturdy erection. 'Mine is hardly as magnificent as yours.' Okiku laughed.

'No, no!' protested Kichibei, still enjoying his role as a woman. He reached forward and the samurai youth's hand guided him between the folds of loosened breathcloth. He felt the crisp hairs at the bottom of the muscular, yet soft belly. But then his fingers slipped surprisingly into a warm, slick channel and were guided downwards between the plump female lips. He strained to push on but was restrained by Okiku. She wanted to enjoy the perverse situation to the full, and she continued to act the role of the man. Her demanding hands explored Kichbei's body while holding his hand prisoner between her legs, where she forced his blunt fingers to masturbate her to the full. At last the game reached a plateau. She seized his erect rod and drew it forth from his robe.

'Why, you're a man!' she said in mock surprise. He strove to move forward, but she restrained him again. She turned away from him, her hand still firmly grasping his erect member. Her pantaloons fell by her knees as she knelt on all fours before him. He rose and lunged, guided by her hand. His turgid cock lodged in the thicket that guarded her juicy cranny. She held him there for a moment, supporting herself on her elbows and rubbing the plum tip against her soft lips. Frantic with desire, he pulled her to him, his body humping like a dog's.

At last, satisfied that he had been raised to a fever pitch, Okiku let him have his way. With a grunt, Kichibei sank deep into her juicy interior. He was about to set to work at once, when she restrained him. She smiled at him over her shoulder, holding him in with her muscles and a restraining hand that commandingly held on to his hairy sack of balls. He felt himself expand in the tight, wet warmth. She let him go, and he began to drive into her with an increasing tempo. His hands clutched at her hips, and then when he directed them, he squeezed her small breasts and their prominent nipples. She moved back against him forcefully, her smooth, tight buttocks smacking against his hard belly. He felt his come rise from the depths of his balls, and he cried out in agony when she squeezed the base of his prick.

Without mercy she pulled at the base of his cock, exposing the cream-lathered length to the cold air. Spasms of pleasure racked her as he withdrew and as she slammed herself backwards onto its waiting length. She came furiously, her insides dripping the honey of her come as he watched helplessly in her grip. Her smooth, tight buttocks trembled before his eyes, and he could feel the walls of her cunt shake as she took her pleasure.

Again she exposed his cock to the night air. She smiled over her shoulder and shifted her grip to the plum tip. She

186

raised the aim of his fleshy cannon and moistened the entrance to her arse slightly with the juicy knob. She placed it properly and inched backwards until the rod was firmly seated in the tiny bud opening of her anus. He felt the muscular ring grip him comfortingly, stronger and more demanding than the entrance he had been in before.

'Now!' she commanded, loosening her grip and positioning her hands firmly on the ground. He needed no encouragement. His cock rammed home into her tight nether orifice. Her ring muscles fought him all the way, constricting his entry and milking the length of his shaft. His hairs rubbed roughly into the softness of her buttocks, and his full weight bore down on her. She let out a breath at the fury of his assault. He rested there for a short moment until a twist of her buttocks reminded him there was much to be done. He tried to withdraw only to find that her muscles had purposely constricted around his length. The withdrawal was slow, milking the length of his cock in a way he had never experienced before. He rammed forward again furiously, and again, each time having to fight his way out, his irritated cock sending messages of exquisite pleasure to his brain. They were both panting now, his hand clutched convulsively at her sides. He pushed in again and this time found relief from the strain. From the root of his manpole he felt the rush of liquids streaming forth. He pumped masses of sperm into this woman's backside, while she twitched and jerked beneath him, eyes closed in pleasure as her own climax mingled with his. Finally they collapsed in a pile on the grass.

'Hey, Kichibei, nice performance, but he should have been on top, not you!' A passing drunk regarded them owlishly, then ambled on into the dark.

'I've ruined your reputation.' Okiku smiled at him, still panting.

'It was worth it. Please do not worry.'

'It certainly was, and I won't,' she replied coolly as she gathered her clothes. 'It was a good festival.'

Rosamund was waiting for her in the booth. Her robe and the grass beneath her were sodden. They walked off into the moonlight, holding hands and laughing together.

'Did you have a good time?' asked Rosamund anxiously.

'Of course. Did you think I wouldn't enjoy myself? He was all I could expect.'

'He? Only one?'

'I don't have the same appetites as you. It was nice and kinky.'

'Mine were too,' laughed the blonde girl. 'There was this one with enormous hairy balls and a rather small prick. . . .'

They waded into the sea to wash. 'Do you think. . . .' they both started saying at the same time, then laughed.

'Yes,' Okiku continued the thought for both of them. 'I'm sure Satsuki took good care of our men.'

They walked sleepily onto the boat.

Chapter Sixteen

The boat slipped down the coast, pulling in as the passengers wished at small villages along the coast. They rounded Cape Shionomisaki and watched a flotilla of whaling boats put out to sea. Their near-naked crewmen waved at the boat while their harpooners, no less naked than the standing oarsmen, stood silent and proud at their prows. Satsuki and Rosamund both had delicious shivers, perhaps from different reasons, when Okiku mentioned casually that the men of Taiji, whence came the best whaling crews, had been equally famous as pirates in the olden days.

Past Oshima Island the seas were rougher. Fantastically shaped rocks marked their passage, worn by sea and wind and the will of the kami into the shapes of demon castles and magical beasts.

They put into the Nachi river. The small village at the river mouth was abustle with life. Banners were flying, and drumming could be heard across the waters. Their usually taciturn boatman grinned a gap-toothed grin of delight.

'The *dengaku* dance! It's the thirteenth of the seventh month; the shrine's festival is tomorrow!'

'We'll not find an inn for us here,' Okiku commented mournfully. She had been seasick for the latter part of the trip, and the others had laughed at her unmercifully.

They strolled through the town in the sunset, shoulder to shoulder with groups of pilgrims who had come to join the festivities. Nowhere was there an empty inn room or, for that matter, barn or shed. They retired to their boat discouraged.

Rosamund woke from a light sleep. Myriad itches assaulted her. The droplets of Jiro's sperm drying on her thighs and golden hair itched, and the weight of Midori's thighs on hers was oppressive. As quietly as she could she slid out of the tangle of limbs and moved off the boat.

Ahead in the dark she could hear the beat of drums and the squeal of a flute. She moved purposely in that direction.

Peering from the dark she could see a long line of dancers circling a bonfire. Onlookers crowded round. The dancers were dressed alike in colourful blue-dyed marine-pattern robes and striped sashes. It was impossible to tell if they were men or women: They all wore black masks, only eye slits showing that living beings, and not dolls, were responding to the music. Above the dancers a group of near-naked musicians pounded their music into the night from a drum tower.

Rosamund looked around. The dancing seemed like fun, and she wished she could join. Under the tower she noted a pile of clothing, apparently discarded by the sweating drummers. It was the work of a moment to steal one of the robes and the mask that lay on it. Dressed for the dance she glided through the night past groups of onlookers — mostly town and village folk, one or two groups of armed samurai — and joined the circle.

Okiku peered into the dark and debated whether to join the dance. Rosamund's snoring had forced her out of the confines of the boat. Her seasickness had worn off, and with its departure had come a desire for adventure. She drifted unnoticed from one group of onlookers to another, using skills developed through years of training as a spy and assassin. She paused behind a group of rural samurai and eavesdropped unshamedly. The men were debating the merits of the dancers, and the tone was not theoretical.

Okiku knew, of course, that some samurai used their immunity from normal processes of law to prey on commoner women, particularly in festival time when youth was at its best. She disliked the idea, but as a predator herself and a realist, she knew there was no changing the world. The local villagers, however, had hit on a device to foil their would-be attackers. Dancers, male and female alike, were disguised by masks. Abducting a pliant village girl was one thing; abducting a violence-inclined young farmer, one who would undoubtedly struggle, who might have friends, another. Moreover, with faces covered how was one to know whether one's intended victim was worth the effort?

The samurai were debating the issue with some frustration, when a malicious thought occurred to Okiku. Their eyes and attention were on the dancers, their ears assaulted by the music. One of the men was standing a little behind the rest. It was the work of a moment for Okiku to strike the samurai's jugular with a pointed-knuckled fist and to drag his unconscious form into the dark.

The young man opened his eyes and tried to groan. A sash bound his jaws, and all he could get out was a mewing sound. He was naked and somewhat cold. He tried to move in the dark, and found he was bound with the cords from his own swords. The one who had tied him was a master of the art of *hojo-jutsu*, by which a captive can be subdued. None of the knots yielded, and his hands remained tied behind his back.

'Enjoy rape, don't you?' inquired a voice above him.

In the dark he could barely make out a shape that straddled him. A cold blade touched his neck, then traced a line down his chest to his belly. He braced himself to die.

'How would you like to go on living?' asked the voice.

Hope blazed in the man's eyes, and he nodded vigorously. Dying gloriously in battle was one thing; dying bound and helpless, quite another. . . .

'Get an erection!' commanded the voice, by now identifiably female. His surprise echoed even through the jaw bindings.

'You heard. Stimulate yourself. Get an erection. I want to see that cock stuck up like your prissy self. Lets get a cockstand, boy — or aren't you able? Think of your wife, think of the girls in the dance, your servant, your hand — I don't care. Or else . . .' The sword tip descended until it pinked the base of his cock lightly, then withdrew.

The samurai lay on his back. His eyes closed, and he imagined every erotic thing he could think of. His first woman . . . a servant at his father's house . . . the pleasure quarters on his one visit to Edo . . . other encounters through the years. His cock rose to its full glory, hovering over his belly.

Okiku looked down at her captive. He was pitiful, she decided, but still, her captive. She raised her robe and squatted, impaling herself on the glowing pole. She let her entire weight down on the man. 'If I'm not satisfied, I'll cut it off,' she said conversationally.

Rocking back and forth on her captive brought Okiku's lust well up to pitch. She regretted that his hands were tied, but she knew he would kill her if he got free. She recalled a similar instance — her first meeting with Goemon — when they had fought with swords and ended fighting with their genitalia. The images conjured translated themselves into a lustful frenzy. She bit and clawed the man beneath her, ramming herself furiously onto his supine body while her lust broke.

She came in flashes of hot pleasure that made the man squeal as his balls were mashed beneath her bottom. She mashed her mouth against his bound lips, then bit his neck and chest in a frenzy. Under her the man twisted in a mixture of lust and terror. When she finished, she noted that his tremours were increasing. Her eyes were glazed and his hips bucked into hers. Notwithstanding the terror of her sword, the man beneath her was sobbing into an uncontrollable orgasm. Maliciously, Okiku rose from above him. A stream of white fluid splashed on his heaving belly, streaking his body with glistening drops.

She laughed and rearranged her clothing. 'Let someone find you like that, my friend,' she said over her shoulder as she walked off into the night. Philosophically, the bound man went over the night's events again, hoping for another miracle to occur.

There was the sound of a scuffle in the dark by a small shed. Cautiously, Okiku peered in. It appeared the samurai had made up their mind after all. Her first instinct was to reach for her weapons, but closer investigation changed her mind. Okiku settled down to watch.

Rosamund had enjoyed the dance. At last she tired and

walked off in search of a drink. Rough hands seized her arms, and a palm went over her mouth.

'I said she was a woman, didn't I?' a voice declared triumphantly. 'She was bulging too much in front.' Several pairs of hands explored her full breasts.

She fought them half-heartedly. She was tired and wanted a drink. In the dark of a small shed she was roughly stripped. Eager hands explored her body amidst cries of surprise and delight at the wonders beneath her robe.

'She's wonderful! . . . Feel those tits! . . . What an arse! . . . Me first . . . Give her some sake . . . Me first . . . Feel that nipple! . . .

For some perverse reason she struggled in earnest. A bottle of sake was thrust at her lips, and she took some grateful swallows before driving her nails into an available face that was licking her thigh. The man cursed and slapped her. Rosamund kicked out viciously and encountered someone's soft spot. He responded with a muttered. 'She's fighting!' and a blow on the nearest available part of her anatomy. Hands tried to spread her legs while someone's fingers wonderingly squeezed the engorged clitoris that stuck out from her soft golden bush like a claw. A mouth fastened on her nipple and she bucked it off. It returned, this time biting into the sensitive flesh and raising the pleasurable pain that she enjoyed. She gave a convulsive heave and managed to slip out of their grasp. Leaping to her feet she made for the door. A mass of musky, male bodies, most in varying stages of undress, bore her to the floor.

This time they were not gentle. Her knees were wrenched apart and a thick male member probed mercilessly between her nether lips. The moisture of her channel was greeted with delight, and the organ's owner sank down upon her forcefully. Her head was seized and a blunt, fleshy truncheon smelling wonderfully of male sperm was thrust at her lips. Her jaws were held apart painfully at the hinges, and the cock made its way into her mouth. She hollowed her lips softly, to accept the proffered morsel. More bodies piled onto her. A blunt cockhead forced itself onto one generous breast and the owner started a quick jerking motion against the soft, yielding flesh. His fingers squeezed her erect nipples.

Someone growled, 'Move over!' and her lips were twisted to one side. The man riding her fell to one side. A cock probed her arse and after a moment found the entrance to her anus. She clenched the ring muscles. The man slapped her backside in frustration, and she refused to yield. His slaps became rhythmic, his breathing heavy, as she gradually yielded to the delightful entry. At last his balls banged against her buttocks and against his friend's balls as the latter pumped away into her cunt. She could feel still other male members, in her hands and rubbing against her back and thighs.

Sooner than she liked, the men started spurting their loads onto and into her body. She felt moiture run down her back and tits and the ramming charge of male bodies as they wriggled like eels on her. Their slaps became less frequent, and she managed to release a hand and aim a few strong, random punches to renew their interest. The man in her cunt withdrew, his cock a shrivelled, pitiful thing. His place was taken immediately by another. Rosamund contracted the muscles of her cunt. The man grunted in surprise. She was tighter than any virgin he'd ever encountered. He pushed at her again and again, more violently each time. Finally he withdrew and probed her with a stiff, hurting finger. Gradually she yielded, her attention only partly on her cunt as the man in her mouth spurted her oral cavern full of his load and was immediately replaced by another and the juices ran down her chin.

The man at her cunt was replaced by another, more vigorous, whose heavy cock tore up her cunt as his teeth fastened on her nipple. She began to come, her whole body shaking in a climax that took subjective hours to die down. The men lay on and in her, exhausted by their own fury, as she twisted and moaned loudly, the waves of pain-filled pleasure finally abating. She lay for a long moment in an exhausted coma.

The men rose from their victim's supine body. One placed a final lingering suck on her softened nipple. Another, the one of the finger, slapped her belly viciously one final time. They hurried off into the night, and Rosamund smiled to see them go.

She raised herself somewhat painfully, stretched and gave a full yawn.

'You look absolutely ravishing,' came a familiar voice from the dark. 'All streaked with pearl juice from head to foot.' Rosamund giggled and touched her sticky mass of golden hair. One of the rapists had impatiently ejaculated into the beautiful soft pile. 'And you'll have some beautiful bruises to explain, too.'

'That's no problem,' said the blonde. 'I'll say it was Jiro. He sometimes doesn't know his own strength. Did you have a good time watching?'

'Not only watching — I had some of that earlier. Actually, I did to him what they did to you.

Rosamund giggled again. 'Then we're even, they and I. I enjoyed it a lot.' She put a hand on Okiku's shoulder. 'I'm glad you were watching over me, though.'

Okiku smiled in acknowledgement. 'Let me know next time? Its better to be safe.'

They left the hut and headed for their friends and bed. Behind them the music died down.

They left the boat early the following morning after paying the boatman off with a handful of silver. He hastened back downriver, anxious to spend the largesse at the festival. They climbed up the long path to the shrine. The way was decorated by vertical banners, the offerings of the devout. They rubbed shoulders with pilgrims in white, villagers from the area in colourful coats, priests in formal robes. In the background, above the sound of drumming and the chatter and hum of the talking and praying celebrants, could be heard a muted roar.

The forest path was bordered by stone plaques and statues, small rest houses, and minor shrines. The sound of music grew stronger, the crowds thicker. They came to the flight of steps heading up to the shrine. They passed through the *torii* archways, painted a brilliant vermillion to the shrine complex. On one side loomed the red-painted structures that had been at Nachi shrine from times immemorial. On the other stood the newly built massive hall constructed at the orders of the Taiko some thirty years before.

Okiku paused in awe. The contrast between the red-painted building and the verdant forest that held it, the background of limitless wooden slopes, brought tears to her eyes. She wished she were a poet, able to express the beauty of the moment in words. Jiro peered over the heads of the crowds that thronged the courtyard. He noted and dismissed several figures dressed in *yamabushi* white or checks. None had the travel-stained look of someone who had been through the mountains. The vermillion building pleased him, but his eye was attracted to a troupe of dancers performing a *dengaku* dance to the sound of flute and drum. The steps were as ancient as the shrine, and his hands and feet twitched in time to the dancers' movements. He wished to join them, knowing full well that his unshaven pate and double swords kept him from the simpler life of the people he saw.

Rosamund could not contain herself. She was bursting with unanswered questions. Her face, well powdered to hide its paleness under her purple coif, was as expressionless as she could make it, but her eyes turned from sight to sight in wonder and awe. The people burning incense and fanning the smoke over themselves were comprehensible to her: In England and the Low Countries, where she had been born and raised, people did similar things to ward off evil. But the strange caperings of the dancers in their gorgeous costumes were out of a dream. She wondered about the interior of the shrine and whether her Buddhist nun's guise would keep her from entering, and she wondered about the white-and-red-clad woman dancing on a stage before a group of men, naked sword and a cluster of bells held in her hand. Other people were busily washing hands and mouths at the water front or tying slips of paper to bushes on the grounds that were laden with paper slips knotted about their branches like exotic flowers.

Goemon, having seen this festival before, watched his companions out of the corner of his eye. Rosamund's eyes were goggling with delight. He hoped their blueness would not be too obvious. Okiku was transported into some private joy of her own, her face held as still as an ivory statue, her eyes glistening with unshed tears. Jiro's eyes were roving over the crowd, observing the people around them, automatically searching for any threat, but his attention kept returning to the joyous movements of the dancers as they sweated and pranced in the sun.

Behind them Osatsuki and Midori stood still, watching the festivities. Osatsuki admired the brilliant red of the buildings, the cool green of the majestic forested mountain range, the tiny bustle of men around her. Her own words were inadequate, she knew, but she wondered about her former husband, killed by her friends. He would have known how to express the proper words for the feelings in her breast. Silently she said a prayer for his soul. Midori watched her elder sister, wondering how she could ever aspire to such elegant carriage.

They drifted eventually through the crowd to the large express-bark-roofed New Hall. Before them in the distance rose a green-covered cliff, bisected by a ribbon of white. From the distant waterfall came the susurrus that had accompanied them from the moment they had arrived. Framed against the blue of the sky and the green of the mountains, the waterfall was the purest white, immobile in the world. They rested and ate a simple lunch in one of the pilgrim rest houses. The dancing ended, and the crowds thinned. They tossed some copper coins into the offertory box before the shrine, and each lit a candle. Busy officials of the shrine in full formal robes moved in and out of the precincts maintaining proper order.

'What now?' asked Rosamund.

Her curiosity had been partially satisfied by her friends while they walked about, but there was still an air of expectancy about the shrine, and she felt there was more to come.

'The main festival is towards evening,' explained Goemon. 'The Fire Festival starts then. There will be a parade of torches and of tabards representing the shrine and the All under Heaven. We must find a good place, overlooking the stairs.'

'Goemon, shouldn't we see the falls first!' Okiku asked.

Rosamund's eyes grew rounder with excitement. 'Oh yes — we must!'

Jiro laughed. 'I too am interested. It is, after all, the main attraction, and I have heard so much about them. But I think that we had better look for lodgings as well, judging by last night's problems.'

They followed the stone-flagged path down through the forest of giant cryptomeria. The giant cedars towered above their heads, receding into the cool dimness of the forest. They clambered down slippery moist rocks, the sound of the falls rising to thunder in their ears. Above the sound they could faintly hear the calls of a conch trumpet as some pilgrim group performed its rituals. The air became spiced with the smell of water, and droplets beaded their hair and clothes.

At last they stood before the falls themselves. A ribbon of water fell almost slowly down the vertical cliff face. At the base it feathered into a rush of water pounding the rocks endlessly. Awestruck, they faced the wall and the pools below it, unable to say a word. Like them, other pilgrims emerged into the clearing and stood in wonder. Later they bowed and clapped their hands in obeisance at the marvel they beheld.

There were several groups of *yamabushi* mixed among the pilgrims about the base of the falls. Rosamund and her friends wandered closer to the thundering water, a silvery sheet that fell forever. Beside them other pilgrims crept closer in awe. The sound and continuous movement were hypnotic, and Rosamund felt infintesimally closer to understanding the people she lived with and the land she was in now.

A man dressed in loincloth and headband was wading through the pool in the direction of the falls. A priest on the bank, unheard in the roar, was gesticulating to him to turn back. A group of travel-worn *yamabushi* on the bank thumped their iron-ringed staves on the rocks in cadence. One of them blew his conch horn again. In another corner a wandering priest was selling charms, near him a monkey trainer displayed his monkey who aped the movements of the *dengaku* dance. They wandered through the crowds, admiring the falls from various vantage points. At last they stopped in a small teahouse and ate rice cakes filled with bean jam and drank large cups of tea. Satsuki admired the contrast of the plain ironware teacup against the red covering of the bench. Midori gamely tried to follow suit, doubting internally the while what was so wonderful about these commonplace items.

'We've still got the problem of where to stay the night;' Jiro cautioned.

Goemon smiled at them all mischievously. 'Are you ready for a long walk? We'll be back in time for the festival.'

'Where to?' asked Rosamund suspiciously.

'Some years ago, when I was playing the part of a wandering doctor, I came to Nachi. High up the mountain, behind the falls, is a small village where I stayed the night. The headman there owes me a favour, as I cured his family of illness. I am sure few people know of the village, and there will be room for us to stay. Let us go and see.'

Several pairs of hard eyes noted their passing as they set off up the mountain.

A narrow trail led through the lush forest. Ferns and akebia creepers grew everywhere. Inedible wild strawberries dotted the green with red. Okiku showed Rosamund and Satsuki how to catch dragonflies gently by their wings. The tenacious insects would then cling for a while to the women's heads. At one point they stuck one, all unnoticed, on Goemon's topknot and giggled as he led them on wearing his peculiar crest.

There were more shrines along the path, though pilgrims were fewer. They worked their way above the massive waterfall and crossed several of the streams that fed it, some of them forming falls of their own. The air grew cooler. After a two-hour walk they came to a large clearing in the forest. To one side was a low cliff over which fell a miniature version of the great Nachi waterfall. At the other end sat a small shrine. Its latticework entrance was closed, but the way between the plain wooden *torii* and the bellpull at the gate was decorated with multicoloured banners.

They stopped to drink, heading towards the waterfall pool. Jiro stopped them with a movement of his hand. Under the crashing waterfall sat a naked figure. His face was creased into a terrifying grimace, his fingers were gripped into a magic power *mudra*.

'Why, that's Master Daisangyoja!' said Satsuki in surprise.

Daisangyoja's hands began to move in strange gestures as he prepared a spell of great power to use against them. Midori looked on in panic. She knew the power of her former master and his vindictiveness.

'Come away!' the chestnut-haired girl cried in anguish. 'Let us get away from here, Elder Sister, before he manages to complete the spell.'

Jiro and Goemon looked at one another. It was clear that Daisangyoja was up to some mischief. Somehow he had survived and arrived at Nachi. Jiro loosened the sword in his scabbard. He would have to finish the business once and for all. Behind him he heard a scream, and Okiku pulled at his arm. He turned to follow her gaze. Midori, fleeing in panic, had reached the line of the forest. Out of the trees leaped a crowd of *yamabushi* bearing weapons. The *yamabushi* moved purposefully towards them. Staves were ready, short swords drawn, ritual axes sharp.

Jiro motioned to Goemon, and the small group ran into the depths of the forest. They would have a better chance there than in the open, where their small number would soon be overwhelmed.

Chapter Seventeen

The *yamabushi* gang outnumbered Jiro's party significantly. There was little time for consultation about tactics. Jiro and his friends drifted through the forest as silently as possible, weapons at the ready, taking up positions as best they could, hoping to split their attackers' forces. Jiro doubled back and circled the small shrine under the spread of a cryptomeria cautiously. Beads of moisture roughened the satiny flesh of his blade. He stepped into the clearing and came face to face with Hachibei and three other men. They screamed and charged. Behind them Daisangyoja started chanting spells again. Jiro parried two cuts at his head and rolled away from a thrust at his belly. As he did so, he tripped on a gnarled root and fell heavily on his hip. Behind him he heard the hiss of a staff descending on his exposed back, its iron rings clinking softly. He twisted desperately, knowing it to be too late. There was a surprised grunt, and then several meaty thuds mixed in with his opponents' cries. Jiro completed his roll and rose to his feet.

Two of the *yamabushi* were lying on the ground. One's neck was at an unnatural angle; the other's cheek seemed caved in. Hachibei and the fourth *yamabushi* were facing Tatsunoyama, both breathing heavily, while the massive wrestler seemed perfectly composed. Keeping an eye on the two *yamabushi*, Tatsunoyama bowed briefly.

'Mr Miura, I see I have the pleasure of assisting you again.'

Jiro bowed in return, smiled, said, 'I am most grateful Tatsunoyama-zeki,' and threw one of his sheath knives. The little throwing knife found its mark properly in Hachibei's wrist. He howled and dropped his short sword. Jiro slid forward almost casually, and his long blade flickered in the forest gloom. Hachibei stood for a moment while Jiro froze in place, his sword guard held near his ear. A gush of blood fountained from the *yamabushi* leader's neck. His torso fell in one direction; his head rolled in another.

The other *yamabushi* had turned to flee when his leader was hit. Tatsunoyama made a prodigious hop. His open hand rose in a short arc and chopped down, followed by the other. The *yamabushi*'s head shook, and he fell silently. Jiro spun and charged. Daisangyoja slid smoothly aside. His fist parried Jiro's blade. His other hand smashed down onto the samurai's wrist. Jiro twisted, and his shoulder knocked the *yamabushi*'s fist off target. Both opponents leaped back, breathing heavily.

A female scream sounded through the woods. Jiro called to Tatsunoyama over his shoulder, 'That is some of my friends. The *yamabushi* are attacking us. Please help.'

Tatsunoyama strode to the shrine and opened the door. He reached inside. A tousselled dark head with a sour expression appeared, followed by its twin. Lady One and Lady Two glared at Jiro's back. They would obviously have enjoyed seeing him slaughtered, but they ran after their massive lover as he strode purposefully into the forest.

Jiro balanced carefully on the balls of his feet. He would not underestimate the *yamabushi* leader again. His sword flickered twice, a cut to the head and then one to the body. The *yamabushi* parried each blow with a clang of metal. Jiro looked at the man's fists. From each side of his right fist protruded a diamond-shaped metal knob. In his left he carried a similar device — a *kongo* in the shape of a crown. The spikes of the crowns could catch a sword blade in time for the right hand to deliver a crippling blow. They circled. Jiro tried a thrust but was repelled. He drew his short sword, holding it unconventionally, hilt forward. He struck with his great sword, once, then again. Daisangyoja anticipated both blows and guarded against them smoothly. He was beginning to smile, showing his confidence, when Jiro managed the unexpected. With an agility unusual for so large a man and a humility exceptional for a samurai, he rolled forward on the ground. His short sword cut across Daisangyoja's shins. The *yamabushi* leader leaped into the air and landed several feet away as Jiro came to his feet and charged.

For a short second the *yamabushi* stared in horror at the spattering of blood that rained from one of his feet. Then, in an almost superhuman display of strength, he leaped back again and was gone into the wood. Jiro breathed deeply, wondering whether to chase him. Then another female scream sounded from the forest, and he hurried to find its source.

Far below them the festival had started. The parade was getting organised before marching to the shrine. Large wooden tabards in the shape of shields decorated with fan-shaped sunbursts were assembled in a line. The torch carriers who would oppose the tabards' progress stood by their massive barrel-shaped torches. Their black gauze hats were set at the proper angle, and the drummers and conchers were ready. In the dancing square the last *dengaku* troupe wound up its act.

Rosamund had been separated from her companions by her ignorance of woodcraft. She wrung her hands nervously. She hated fighting. The emotions it roused were ones she felt uncomfortable with. She cowered by a tree, licking her lips and wondering what had happened. A sound intruded on her thoughts. She raised her head and could not forbear a scream. An unshaven face under a pillbox hat was leering at her around the bole. Seeing she was alarmed and alone, the *yamabushi* stepped around the tree and reached for her. She reacted instinctively. Pulling back, she lashed at him with her hand. The *yamabushi* grinned and grabbed at her robe. The weighted end of the chain she kept in her sleeve hit his forehead above his eyebrow. The front of his skull caved in, and his eyes turned in his head. Rosamund's breath whistled beneath her teeth as she turned to seek more enemies.

Osatsuki knelt in a clearing, admiring the hint of white seen between the trees. The sound of the waterfall was muted by the tree boles. Beneath her the velvety moss cushioned her knees and stained the hem of her robe a bright green. There was a poem on the subject, she remembered, but the lines would not come to her.

Tsuneyoshi stepped out of the forest and stopped beside her. His handsome, aristocratic face was sad. 'You should not have betrayed us,' he said.

She bowed slightly, looking sideways at him, her head tilted to one side.

'The Master has indicated you are no longer acceptable. I am sorry, but my duty is to him. I could have loved you, but instead . . .'

'What would you do now?' she asked softly.

'I'll go into the mountains. I can no longer serve him.'

His sword was resting lightly over his shoulder. He raised it higher, and she noted that it was a heavily curved sword of ancient style, no doubt a relic of his family. There were many such men, scions of great families brought down by the politics and wars that had ended at Osaka with the fall of the Taiko's heir. She leaned forward and shrugged out of her embroidered outer robe, tucking the ends of her sleeves beneath her knees so as to fall properly. He looked at the back of her neck, and the memory of her beauty on their travels rose in him.

'I shall pray for your repose in the afterlife,' he said, and raised the blade two-handed.

'And I for yours,' she said softly, and drove the sharp steel hairpin she had drawn from her hair through his ribs and into his heart. Far below them, conches and drums announced the start of the parade.

Okiku crouched on a branch, motionless. The stalking *yamabushi* crept closer. Midori's keening teased him on. When the man was directly below her, parting the bushes that hid the brown-haired girl, Okiku slipped from her perch silently as an owl. The *yamabushi* died with a snapping crack of the bone in his neck. Okiku stepped off the warm, twitching body, then immediately leaped high, tumbling in the air as she rose. A second mountain ascentic slashed down at the spot on which she had been standing. Her feet hit the ground, and she flexed her knees and leaped again. The *yamabushi* leaped high too, and they met in midair. His hands moved swiftly and a bright length of steel whispered through the air as it was withdrawn from concealment in her pilgrim's staff. The *yamabushi* shrieked and fell in a heap. Midori ran to Okiku's side. Her sash was off her waist in a flash as she tried to stanch the bright stream of blood that gushed from Okiku's arm and side.

'Are you all right? Mistress Okiku, are you well?'

Okiku grunted. The cuts were superficial, but her arm and side would soon stiffen. Another *yamabushi* ran into view and headed for the two women. Midori hastily interposed herself between Okiku and the attacker. Hands extended into claws, she tried to block his approach, screaming incoherently. The *yamabushi* batted her aside, concentrating on Okiku's blade. Midori swung her head, and her fine brown hair blinded him for a critial instant. The man hesitated. There was a double whir through the air. The *yamabushi* screamed. His eye sprouted a metal star, and his throat gushed scarlet.

Goemon slipped patiently from shadow to shadow, one tree to another. He wanted to entice the *yamabushi* chieftain into the forest. It would be better to dispose of him quietly, if at all possible. A group of the mountain men patiently tracked him, and suddenly Goemon found that all his wiles were in vain. Daisangyoja stood before him, a mocking smile on his face. Between them stood five fierce-looking *yamabushi*. Goemon stood quietly in the clearing, his mind cool and alert. He smiled at the five men as they surrounded him. His calm enraged them, and they made trembling attacks in his direction. He took the fan out of his sash and fanned himself patiently.

One of the *yamabushi* lunged, and Goemon easily avoided the attack. A second cut at his head, and he parried neatly with the fan. The steel ribs clanged on the sword metal. Goemon threw a handful of powdered pepper into the attacker's eyes, then slid beyond him and hammered the edge of the fan into another attacker's wrist. The man's weapon fell from his grasp. Goemon seized his lapel, twisted, and threw the struggling *yamabushi* easily onto two of his companions.

Goemon kicked high and his foot connected with a *yamabushi* chin; then he spun, grabbed a sword hand, and twisted. The *yamabushi* fell to his knees with a broken wrist. Goemon attacked again, opening the fan one-handed and cutting at a rough face. The sharpened steel edge of a rib sliced through a black pillbox hat and tore at a scalp. The *yamabushi*, blinded by his own blood, did not have time to react as his own sword was twisted from his grasp and plunged into his belly. The attackers, those still able to move, were in a panic. They turned to flee, and all but one fell victim to their cowardice. Using the borrowed sword, Goemon cut them down as they fled. He turned to deal with their leader, and threw the sword with disgust at Daisangyoja's retreating back.

In the shrine complex below, the tabard bearers advanced, their devices held high. Conchs, flutes, and drums heralded their approach, and the torches were raised to oppose them.

Goemon heard a crying sound, and ran rapidly through the forest seeking the woman's voice. He charged into a clearing in time to see a wild looking *yamabushi* aim a cut at Okiku, who was leaning painfully to one side. Goemon's fan spun through the air just as the *yamabushi* raised his sword and attacked. A steel star sprouted from the mountain man's eye. The fan's jagged edge sliced through the exposed great artery in his neck. Goemon passed him at a run and retrieved the steel-ribbed fan. Okiku smiled at him through the pain and pulled the steel throwing star from the *yamabushi*'s gory eye, and the three of them set off to find more enemies.

They all met again in a clearing in the forest. Goemon looked at his friends, then ruefully at the pile of bodies in the clearing. None of the three bodies bore any wounds, but their necks all rested at curious angles. A heavy man was sitting on a rock. He had a minor cut and was being tended by two young women, twins, who were dressed as itinerant actors.

Goemon's face twisted in momentary disapproval. Actors should not involve themselves in important affairs. Then his natural good humour reasserted itself, and he considered his own actions ruefully. Jiro stood near the wrestler, eyes raking the forest. Only Okiku and the wrestler were wounded. Considering that the wrestler was completely unarmed, Goemon thought his survival a miracle. The riffraff that made up a mountain beggars' band was hardly a threat to him, Jiro, or Okiku, all of whom were armed. Rosamund had found Satsuki and the two of them had hidden the best they could, coming out when Jiro's powerful bellow had announced the *yamabushi*'s defeat. They counted seven bodies and several trails of blood. Daisangyoja's body was not among those found.

'They'll attack again,' Jiro said stolidly, wiping his long blade. He sheathed it in one smooth motion, his eyes never leaving the wrestler's.

'Good,' the wrestler grunted. 'I do not care for those people.'

'No, I am sorry.' Midori moved her open hand in negation. Her voice was soft but firm. 'They will not return.'

'How do you know, dear?' Satsuki's mild rejoinder seemed to give the *yamabushi* girl confidence.

'I know the bands. Daisangyoja has failed them too many times. They will not obey him now. His dreams have come to naught. We have nothing to fear from him. He will be replaced by one of his seconds.'

'I saw Hachibei's body on our way here,' Satsuki said in a low voice. 'And . . . I am afraid I killed Tsuneyoshi myself. . . .' She looked somewhat abashed, her eyes held low.

'Nonetheless,' said Goemon, 'we will be very careful. They will probably search for us at the festival. We had best reach the village before nightfall. It is small, and there will be no crowd to serve as a blind for them to stalk us. I would rather meet them in the open.'

At the far-off shrine the lit torches met the advancing tabards and opposed their entrance to the precincts. The excited crowd watched as the tabards advanced again and again, only to be repelled by the blazing wooden barrels. The bearers' faces ran with sweat. The crowd drank and called out excitedly. In the darkening forest several dead men lay quiet, uncaring. Ferns caressed their faces.

Evening fell as the party from Miyako tolled up the path. Across the valley they could see the last glow of the torches from the festival. Above them the stars shone through the growing night. Somewhere below them in the dark they could hear the endless sheet of the roaring waterfall. They sought the headman amidst the quiet cluster of thatched houses.

The formalities were soon concluded. Food was brought, and they were apologetically shown to the only free room the grateful headman could offer them, the main room of his house. The meal was a simple one, rice, grilled ayu whose flesh was sweet and redolent of pure mountain streams, fresh mountain vegetables, and delicate-flavoured pine mushrooms. Exhausted, not even blowing out the lamps, they crawled into their bedding. Not even Tatsunoyama's mountainous snores could keep anyone awake.

Midori awoke to a delicate touch on her thighs. She opened her eyes and looked up into a cloud of golden hair. Rosamund smiled down at her, then leaned forward and kissed her passionately. The blonde's inquisitive tongue searched Midori's mouth expertly, and Midori surrendered to the feeling.

'I've been wanting to have you alone for some time now,' whispered Rosamund. Midori hugged her to her breast. Her nipples, she noticed without surprise, were rock hard, almost painful with her desire. Rosamund's mouth moved downwards silently. She engulfed a nipple, then sucked the entire small breast into her mouth. Midori sighed a ghost of a sound. Her hands lightly touched the fall of golden hair against her chest.

'I've been wanting to do this for soooo long. . . .'

She tugged at the hair gently. It was softer than hers, and unlike any other she knew, it fell in ringlets that resisted straightening.

'Harder!' said Rosamund.

Surprised but obedient, the former *yamabushi* girl complied, forcing the blonde's mouth to dig deeply into her breast. She was rewarded with a flickering tongue that laved the painful nipple. Rosamund's mouth shifted to the other side, and her fingers sought the soft, downy hair of Midori's pussy. Midori obligingly spread her legs. Her hips rose without conscious command to meet the probing digit. Rosamund cupped the soft, downy mound with her hand. She squeezed the slimmer girl's lips between the three middle fingers, rubbing the slick clitoris fiercely. Midori grinned and showed her teeth, and her hand squeezed Rosamund's full breast harder than she intended. She was about to apologise, when Rosamund kissed her deeply, then muttered, 'Again!' The brown-haired girl squeezed harder and was rewarded with another soul-searching kiss. The blonde's expert tongue licked out and laved the inside of her mouth, then nibbled the length of her neck, descended to her shoulders, and then sucked hungrily at her erect brown nipples. For a moment Rosamund raised her head and peered through the dark at Midori's face.

'Hard! I like it hard!' she said. There was a note of pleading in her voice. Midori obligingly squeezed the beautiful full breast before her. The erect pink nipple burned against her palm, and her strong trained fingers sank deeply into the soft flesh. She was rewarded by a muted groan and another deep kiss from the blonde. Intrigued and somewhat mystified, Midori experimented. She took one perfect soft nipple and pinched it roughly. Far from having it pulled back out of her grasp, she found Rosamund's body covering her and the blonde's mouth laving her with kisses.

'You *like* being hurt while fucking?' she asked in a whisper.

Rosamund giggled softly. 'Goemon, Jiro, and Okiku all raped me when we first met. I've loved it ever since. Hurt me — please hurt me.'

For a moment Midori was shocked to the bottom of her soul. Lovemaking was for fun and enjoyment. She had seen the result of rape, and no one she knew who had undergone the experience enjoyed violence. That was a thing for men, and not of the best sort. Then she suddenly recalled whom she was speaking to. Of course, Mistress Rosamund was a foreign devil. . . . Their customs must be so different, and one could not expect their reactions to be completely human.

No girl would enjoy that sort of thing, but among the *kebozu*, the hairy devils, it must be the norm.

Meantime the friction of the blonde's fingers on her cunt was getting to her, and she felt obliged to return the pleasure she was receiving. She stiffened a finger and drove it into Rosamund's shoulder. She had been taught finger massage by one of her former band, and the pressure points could be used for ill as well as good.

Rosamund yelped and ground her hand into the chestnut-haired girl's cunt. Her body wriggled with abandon on the slimmer body below it. Her full breasts were mashed against Midori's smaller ones, and both women joined their mouths in a passionate kiss.

'You must be quiet or the others will wake up,' Midori whispered.

'No, they're too tired. In any case, they'll just join the fun. . . .'

Suddenly it occurred to Rosamund that she would rather have Midori to herself for a while, and she whispered half-reluctantly, 'Actually maybe you should gag me somehow. I usually yell a lot. . . .'

Midori, still somewhat unsure of herself, removed the silk scarf that Rosamund used to tie her sleeping robe. She gagged the blonde, not too tightly, then looked into Rosamund's eyes to be sure she was doing the right thing. The blue eyes, almost invisible in the gloom, looked at her with a hint of mischief and expectation. Midori spread the blonde beneath her and set to work with her fingers and tongue. The strong, practiced digits dug into the blonde's soft breasts, eliciting muted squeals. Midori kissed each painful point carefully, before moving on to the next, descending gradually.

Rosamund found herself enjoying one of the most pleasurable fucks she had had. At first Midori was gentle with her, carefully not to hurt her too much. But gradually as she got into the spirit of things, the light blows turned harder, the pain from the probing fingers more lingering. Midori's mouth sucked on her skin, bringing pleasure with the pain, and Rosamund started shivering uncontrollably.

Her hands, which had been guiding Midori's head to the places of her greatest pleasure exploring the slim girl's smooth body, now flailed aimlessly. Midori paused a moment, and a bold idea occurred to her. She slipped off the blonde, flipped her over, and rapidly tied Rosamund's hands together behind her back. Rosamund did not object, merely waiting for what was to come.

The sight of Rosamund's magnificent backside beckoned to Midori. The smooth, pale hills rose in a perfect curve, bisected by a long, sweet line that separated the two halves like a peach. She kissed each buttock separately, then dug her fingers viciously into them. There was another muted squeal, and she set to work in earnest, her teeth nipping the smooth skin, her fingers digging into the soft flesh. Rosamund's trembling increased, and she agitated her bottom in circles, unsuccessfully trying to evade the painful touch.

Midori separated the two halves, exposing the length of the crease, the tiny bud of the arsehole, and the beginning of the blonde forest below. She bent close and wondered whether any man had penetrated that little hole. Her fingers explored for her, and Rosamund's bottom jerked up to greet her. She dug her fingers in in earnest, then shifted some of her attention to Rosamund's cunt. As soon as she touched the slick lips, she was rewarded by a flood of moisture that overran her fingertips. She forced the beautiful legs apart and her tongue licked out to collect some of the honey. Rosamund trembled violently, and her hips bucked, throwing Midori's head backwards.

She turned Rosamund roughly over and crouched over her body. She was surprised at the size of the blonde's clitoris, which stuck out like a tiny fleshy claw. She sucked at it, at the same time forcing her cunt down onto the blonde's mouth. Her tongue licked the length of Rosamund's cunt; then she settled down to sucking hungrily at the large clitoris, her fingers digging into the muscles of Rosamund's thighs.

The combination of the demanding mouth and knowledgeable fingers was too much for Rosamund to bear.

Over her nose she could smell the musky perfume of Midori's cunt. She wriggled her wrists, and the sash on her wrists fell away. She ripped the gag from her mouth and reached for the slim girl's arse. Her mouth and nose were covered by the flagrant forest of Midori's soft hairs, and she began licking and sucking hungrily.

Both women were exhausted before long, their faces covered with one another's juices, their insides rippling with the number of times they had come. They stopped with mutual consent, and Midori rolled off Rosamund, touching her sleepily. Both smiled in the darkness as they composed themselves for sleep.

Chapter Eighteen

Rosamund's hair lay spread on Midori's flat brown belly. Their fingers were entwined while the others slumbered on. There was the sound of stealthy movement in the room. Two silent figures rose and cautiously stalked around the group of huddled sleepers. Tatsunoyama's snores hid the quiet sounds of their passing. Feigning sleep, Rosamund was not surprised to see that the figures were those of the twins, Lady One and Lady Two. Their faces were set, and their eyes glared.

Rosamund's chain and Midori's pilgrim's staff lashed out together. The chain wrapped itself around Lady One's leg and brought her down with a crash. Midori's staff smacked into Lady Two's exposed rump with a sound that brought Jiro and Goemon to their feet, weapons in hand. Tatsunoyama snuffled and grunted, coming awake in his own good time.

They sat around the two miscreants, Jiro giving mighty yawns. Tatsunoyama was furious. He harangued his charges, slapping exposed portions of their anatomy freely. Okiku noted with amusement that none of the blows were as powerful as those he had landed during the fight. The twins scowled and yowled occasionally, but it was clear they expected the treatment – and worse.

'How can I apologise, Mr Miura? Their behaviour is inexcusable.' The wrestler was almost incoherent with fury. 'I shall give them to you to dispose of. Kill them if you choose.'

'Why are they trying to kill Jiro?' Rosamund intervened in the harangue.

'Yes, why?' The sumo wrestler glared at them.

'He killed our master!'

Rosamund, Okiku, and Goemon exchanged glances. They too had participated in that killing, when the twins' master,

Lord Matsudaira, had conspired to unseat the Shogun, effective ruler of all the Japans. The twins evidently did not know that, though they remembered Jiro's face.

Okiku was looking at her companions while the debate about the girls' future was going on, Tatsunoyama insisting on handing them over to Jiro, the latter refusing to dispose of them. Rosamund and Midori, she noted, were both flushed. The blonde's disarray indicated more than the normal dishabille of sleep. An idea struck her. It arose, she knew, not from her head, but from her emotions.

'I have an idea,' she cut into the conversation. Heads turned in her direction. Jiro and Goemon looked at her sideways, like shy horses. Both knew her powers of invention, and the silky tone she was using meant an interesting, if exhausting time for them.

'Tatsunoyama-zeki, why don't you turn them over to Jiro? Since he does not want to kill them, let him exhaust them in punishment instead.' She slid a hand up the nearest twin's smooth calf, avoiding the half-hearted kick aimed at her. She flipped the actor's short robe aside, uncovering the downy expanse of her cunt.

Tatsunoyama leaned back and considered. He smiled broadly. 'That may indeed be their problem. You see, they have not felt the weight of a man on them for some time now.' He grinned. 'I am not exactly built for that, and they may be getting above themselves simply because they are above *me* some of the time.' He laughed at his joke.

'How about it, Master Jiro? Do you think you can exhaust them into submission? I tell you what − let Master Goemon assist you.'

Goemon licked his lips in agreement.

Sullenly the twins submitted to being stripped. They were alike in every detail, Okiku noted. Their skin was smooth and brown, and their elfin faces showed identical scowls.

Jiro was clearly embarrassed, but Okiku was not to be put off. She squatted between the two twins and examined their figures curiously. As far as she could determine, there was not a point of difference between the two. She laid a palm on either flat belly and stroked downwards. The twins

220

kept their legs stubbornly closed. She pulled at the black smooth hairs that rimmed the bottom of their bellies, and they merely scowled at her.

'Open your legs!' she said pleasantly.

They clenched them still tighter, their looks becoming murderous.

'Open your legs,' roared Tatsunoyama in his hoarse voice. They obeyed with alacrity. 'Do whatever she tells you to! Do you understand me?'

'Yes!' they chorused in unison.

Okiku fingered their smooth, tight cunts. Both were dry, intent on not participating. She smiled at them, then jabbed her fingers into the knuckles. The twins grimaced with pain but merely tightened the muscles of their inner channels.

'I think you will like them,' said Okiku cheerfully to her men. 'They're almost as tight as virgins.'

Tatsunoyama laughed. 'Maybe I do not use them enough, eh?'

Goemon merely licked his lips. Rosamund looked on with interest. The entertainments Okiku put on were always interesting and innovative.

Okiku rubbed her palms against the twins' soft mounds, one finger still in each cunt. Gradually, against their will, the walls of their cunts responded to the treatment and their insides turned slick with their interior moisture.

'Will they obey all my commands?' Okiku asked sweetly.

'They will do anything you command?' said Tatsunoyama forcefully. His tone softened somewhat. 'They are, for all their faults, extremely obedient.'

Okiku turned to Goemon and Jiro while she laughed lightly. 'You poor things. You've had to make do with us alone for so long. Come here.'

Obediently, as if hypnotised, the two men positioned themselves between the spread legs of the twins. Okiku exposed both erect cocks, Jiro's tremendous one and Goemon's which was no shorter, though it was thinner. She shook them in the air, offering the prone twins a full view of the stubby branches that were soon to be inserted in their soft bodies. Then Okiku guided both staves home, stopping only when the two tips came into contact with the two delicate pairs of lips, framed so pleasingly in black hair. She rubbed the tips up and down the length of the girls' cunts, spreading the lips ever so slightly, lingering over the clitorises, dipping them slightly in the direction of the clenched anuses. Then, with much delight, she gradually led both cocks into the waiting bodies. The two fleshy swords gradually sank out of sight.

Rosamund was charmed by the picture. The two slim figures of the women, alike as mirror images, lying flat on their backs, and the contrasting figures of the men. Between them a guiding woman, who obviously enjoyed her work. The two men started to work away with a will. Their hands clutched the two arses beneath them and then started moving over the captive figures. The twins were soon gasping, their legs contracting around the muscular figures covering them, whether from the weight or from real enjoyment. The men too were soon reaching a climax, as could be seen from the rapid oscillation of their buttocks and the strain that showed in their faces.

'Stop!' Okiku's imperious command was not immediately obeyed, but two strong slaps to the men's backs slowed their motion.

'Change!' she ordered. Goemon looked at her uncomprehendingly for a moment; then a grin split his face. He pulled his slimy cock from Lady One's sopping cunt and nudged his friend. The giant withdrew too, trailing a streak of froth. The two men changed places and recommenced.

Rosamund could not restrain herself. 'Is there any difference?' she asked Jiro, who was closer to her.

The young samurai was too dazed to answer. He mumbled something and returned to sucking the supine girl's nipple. She moaned and her head thrashed from side to side. Lady Two was as deeply sunk into a trance as her sister. Her face was as contorted, her hands and heels clutching at Goemon's back, kneading the muscles, pulling more and more of the delightful morsel into her.

'It's time to play *kemari*,' Okiku announced. Satsuki looked at her in surprise. *Kemari* was a court game in which a ball was kicked from point to point within a courtyard garden while the players recited verses appropriate for the season and the garden. This was hardly the place or the season, and in any case, the only balls were firmly attached to the men.

Okiku laughed at their puzzlement. 'In court *kemari*, the ports are immobile while the ball is kicked from one corner to another, not being allowed to fall to the ground. In *my kemari*, the balls will be stationary while the players will rotate. She stood up and stripped, motioning Rosamund to do the same. They stood there for a moment, allowing their audience to admire their beauty. Even Jiro and Goemon, used to the sight, paused at their efforts. The twins looked on, a look of envy in their eyes. Both women were impressive. Okiku's figure was smooth and without blemish. The heart-shaped fur of her pussy complemented her slim figure and her delicately shaped breasts. Long black hair fell past her shoulders. She ran her hands suggestively over her body, cupping her breasts for a moment, then slipping a finger momentarily between the delicate lips of her cunt.

Rosamund was no less beautiful, though a complete contrast. Her figure was lush and full, and the golden hair at the juncture of her legs fluffed out provocatively, setting off the pale alabaster of her thighs, the bold pink of the slit between her legs, and her prominent nipples. Her breasts were full and stood proudly away from her chest. They trembled as she strode forward to stand before her friend. They knelt together over the twins' faces, and the two miscreants knowing what was expected of them, began licking the two expectant cunts lustfully. Rosamund and Okiku sighed happily and settled deeply onto the twins' faces.

Goemon and Jiro resumed their labours, pausing now and then to touch or tongue either of the girls before them. Goemon promptly leaned forward as far as he could and shared the task of laving Okiku's cunt with his twin, stealing delicious licks of the busy tongue at the same time.

The treatment soon brought all participants near a climax. Okiku, alert for the signs, promptly stopped them. She rose and pushed Rosamund from her position on Lady One's face. Rosamund, seeing the game dispossessed Jiro of his place, and Jiro pushed Goemon. The latter found himself kneeling before Lady Two's head. Gingerly he inserted his long, thin prick into the twin's mouth, forcing her neck back to accommodate him. His cock slid into her mouth with ease, somewhat to his surprise, but rather than biting it, she wrapped the length of the shaft with her tongue, then closed her lips gently around it. He was soon pumping wildly into her, anxious to relieve himself of the pressure growing in his balls before Okiku could remove him from the sweet, hot furnace of the girl's mouth. His hand shared Lady Two's breasts with Jiro, and he leaned to one side and bit Rosamund forcefully on her shoulder. His consort screeched her delight.

Okiku spread Lady One's thighs farther, then spread herself so that one of her thighs lay under the supine girl's upper thigh, the other over her belly. She pushed forward until their hairs and lips meshed. Rubbing herself back and forth feverishly, she experienced the indescribable thrill of their slick lips sliding together. She continued for a while, lost completely in her pleasure, then focused on Rosamund, who was riding Lady One's face with abandon, squeezing Goemon's face into her bobbling tits the entire while. With a suppleness possible only to one who had exercised her body since childhood, Okiku doubled her body and joined her lips to those of Lady One. Together they licked Rosamund on.

Tatsunoyama regarded all the foregoing activity with impassive bemusement. His mask of impassivity was starting to slip, however. He wet his lips with his tongue and opened the front of his robe. The bulge in the robe was very apparent. Satsuki, who had enjoyed the show so far, returned immediately to her professional and personal courtesy.

'Tatsunoyama-zeki, pray forgive me for not offering myself immediately, but I imagined you would wish to regale your eyes before anything else − is that not so?' She bowed to him a second and then motioned to Midori. Together the two rapidly stripped the massive wrestler. To the undiscerning eye, Satsuki thought, the wrestler might appear monstrous. His belly was a massive dome overshadowing his erect prick, which was bent almost forward under the shelving. His hams were as thick as logs, his hands the size of shovels. And yet, she noted, he sat fully erect, and his shoulders were firm, smooth, and broad. His belly, far from sagging with fat, was a mountain of muscle. She contemplated him for a moment, while Midori crouched before his belly and delicately sucked his cock into her mouth. He regarded the crouched figure before him benevolently, his huge palms resting lightly on her back.

Satsuki smiled at him. He was the best possible customer expecting her to arrange his pleasure to the best possible advantage. She rose and helped him recline on his back. His flexibility was such that he could do so without moving his legs and disturbing Midori, who continued suckling at his aroused manhood. Satsuki opened her robe and exposed herself to his gaze. She stood so for a time while he minutely examined her figure. Just before she judged the sight was about to pall, she moved from his view. She crouched over him, lightly teasing the muscles of his belly until they quivered with anticipation; then Midori guided her down onto the waiting shaft.

She did not have Rosamund's control of her inner muscles, but she was very accomplished nonetheless. First she glided up and down the extended shaft, the panting and sighing from the others in the room lending cadence to her moves. The tempo increased, then changed as she ground her bottom onto his prick, then contracted herself forcefully around the base of the shaft. Midori was leaning over him, nibbling the massive muscles of his chest, stroking his arms and belly, her light fine hair tickling his skin to a climax. He came almost without moving his body, and Satsuki supplied the necessary movement, urging him on with wild gyrations of her hips. He grunted happily as he felt the last of his sperm gush out and fill her cavern. She rose slightly to change her position, and instructed Midori to place cushions behind his back so he could see as well as feel.

Okiku signalled another change in the ballgame. This time she straddled Lady Two, then lowered her backside so that her cunt lips barely kissed the other girl's. Slowly, then with increasing tempo, she slid the lips together in an extended kiss. Lady Two welcomed the delicate touch. Her mouth was extended fully by Jiro's gigantic cock. She sucked as best she was able but finally found the solution in relaxing her mouth and allowing him to fuck as he would. Mindful of his size, Jiro inserted only the broad head of his member. Touched by his gentleness, notwithstanding the enmity between them, she found herself lightly cupping his massive balls, stroking the length of the shaft that could not enter her.

Goemon positioned himself over Lady One's face. He looked down at the inverted woman, and a new fancy struck him. He gathered her small tits together, squeezing them delicately. Then he leaned forward and placed his sopping penis in the channel between the two breasts. The sensation was nothing like that supplied by Rosamund's. The blonde looked on approvingly.

Rosamund was not as flexible as Okiku. Rather than try to emulate her friend, she stretched out on Lady One's body. She engulfed Goemon's prick with her bright red lips, and her tongue caressed the length of the shaft until the tip touched her uvula. Her head bobbed up and down as Goemon fucked slowly through the channel of Lady One's breasts and into his mistress's mouth and throat. As he moved he felt the young woman lying under him surrender completely to the discipline imposed by her wrestler. Diffidently, almost shyly, Lady One began licking his balls as they passed above her mouth.

Satsuki sank deeply onto Tatsunoyama's cock. Her bottom rested comfortably against the bulk of his belly, and she luxuriated in the feeling for a brief moment. He was indeed as pleasurable as she had thought. Then she raised her arse slightly and bowed forward, knowing how charming a picture her upturned behind showed to his eyes. He slid his hands in appreciation down the perfect half globes, lingered for a brief moment on the tiny pursed bud of her anus, then briefly stroked the forest of damp hairs lower down. Midori knelt before them, parted Satsuki's legs, and laved the length of his shaft and her slit as the strong male member briefly appeared then hid again. The six on the floor before them continued obliviously towards a climax, while the two professionals slowly and surely reached the expected outcome of their pleasure while watching amateurs perform.

It was a glorious morning. Rosamund awoke and stretched. Her friends were around her, sleeping deeply. She poked bits of bare skin experimentally. There was no response from female or male except groans or grunts of sleepiness. Annoyed, she fingered her glowing golden fur. She was just ready for another round, but none of these weaklings could supply her, she decided. She rose quietly from the tangle of limbs and knelt by the toilet table. Her face shone at her from the silver travelling mirror. Her hair was a golden cloud framing her large blue eyes and blooming cheeks to perfection. Idly she brushed her hair. The strands crackled with suppressed static electricity. She felt the same, still tensed up from last night's events.

She smiled wickedly and moved the brush downwards. With steady strokes she brushed her golden bush. The sensation was titillating but not sufficient. She pushed harder, then sighed with frustration. Being the mistress of a rich and importnt lord had its disadvantages. The brush, for instance, was soft and smooth for a lady but too soft for her needs, which at times, like now, were violent. Her companions were still asleep, so she hastily dressed, not bothering with undergarments. A white robe and over it the violet cloak and hood of her disguise would suffice. She tucked her *manryukusari* chain in her robe and slid the shoji doors open. She closed them quietly and turned to face the glorious world without.

The enormous cedars towered around her, their tops hidden in mist. The roofs of the houses were likewise wreathed. The mountain rose beside her, covered with forest and mystery. Not really thinking about it, she turned her steps to the slopes and started climbing, wishing to exorcise sleep from her bones.

After a stiff climb she could no longer see the roofs of the small hamlet below her, nor of the headman's house where her lovers lay sleeping. She turned and breathed deeply of the scented air. The sound of a small brook came to her through the mists. Suddenly thirsty, she headed for the water. The stream was small and deliciously cold. She followed it up to a small widening in the course. A waterfall fell from the cliff above.

She stripped and slid her hands caressingly over her body. Her nipple stood erect in the cold, puckered slightly. Her thighs were white and firm. She spread her legs and bent forward to examine the rose on her inner thigh. Kissing a finger she said. 'Poor little rose, no one has kissed you for ever so long,' and put the digit to her mossy grove. Then she plunged into the pool.

The cold bit into her like a knife. Her nipples puckered more than before, painfully. She gasped with the pain, finding in the freeze an element of pleasure that raised inner warmth even as the external cold raised goose bumps on her flesh.

She paddled to the end of the pool near a large bush which grew from the rock and pulled herself up. She shook herself, then noticed a small niche behind the bush. She peered into the darkness. Something glittered on the rock. Heedless of the scratches, she forced herself through the bushy barrier. On a rock before the niche rested a lacquered wooden bowl and a short metal handle with two diamond-shaped ends. The joining handle would have been well covered by a man's fist. She had just bent to pick it up, when something loomed out of the darkness of the niche. She suppressed a scream. The figure in the gloom of the niche was Daisangyoja, leader of the *yamabushi*.

Chapter Nineteen

The leader of the *yamabushi* band seemed asleep or dead. There was no colour to his face, and his eyes were closed, his muscles slack. She examined him closely, unsure for a moment of his identity. It was indeed Daisangyoja. He was dressed in white, weaponless and seeming harmless. A man peacefully dead. No, she decided, he must be meditating. He was seated in double lotus, his feet resting on his knees, his hands twisted behind his back and joining in front. His broad chest was stuck out as he held his own feet. She drew back, intending to run for help, fearful of his awakening.

Her movement was arrested in midmotion. Unconsciously while she thought her hand stirred the thicket between her legs. Slowly, resolution budded in her. She turned away, only to return with her sash and the weighted length of chain that had served her so well as a weapon. It was work of a moment to tie him hand to foot. She stood back and admired her handiwork.

Neither a foot she shoved roughly into his face, nor cold water dashed there seemed to wake the man. Rosamund stood back and considered. She spied his sword leaning against the inside of the niche and cut his clothes from him. As Satsuki had noted, he had an impressive physique, though somewhat stringy for Rosamund's taste. She leaned forward and warmed her hands on his genitalia. The cock was flaccid for a while, the balls in their silky bag warm to her touch. Her hands and his natural reactions, warmed up at the same time, as his cock rose slowly to full erection. She fondled it for a long moment, then bent forward and licked the tip slowly and sensuously. The rate of his breathing increased, she noted. Her treatment, she well knew, would bring any man out of a trance.

Now for the final act. She straddled the seated figure. The walls of the niche were narrow and scraped her sides, but she managed to lower herself onto the waiting pole. She teased herself for a while, not allowing the desired mouthful to penetrate her lower lips; then with a sigh she relaxed her thigh muscles and tensed those inside her. Gravity alone impaled her with exquisite slowness on his turgid erection.

She bounced for a while, making herself comfortable and not incidentally putting pressure on his hands and feet. His breathing quickened, and his eyelids began to flutter. Without warning she squeezed her inner muscles. His eyes snapped open, and he looked into her face. Instinctively he pushed forward, and the juices in his balls sped upwards. He jerked in surprise as his orgasm splashed warm liquid into Rosamund's waiting channel. She leaned forward and bit his lips, sunk in her own pleasure.

He tried to heave her off, then discovered his bound condition. She slapped his cheeks playfully, then, in a more serious vein, contracted the muscles of her interior. He glared at her, trying to scare her away with his fierceness.

She laughed heartily at him.

'I am Daisangyoja, the living incarnation of the mighty En-no-gyoja. Who are you to disturb my meditations?' His breath quickened, and he writhed, trying to free himself from the caverns of flesh and rock that engulfed him. She smiled sweetly, then clenched her vaginal muscles spasmodically. He winced with the unexpected pain.

'You do not know who *I* am,' she said triumphantly. 'I am the friend of one whom you sought to bury alive in your unholy rites. One of those you tried to kill yesterday.' She glared at him, no longer amused.

'She would have won everlasting life!' he shouted. His shout was ended with a yelp as once again she applied her slick, well-trained insides to his member.

'No! She would have won death. Now *I* will try you. I will strangle you to the death you wanted with my bare . . .' She paused to giggle as the sense of what she was saying broke through to her. He stared at her in horrified fascination, and she emphasised her meaning by squeezing once again.

'But . . . but . . . that is unnatural,' he said. 'The female principle must not be dominant! I'll never be reborn in my proper shape!'

'Too bad!' She smiled at him again. 'In any case, you're wrong. I *am* dominant. You will see. . . .'

She set to work on him in earnest. Her milk-white hips moved her heavy arse up and down his cock. The slick insides of her cunt laved the length of his heated shaft. He tried to ignore the sensation, starting the complicated words of a ritual to exorcise demons, but the sensations of her cuntal tissues penetrated the words and broke him out of his trance. Unwillingly, unable to control his traitorous body, his hips began to respond to her movements. The pain was terrible. He was used to sitting in the position for hours, but not chained and confined the way he was.

The pulse beat in his head, and his cock throbbed with painful anticipation. Way below, at the bottom of his scrotum, uncontrollable forces gathered. He gritted his teeth, and she laughed in triumph. She leaned back and gathered her rosy-tipped breasts together, raised them to his face, and rubbed them across his unshaven jaws. He snapped at the perfect white mounds, capturing a bit of skin and biting down hard on one of them as she jerked the tempting mouthfuls away. She yowled as a drop of blood appeared, and squeezed his prick with such force that he groaned. He groaned again as a rush of sperm from his balls spurted the length of his cock and flooded her insides. Again and again, like a hooked fish, he drove uncontrollably into her. The waves of pain and pleasure subsided at last, leaving him only with a feeling of heaviness and a reminder of pain. Surprisingly, her versatile cunt still held him in a crushing grip.

'You have won, this round at least,' he said. 'I shall have to meditate for a long while before I am pure enough to try the Way again.'

She shook her head, and the golden fall of her hair swirled around her face. 'No. I am not finished with you.' Her inner muscles began milking his rod with renewed fervour. To his horror he found himself responding again. This time the orgasm was slower in arriving. He twisted in her arms, trying

233

to shake her free. Waves of pleasure swallowed up his will, and the struggle turned to forceful thrusts as she bounced over him. He cried out as a thin stream of come spurted from the tip of his member, joining the rivulets that made their joining parts a humid swamp. His head sagged, but within, he knew she could not tempt him again.

He was wrong. Without cease, and against his wishes, Rosamund brought him again and again to climax, until the dusty floor he sat on became a morass of mud. Finally he knew he could not go on any longer. Rosamund looked down into his eyes, fierce blue eyes, unnaturally large and round, looking into the eyes of the would-be sage. She laughed, and her body shook. Even in his exhaustion and humiliation he found himself unable to ignore the beauty of her full white breasts as they billowed before his eyes with her full laugh.

Rosamund's hands began stroking his body sensuously. Her fingertips ran over his exposed skin, leaving trails of electric thrills behind. They descended lower, scratching at his pubic hair, then somehow insinuating themselves lower, ticking his exhausted ballbag. Her lips and teeth nibbled at his ears, his shoulders, his neck, his chest. Inside her, he felt his flagging prick revive. Be *still*! he commanded his mind, but the rebellious member, detached from thought, raised it head again. Her smooth inner muscles milked him incessantly, and to his horror he found his whole body responding once again.

The woman riding him showed signs of arousal too. She twisted incessantly in his lap, gouging sharp edges of rock into his behind. She threw her head back, exposing the pale whiteness of her throat, emphasised by the faint blue of her veins. He leaped forward with his teeth. Rosamund jerked the head back just in time, though the sharp nip of his teeth grazing her skin brought added and unexpected pleasure. She let herself go fully now. Her cunt squeezed his cock forcefully, urging it more fully into her. Her hands and teeth were busy as his fettered body, urging it on to a final climax that was already building inevitably in her own downcovered mound.

The climb to a climax was slower this time. Daisangyoja was almost detached from his labouring body. His breath, coming in gasps, was that of a cornered animal. Their approach to the peak she sought and he avoided was slow and torturous but speeding up with every move and every moment.

She squeezed now in earnest. His cock was in a soft, infinitely strong vice. Stronger than the power of his magic, softer than the infinity he had sought before in the Way. His throat was too dry, his power too exhausted to control himself. Veins bulged in his face. His eyes rolled back in his head, and spittle tinged pink with blood emerged from between clenched lips. Racking sounds came from his throat. He heaved convulsively, once, and again. The second heave was so strong that Rosamund was flung off her perch. He let out one final yellowing growl and collapsed. His body fell sideways, seeming to collapse in on itself.

He was dead. There was nothing left of the feared Daisangyoja but a dry husk of a man.

Rosamund staggered erect and looked at him long and tiredly. Then she bent and did what had to be done.

'We were terribly worried!' Okiku said as she greeted Rosamund. 'Where have you been?'

Rosamund smiled and said nothing. Okiku shook her head in despair. Her foreign friend sometimes had these moods. Willful and headstrong, she was unwilling or unable to explain them to anyone.

Rosamund went into the house. The villagers had provided them with food, and she ate ravenously. Satsuki was sitting on the veranda, admiring the view when she finished. Okiku had gone off to tell the men Rosamund had been found. Without a word Rosamund took out a small folded kerchief from the bosom of her robe. She placed it on the floor before her, then unwrapped it and pushed it forward to Satsuki. On the white kerchief rested a bunch of short, dark public hairs tied together by a longer strand of head hair. Through the bundle was stuck one of Rosamund's elaborate hairpins.

Satsuki touched the bundle with her fingertips, then looked at Rosamund's face.

'Thank you,' she said, and turned again to watch the view. There were faint smiles on both women's lips.